T0167225

A Tale, Nearly True, of *Richmond, Virginia*

R. M. Ahmose

iUniverse, Inc.
Bloomington

A Tale, Nearly True, of Richmond, Virginia

Copyright © 2012 by R. M. Ahmose

*All rights reserved. No part of this book may be used or reproduced by
any means, graphic, electronic, or mechanical, including photocopying,
recording, taping or by any information storage retrieval system
without the written permission of the publisher except in the case
of brief quotations embodied in critical articles and reviews.*

*This is a work of fiction. All of the characters, names, incidents,
organizations, and dialogue in this novel are either the products
of the author's imagination or are used fictitiously*

iUniverse books may be ordered through booksellers or by contacting:

*iUniverse
1663 Liberty Drive
Bloomington, IN 47403
www.iuniverse.com
1-800-Authors (1-800-288-4677)*

*Because of the dynamic nature of the Internet, any web addresses or links
contained in this book may have changed since publication and may no longer be
valid. The views expressed in this work are solely those of the author and do not
necessarily reflect the views of the publisher, and the publisher hereby disclaims
any responsibility for them.*

*Any people depicted in stock imagery provided by Thinkstock are models,
and such images are being used for illustrative purposes only.*

Certain stock imagery © Thinkstock.

*ISBN: 978-1-4697-0033-5 (sc)
ISBN: 978-1-4697-0035-9 (e)
ISBN: 978-1-4697-0034-2 (dj)*

Library of Congress Control Number: 2011963510

Printed in the United States of America

iUniverse rev. date: 1/24/2012

Contents

Chapter One

WHILE ZATORAH LEEMAN slept uneasily in the adjoining bedroom, Peter clicked through the available TV channels, for Cambridge, Massachusetts. To the Leemans, the *public broadcasting stations* seemed, at times, the only networks offering programs with real entertainment value. The large, wall-mounted screen flashed one broadcast after another, upon Peter's selection. At the last channel displaying, he took note of the show's content, with unease.

The thirty seven year old dentist of ten years practice was mild and even-tempered—nothing like the model of the "aggressive surgeon" that haunts the imaginations of some. For his tolerance in dealing with peers and patients, the reward was premature graying about the temples. But, he always tried to balance his tendency to internalize daily concerns, with a shameless show of the deep affection he felt for his wife.

Pausing, Peter whispered to himself: "I don't believe this— yet another reference to Richmond, Virginia. This has to be the twentieth time this month. Sheesh. I'm glad Torah isn't awake to see this one." He then clicked pass the channel he had viewed.

"The last thing Torah needs," he continued in his musings, "is another reference to Richmond—enough, already."

"Apparently, *not yet* enough." It was Zatorah Leeman's utterance, in response to her husband's comment.

The listless voice breaking the silence behind him gave Peter a small start. He turned to face the ghostly specter in the dark bedroom doorway.

"I dreamed it again, Peter." Zatorah's face was pale, her eyes sleepless, her nightgown appearing fragile and powdery white like a butterfly's wing. "And, again, it was Emrich. This time I was riding as a passenger with him, as he drove up and down, along this rolling highway. The big green destination signs overhead, one after the other, informed of our increasing nearness to...Richmond.

"Peter, just as before, he wouldn't say a word—Emrich, I mean. He just drove in what looked to be a state of utter distress. God, it was so scary. It was like riding in a rollercoaster car beside someone who is dead and, somehow, still operating the cars."

As Zatorah approached, Peter rose from the sofa, and in a gentle, caressing gesture, urged his wife to sit beside him. The concern in his voice matched his serious expression.

"I don't suppose, at this point, I can keep telling you it's all coincidence—these *Richmond* references—and will pass. But, Torah, you know how I feel. I just don't believe in premonitory dreams...and signs...and...."

"And the *paranormal*," Zatorah said, completing her husband's thought. "Peter, I'm not blind to your view of the subject, although you've been a dear about treading so gently when the topic comes up. But, more and more, I'm being shown that it is to be my next area of research.

"For the past semester, at the university, as you know, those within the new department have so strongly solicited my participation. I resisted, asking for time to give it more thought. Then, the next thing I know, they're telling me of a newly reformulated plan for collaborative work outside of Cambridge. And, *where*—? It's none other than the city of my birth—Richmond, Virginia.

"But nooo," Zatorah continued dramatically, "even *that* wasn't enough. Next, the father with whom I've had no parent-daughter involvement, over my entire life, *dies* and begins to haunt me with *dreams* concerning Richmond."

"It's funny you would have dreams about him, having barely known him."

"Even that's an overstatement, Peter. I didn't know him *at all*—not really. Emrich just kept on-and-off communication, through the years—phone calls and letters—always mysterious about his intentions and whereabouts."

"Then—what was it, a couple of months ago?—your mother gets a call from some government agent, saying Emrich has passed on...a mystery man to the end." Peter had a perplexed expression as he spoke.

"And, as you know, from that time on, one Richmond reference after another has popped up, from various sources—not one of them *our* Richmond, here in Massachusetts."

"Torah, I'm feeling just a little guilty about my intention, seconds ago, to conceal something. Just before I heard you in the doorway, I switched the TV channel, not wanting the program to play, even with you asleep in the bedroom. I planned to keep it hidden. But, deception, even one of *best* intentions, just won't work as feature of our marriage." With that revelation, Peter turned back to the TV's previous channel.

Gazing at the screen, Zatorah clasped her husband's hands in mild wonderment. When Peter increased the set's volume, the couple listened to the announcer's continued description of *Hills and Lowlands of Richmond, Virginia*. It was both the title and focus of the documentary.

That same night, five hundred miles south of Cambridge, a section of Hill Street, in Richmond, Virginia was experiencing unrest. The street was part of a network of brief roadways crisscrossing a public housing area known as "Gilpin Court." Several such project complexes within the city were, and are, operated by the Richmond Redevelopment and Housing

Authority. But *Gilpin* had a special distinction: It sat within a district of Richmond with unique historical significance.

Just after the Civil War, Richmond contained three voting districts, or *wards*, each named for a renowned Virginian. Soon, the number increased.[1,2] In 1871, a sixth ward was carved out of the north-most sections of five existing at the time.[3] Predominantly black, this sixth ward soon contained nearly half the registered voters of African American descent, in Richmond.[4]

Jackson Ward, as the section came to be known, developed into an area replete with black entrepreneurs, the largest district of the kind, in the South.[5] Businesses and upscale homes of these enterprising souls lined the various streets, within the district. The economic success of "the Ward," to the first quarter of the 20th century, earned it an impressive distinction. By the 1930s, however, its glory days were fading into the past. Years later, north-most Jackson Ward was selected for erecting the sprawling public housing complex of *Gilpin Court*.

Some of Gilpin Court's unrest this night centered on a street-wise hustler named Merquan Paler. He resided with his girlfriend of two years and had no employment that could be viewed as "usual." Through translucent curtains, he looked out on Hill Street, from a front window. Darkness of night obscured the view outside the housing unit he occupied. With mounting vexation, Paler tracked the movements of some community menaces, as they paced back and forth between ends of the block.

From St. John Street, at one end, to St. James Street, at the other, public housing residents and their visitors stood in doorways or watched the street through open windows. Word was that the five young men making a brazen show of their contempt were looking for confrontation. Symbolically, their acts challenged Merquan Paler, or *Merk*, as he was called in "the hood," to come outside and face them.

Each of the five men "seeking audience" with Paler had a criminal history. On the surface, it seemed odd that they were so tentative in their approach, tonight. However, the circumstances were not at all puzzling to those with any familiarity with Paler—which was most in Gilpin Court. The community, whose residents included the five trouble-seekers, drew consensus on a certain belief: Anyone *in the hood* scheming to make an adversary of *Merk* Paler should do so with care. In addition to many friends in the community, Paler seemed endowed with a sort of *luck* that gave him an edge in conflicts.

Across the street from where Paler stood at the window, and down the block, Trayon Twine stood in a doorway. Alongside him was his cousin, Neil. They had strongly advised their girlfriends, the unit's legal residents, to stay inside and watch through a window. If any shooting started, stray bullets might well find anyone not able to duck quickly behind a wall. Indeed, Trayon, himself, packed a nine-millimeter weapon at that very moment.

Throughout Gilpin Court it was joked that similar facial features gave the cousins more the appearance of brothers. Countenance, complexion, and composure, however, were where likeness between the two ended. Squat and boisterous of voice, Neil was thought to be a typical, take-charge "Virgo." Conversely, Neil was of average size and height and possessed the more *reserved* nature Gilpiners attributed to "Pisces." Watching activity in the street from their lair, Trayon listened to Neil's excited mutterings:

Neil: "Tray, man, I hope *Merk* don't come out. But, you can tell they gon' start hollerin' for him. They been at this shit for damned near a hour. What's wrong wit' Dre' and them niggas, anyway—five against one?

           "And you know *Merk* ain't got no *heat*—not the way Treecie be hatin' on guns in the house.

What's wrong wit' them niggas? Why they beefin' wit' *Merk*?"

Trayon: "They *haters*, Cuz—haters. I think they figure they can boost their own respect, if they can put *Merk* in the curb, in front of everybody. But, you know *Merk*, man. That nigga is crazy, too. He gon' come out, if they call him."

Neil: "He can't take no five against one. They might start one-on-one, but that ain't gon' last, once *Merk* lays big Dre's ass out."

Trayon: "Yeah, like he did that summa-bitch, *Hawk*, that time. That shit was funny as a bitch. Nigga layin' there pretendin' his back was out."

Neil: "Man, this shit ain't lookin' good over there, man."

Trayon: "Don't sweat it, my nigga. We got this. You gon' see some shit in a few minutes."

Neil: "That's the thing. I ain't feelin' this shit tonight. I hope he stay *inside*. Ain't no tellin' how far this ol' *monkey shit* might go. I knew I shouldn't'a lent my *piece* to Bone yesterday."

Trayvon: "It's all good, Cuz. I told you before: *Merk*'s got *luck,* or some'em, with 'em. You watch and see if Dre'-and-them don't fuck around and wait 'til *the Greeks* roll up.

"Anybody else—the shit should'a gone down by now. You know what I'm sayin'? If it was anybody else, the *throw-down* would'a already happened. But that *Merk*...he got some'em *watchin'* his ass. And it ain't just me and you."

Neil: "Did you say *Greeks?* What Greeks? ...Oh, shit! It's starting! They callin' him out! It's 'bout to get crazy!"

Trayon: "Ooooh...what the fuck did I tell you?! Look! 'Comin' *both* ways down Hill. Look at them *Mack-ass* limousines! What the fuck did I tell you, Neil?! *Merk* is one lucky somma-bitch! Seven fuckin' limousines—and just when them five clowns start callin' Merk out."

Neil: "What the hell?! Oh, shit—is that...?"

Trayon: "You goddamn right! It's *the Greeks*, my nigga! I called 'bout twenty minutes ago when I saw the shit shapin', out here. I saw what was comin'—everybody did.

"Lucky, the shit happened on *this* night. Any other night, this would'a been some bad shit. What are the fuckin' odds, man, that it went down *this* night, when them bad ass *Greeks* is in town?

"Check it out, this how it went down: Priola just told me Wednesday they were havin' the convention for a week. He was all *hyped* and shit like he can get. He said, *'We got muscle down here, Tray. You got no idea.'* You know how he talks in that fuckin' *Jersey* voice.

"On the real, though, he *been* told me if *Merk* get in a jam, call 'im. He say *Merk* done helped to keep him and some of his people out'a jail. Don't ask me how. I just do my part, workin' for him, just like you do your part, and I don't fuckin' ask too many questions."

As the cousins watched from half a block's distance, black limousines came to a slow halt, lining a block of Hill Street in two directions. By now, the sidewalks and blacktop of Hill Street were vacant of all strollers. All observers watched from doorways, open windows, or peered around corners.

From three of the vehicles five men stepped out. Each, with deliberate discretion, held what appeared to be an *Uzi* machine gun. In the block of Hill Street between St. John and St. James Streets, they stood in formation around the parked limos. A sixth man, whose car stopped in front of the housing unit inhabited by Merquan Paler, emerged from the opening car door. When he had straightened his posture he saw Paler standing outside the doorway of a housing unit.

The two men stood alone on the sidewalk of Hill Street, in full drench of moonlight. In view of spying eyes—upwards to forty pairs—they grasped hands and executed a brief cordial embrace. Each appeared in striking contrast to the other. Paler was tall and wiry, a creature of the Gilpin "project." The pudgy, ruddy faced fellow posturing before him was "Lew" Priola, a man who mingled regularly with businessmen of downtown Richmond. The two talked as freely and cavalierly as they might have, in a country club setting.

Suddenly, on advice from a radio transmission, audible in the still coolness of that April night, the armed men quickly re-entered the cars. Coming from both directions on Hill Street were police cruisers. The arrival did not result from a call about a disturbance witnessed. It had more the look of routine investigation of an unusual spectacle. One of the patrol cars pulled up to where the fifty-ish businessman and the twenty-two year old hood hustler stood. The older man spoke:

"Hello, officer. It looks like my *convention* buds and I took a wrong turn off I-95. This pleasant young fellow, here, tells me our 3rd Street exit was a little ways south of where we got off."

The officer responded casually from inside the cruiser: "You must have taken the Belvidere exit. To wind up here, you folks had to do some fancy maneuvering, after taking that turnoff."

He gave a brief chuckle and continued. "I'll bet if you had been *trying* to find this section of the city, at night, without a map, you'd have been circling around until daybreak, looking."

"You're right. To tell you the truth, I don't think a single one of us could retrace the route, backward, to the highway."

"Well, you're not far from 1st Street, assuming you're trying to get downtown. Where are you-all headed?"

"The *Omega*—between Cary and Canal?"

"Not a problem. Just have your group follow me down the block to 1st Street, where we'll hang a right. We'll cross over I-95 and then work our way to 3rd, where you were headed originally. Fair enough?"

"I'll say. Imagine getting lost and given a police escort, in minutes. My guess is: only in Richmond, Virginia."

Merquan Paler stood at the ascent of steps outside his girlfriend's unit, until the street was clear of limousines and police cruisers. He then walked casually up the stairs and opened the door seconds after hearing the lock disengage. Once inside, he folded his arms and prepared to face Patrice's inevitable drilling.

In height, Patrice stood seven inches below Merquan's six-foot-one stature. The three years of age she had over him was in no way apparent. Like him, she, too, was slim of build, but her complexion was muffin brown, a few shades darker than Merquan's. Her eyes, spaced attractively far apart, retained almond shapes characteristic of youth. They appeared childlike when she was unhappy about something, as she was at present.

Patrice:	"You were still going out there to fight, even while I'm begging you *not* to."
Merk:	"Who…me?"
Patrice:	"Yes, *you*. Who do you think I'm talking to?"
Merk:	"What—you really think I was goin' out there to *dance* with those clowns? *No-way.*"
Patrice:	"*Merk*, you had unlocked the door and you were pulling on it, with me standing against it."
Merk:	"Huh? Nooo, sweetie girl, I don't think I was doin' *that.*"
Patrice:	"So, what am I, crazy? Why do you want to play *head-games?*"
Merk:	"Head games? Oh, no, that ain't *even* me. I just don't want you to be upset over some'em that turned out all right.

"This is how it works: In life, when things turn out okay, you let it go. Roll with it. You swat the fly, let 'im fall on the floor and die, and don't keep sweatin' that 'nigga'."

Patrice: "*Merk*, you showed that you didn't care about how I feel."

Merk: "Nooo. You just *think* I was showin'…that. *On the real*: I always care how you feel."

Patrice: "You got a strange way of gettin' it across—pushing me out of the way to get the door open."

Merk: "Whoa. I just sliiid you aside…smooth and gentle."

Patrice: "Liar. You just wanted *out*, regardless of me."

Merk: "You know, I almost believe you mean that. You think I'd do some'em, knowin' it would upset you? Nooo…no way. *And*, I know *you know* me better'n that."

Patrice: "So, what are you saying—it was all an act?"

Merk: "Uuh, *yeah*. How *could* it have been real? You know I care about your feelin's. In fact, I care about 'em more than anything else I can think of. More than *hot wings*, baby. And you know me and *hot wings*—get that cold beer goin', girly-girl. Shaaat!"

Patrice: "Man, you are as slippery as grease."

Merk: "*Grease?* I hope you mean *olive oil*. Grease is some bad shit—go straight to the veins and arteries is what they tell me. …Hey, you know the *Merk*. I got to make a joke, when I can. What can lighten a mood better than a good ol' *jokey-joke?*

"Treecie, believe this: You got a nigga so he can't *think* straight, half the time. You got my heart *and* my soul. It's good that I can make light *er'y* now and then. You don't want no nigga

	act like he a *love sick puppy* all day. Women get tired of that dumb shit, ain't it—?"
Patrice:	"Oh, God. Just stop it. I don't know why I put up with some of your ways—like now, when you're trying to fluff stuff over.

      "Now, let's skip that oily talk. ...I'm sure you know what's next: *Who...the...hell...*were those *limousine people?!*"

Back in Cambridge, it was the end of the spring semester at the university where Zatorah Leeman taught. Now, with the posting of students' grades complete, a cadre of professors gathered for discussions. Free of instructional obligations, their full attention could be focused on research, planned for summer. They comprised a unique collection of higher-level educators within the state of Massachusetts. In addition to being psychology professors, each had a special interest in the *paranormal*.

Zatorah was new among the group of four. Accompanying her at the discussion table were Drs. Emily Noam, Mitchell Barcotti, and Adam Price. Dr. Zatorah Leeman's solemn commitment to the project to be undertaken was just three weeks old. By now, only the slightest doubt remained with her, as to the wisdom of her decision to join the collaboration.

Three factors accounted for Leeman's relative conviction that the course she'd chosen was justified. The first concerned scores she attained on the *PRI*, as administered and interpreted by developers of that so-called *Paranormal Receptivity Inventory*. On it, she was deemed a good candidate for conducting research in the field. The second factor involved a reading she received, in consultation with an East Cambridge *psychic*. Third, was the fact that the research was to be conducted in Richmond, Virginia. She felt, somehow that Richmond was beckoning her.

Emily Noam's excitement seeped through her composed demeanor, as she spoke to the other professors. As a group, they felt the classic élan of explorers about to embark on a mission.

"Our Richmond counterparts got the nod from their *appropriations* people yesterday. So, the project has official approval on both ends, now. Can you believe it? It's finally a definite *go*."

"Outstanding," Dr. Price added. "After two years of preliminary investigation, planning, and wrangling at board meetings, it's gotten official approval. So, I guess the gamble of leaving all our equipment in Richmond paid off. Having that stuff driven back and forth would be a pain. All that's left, now, is to plan for the flight. I assume the school in Richmond is committed to our complete accommodation."

"It had better be," responded Dr. Barcotti. "It's all covered in the project proposal."

Dr. Noam gave assurance: "Everything's set folks. So, Zatorah, are you as jazzed about this venture as the rest of us? I see you've been following but you haven't said much."

"If *jazzed* includes *quietly thrilled to the bone*, then I'm there. I'm still dealing with the honor and wonder at your group's having chosen me as a research partner."

"You fit the bill, *Z*. We think you conform to the proverbial 'mold,' *and* you passed all the tests. Rest assured it wasn't *eny-meny-miny-mo*. What's more, you have a Richmond connection. Who knows what, even small, benefit it might accrue?" It was Barcotti speaking.

"Oh, and Em," he continued, addressing Dr. Noam, "Mitch, here, tells me you've actually spoken to the guy in Richmond who is to be our collaborative *spiritual guide* in the project. What, *sense*, at the risk of sounding overly immersed in the *paranormal*, did you get of him?"

"Over the phone, our Mr. Evan Nesset comes across as the typical *spirit-hunting* eccentric. The project's interest in him, of course, lies in his notoriety in Richmond as a 'channeler' of the energies of *spirits*, to and from the *spiritual* world. Each of us is familiar with one aspect of his credentials—his having helped local police with unsolved crimes."

The passing of a month did little to dim the memory and awe of witnesses, in Gilpin Court, to the limousine spectacle that night. As for the rest of the city-housing residents, fanciful and excited descriptions of the event kept the imagined scenes alive in their minds. At one extreme, accounts placed Merquan Paler in fraternity with some number of Richmond police officers. At the other, he was aligned with mid Atlantic mobsters respected by police departments along the east coast, including Richmond.

Had someone else in Gilpin Court been at the center of the witnessed event, interest in it may have faded sooner. But, to many residents and occupants in the community, Paler had a sort of exotic air about him. Even at a youthful 22 years, he was, nevertheless, a man of contrasts. He seemed equally comfortable in the company of Gilpin's worst criminals *and* with those working hard to improve their condition. The quality of being both *hood -typical* and *-atypical* inspired mild enthrallment in those around him.

In addition to the gifts of charisma, intellect, and loyal friends within Gilpin, Merquan had two other attributes that fascinated observers. Some number of people saw what they took as evidence of a strange sort of *protection* accompanying him. Paler's periodic escapes from tight scrapes had been events much marveled at, within the community.

At the less fortuitous extreme, the occasions of epileptic seizure Merquan Paler underwent were also widely known. At the age of eight, he began to experience those episodes, and, to date, they remained sudden and unpredictable. In Merquan's sixteenth year, his Medicaid physicians issued a stern warning to his mother and him. Until the seizures were under control, Merquan must never operate a motor vehicle.

When Merquan had to travel an appreciable distance beyond *Jackson Ward*, he did so, usually, by bus. This was one such day. With bus fare that Patrice provided, he walked to a stop on Chamberlayne Parkway. Situated west-of-center, within north Jackson Ward, the street allowed transit, north, along busy, Chamberlayne Avenue. A southward commute took travelers to, and beyond, one of the city's most central roadways: Broad Street. It was in the latter direction that Merquan designed to go.

That which prompted the excursion was a call that came two days prior. Lew Priola had another "job" for his valued *Pisano*. Always he got Merquan's agreement to proceed, days in advance of a meeting date. It illustrated how important it was that Merquan be certain of his availability, at the desired time.

The service Priola paid for always took place at lunchtime, within the Omega Hotel's *Omega Café*. Paler's attendance and performance on these occasions assured that he'd walk away with about a *grand* in twenty and fifty dollar bills. The money, Paler knew, must be managed judiciously, as the "job" only came up, on average, every four to six weeks.

When his bus turned onto Broad Street, Merquan took note of two familiar figures among a group waiting at the next stop. Boarding the bus, it was not long before the nearly inseparable cousins saw *Merk* sitting at a window, in the back. Trayon Twine began the greetings:

Trayon:	"Hey, my nigga! What up?"
Merquan:	"Chillin', chillin'. Goin' down to do a job for the man with the *paper*. On the real, I'm just livin' day to day. "Hey, Neil...what's up wit'cha? You still holdin' it down?"
Neil:	"I'm *bum*, baby. Just tryin' to be like you, when I can."
Merquan:	"It ain't hard. Smoke a little more weed, you'll be there. Y'all niggas headed for *Omega*, too?"

Trayon:	"Yeah, we cleanin' Priola's limos again this week. One thing about that bastard: If he trust you, he'll pay you good. Grouchy somma-bitch, though. Can't tell 'im shit—think he know every fuckin' thing."
Neil:	"Sure got niggas' attention, when Priola and them *GQs* that Tray call *Greeks* rolled up in the hood that night."
Merquan:	"That was some decent shit you did back there, Tray. Ain't nothin' like havin' your homies watchin' your back—like you and cuz. This weekend—I'm'a hook y'all niggas up with some potent shit. Belie'e dat!"
Trayon:	"We always *down* for some good smoke. But it wasn't nothin'. Like I tell Neil: you born with them *nine lives*, my nigga. Some'em would'a come up, one way or anotha'."
Neil:	"Even with *nine lives*, I think you should start *strappin'* a *nine-millie*, just in case."
Merquan:	"I don't know about them *nine lives*, but this is *fo'sho'*: If there *is* such a thing as *guardian angels*, that nigga couldn't be more *Mack-dog* than y'all two *chillers*. Belie'e dat! ...And that *nine*, Neil? I'm gon' say you probably *all the way* right."

Once it reached Cary Street, the bus ridden by the three stopped a half block pass their destination, the *Omega Suites* complex. At a corner of the massive hotel building, Merquan and the cousins parted ways. Paler continued on Cary Street to a front entrance. Detouring along one of Richmond's numbered streets "Tray" and Neil headed to a utility access-point of the hotel. When they reached their usual entrance, Neil inquired:

"What you think it is, *on the real*, that *Merk* be doin' for Priola?"

"I ain't never figured the shit out," answered Trayon. "Like I said before, you can tell he don't want to talk about it, if you bring it up. So, I just let it go. Fuck it—who cares? Sometimes a nigga just got'a mind his own business. You know what I'm sayin'?"

"I *feel* you, Cuz. Must be a good hustle, though—only last a hour or two. He said that, his-self. Next thing you know *Merk*'s spottin' niggas a *c-note* here and another *ball* there and sharin' in the profits, plus his money back.

"And me and you," Neil continued, "we come in here at twelve, bustin' our asses, cleaning them limousines, inside and out."

Trayon replied in low voice: "Yeah, we cleanin'. And anything we find that look funny, we only need to be smart enough to take it to Priola and let him deal with it. And for doin' that, the fat man makes our checks a lot bigger than they'd be if we was washing cars somewhere else. Am I right?"

"Right as a discount *brick*, my nigga."

Chapter Two

I N THE YEAR prior to induction of its newest member, the research team investigated eleven U.S. cities, at night, for *paranormal* activity. After the tenth exploration, which involved Richmond, Virginia, the decision had been virtually made. In each case, the objective was to detect ghostly presences, lasting more than a few fleeting seconds.

As with other cities, a week of monitoring Richmond locations transpired, using research vans outfitted with *paranormal-energy* detection equipment. At the end of that week, the researchers all but declared the preliminary *search* phase of the project terminated. Richmond, above all other cities studied, was chosen for formal research. But that was several months past. Now, in the last week of May, the Cambridge and Richmond teams were a day away from uniting, to start their work, in earnest. The investigators worked diligently to bring their project to its next stage.

On this Monday, the Leemans completed the final stages of packing Zatorah's luggage. Peter took part of the day off from work to be with his wife, in the final hours before her flight. All that remained of his "labor of love" this morning was for him to drive Zatorah to Logan Airport and be with her until she boarded the plane.

When the house phone rang, Peter answered and gave cordial greeting to Zatorah's mother, Torasine Heinz. After a brief chat, he passed the phone to Zatorah. Positioned in "hearing distance" of Zatorah's voice, he took in one side of the conversation between mother and daughter.

Torasine:	"So, it's *full speed ahead*, I see. My one and only child has no regard for her mother's advice."
Zatorah:	"Now, Mother, you know that's not true. I've always listened to you and almost always obeyed. But this time…I just have to see where this will lead."
Torasine:	"You couldn't stay in East Cambridge and hunt for ghosts? You have to go to Richmond, Virginia? We have a *Richmond* right here in Massachusetts, you know. I'm sure our *spirits* are a far more sophisticated and engaging *lot* than those tired old souls, in Richmond, Virginia."
Zatorah:	"Mother, you know it's not just study of the *supernatural* that draws me there. Richmond, Virginia is where I was born. I feel a *connection* with the city. I've *always* felt it, but I never before had a compelling enough reason to visit.
	"And Lord knows, whenever I broached the topic with you, you always said revisiting Richmond was a great waste of time and money."
Torasine:	"I applaud myself for dispensing such good counsel. Shame on those nutty *ghost hunters* for inducting you into their farce."
Zatorah:	"Mother, you know, the more I think about it, the more convinced I am that you are keeping something from me, where Richmond is concerned. As Shakespeare's Hamlet said, *'Thou dost protest too much.'* It makes me

	suspicious. I just get the feeling there's more to our connection to Richmond than you tell me."
Torasine:	"Well, my poor misguided daughter, you're mistaken. If only I had a quote from *Shakespeare* to underscore it. But, I repeat: There's no more than what I've always told you.
	"I got married in Richmond during a brief stay in the so-called *river city*. While there, I gave birth to a beautiful, wonderful, curly haired angel. Soon after, I discovered the cheating ways of your despicable father—may he rest in peace. And, not very long after that, I left that uninspired municipality—never to return. End of story.
	"Richmond was a dreadful—and fortunately brief—interlude. It has the sole significance of a bad memory."
Zatorah:	"I want to visit the places you traveled about, in Richmond, with me in tow. ...Why?—I don't know, but it seems important. The place I was born, the home you brought me back to, the streets you walked carrying me, stores, homes of friends, restaurants—you must remember most of them.
	"You know—you ought to come to Richmond, while I'm there, and let's visit those places together! Wouldn't that be fantastic?!"
Torasine:	"You want to drag a tired old woman through the avenues of her torment, of thirty-two years passed?"
Zatorah:	"Oh, Mother, people mistake us for sisters sometimes, and you're no more tired than I am."
Torasine:	"I would think you'd be invested in keeping it that way, rather than put me through a *trial of*

reminiscence that is sure to turn my hair white, promote wrinkles, and brittle my bones.

"But…if you simply care nothing for my health, my fragile emotional state…."

Zotorah: "Okay, okay…you win. I won't have your self-induced deterioration on my hands. …So, may I go out on a limb and ask what our address was on the day of my birth?"

Torasine: "Why, of course. I'm not totally unreasonable, Zatorah. It was in the 2100 or 2200 block, even, of Monument Avenue."

Zatorah: "Gee, that's it? No specific address?"

Torasine: "It was thirty-two years ago. Work with me here—the old girl is doing the best she can. … Oh, you never finished telling me about that session with the *psychic*. Believe me, I'm not sure I even want to ask, but curiosity has taken hostage of my *reason*.

"So, you were given a reading, and the *charlatan* claimed to get a *vision* of you inside a Richmond hospital. Seems to me, that should have deterred you, rather than fuel your resolve to push forward."

Zatorah: "Not *inside* the hospital, Mother—outside it. She saw me among a crowd of people watching someone enter that hospital. But the building was filled with staff and patients who were, uh, both dead and alive at the same time."

Torasine "And, Zatorah, that isn't enough to tell you that you were listening to a crackpot? *Dead and alive at the same time.* I could have come up with something better than that, in my first day *training* as a sorcerer. And which of Richmond's hospitals was it? Was the Gypsy astute enough to name names?"

Zatorah: "Well, that's sort of a problem, too. She gave the name St. Philips Medical Center, but I checked with the researchers there, in Richmond. There's no such center or hospital listed."

Torasine: "Now, you see what I've been telling you? Richmond is full of *dead-ends*—past and present. But, you know, dear, I feel inclined to make a sort of peace offering.

"I have an old map of Richmond I used to use, way back then. It was printed sometime in the 1970s. For what it's worth, it'll show Richmond before whatever recent changes in topography were made."

Zatorah: "The point?"

Torasine: "Well, you're partly going there in search of 'the way it was.' In spite of my lighthearted disparagements, I'm aware that Richmond has changed a lot, with many improvements, over the years. A thing like that is bound to throw camouflages into your search."

Zatorah: "Well, as much as I appreciate the map, it doesn't quite match an agreement from you to accompany me, at some point, in our former *city on the James*."

Torasine: "See? There you have it. I offer you my favorite old, paper, *street* map, and you regard it as having less value than an ill-tempered escort."

Zatorah: "What *was* I thinking?"

Two hours later, at the Logan terminal, the Cambridge paranormal studies team convened. In another half hour, they would be boarding the flight to Richmond, Virginia.

Patrice Keeper and her seven- and six-year olds, Shar`dey and Markee, un-boarded the transit bus, just ahead of Merquan. Together, from the stop at the 400 block of North 9ᵗʰ Street,

21

the four headed to their destination. The short walk took them through a shaded and manicured expanse, with areas for sitting made of marble and concrete, and with paved walkways. Those frontal grounds belonged to Richmond's central Department of Social Services. Patrice had an appointment to visit with her caseworker there.

An hour later, the Keepers and Paler were on their way east, on Marshall Street, from the Social Services building. Their destination was one of Patrice's favorite street vendors, before it packed up and left for the day. Having arrived in time to make the desired purchases, the group walked to a nearby lot on Marshall Street. The concourse sat midway between 12th and College Streets and was provided outside structures of stone, for sitting. Suddenly Merquan began to get the familiar sensation that came over him just before onset of epileptic seizure.

Over the past two years, Patrice and her children had learned to be subtly vigilant of signs that presaged one of Merquan's seizures. Noting his pause, in walking, they went into practiced action. Their combined efforts prevented him from falling, un-braced, to the hard pavement.

The Keepers held onto Merquan as best they could, setting down their own food and drink, and guiding his descent. Around the four, numerous passersby stopped or slowed their gait to get a sense of what was happening. Toting Merquan by his armpits, Patrice and her children impelled him toward a nearby bench. To the gathering onlookers she uttered an explanation:

"He'll be all right in a minute. He has these seizures once in awhile. If someone can help us get him on the bench—. He always comes out of it after a minute."

Ascending the incline of East Broad Street, the airport taxi-van rode westward, from its previous turnoff from Interstate 95. The destination of its occupants was a site among a complex of school and medical buildings, nearby. These edifices serve the designs of joint institutions called Virginia Commonwealth University (VCU) and the Medical College of Virginia (MCV).

Familiar with Richmond streets, the taxi driver determined that the best turn-off, into the MCV-VCU maze, was onto College Street. A left turn, next, at Marshall Street, brought the taxi riders to a corner of Marshall, where 13th Street once intersected.[1] There, the driver stopped briefly.

The aim was to provide his passengers a view of the scene playing out in the open expanse on the opposite side of Marshall Street. After some seconds, Zatorah Leeman requested to un-board the van to view more closely the person whose welfare garnered concern from the crowd.

The scene within the small concourse triggered a recall for Zatorah. Back in East Cambridge, Massachusetts the *psychic* had described a lot where two hospitals joined, forming a 90 degree angle. In front, were circular patterns of paved walkways and a grassy area, ascetically designed and maintained.

A man, Madam Lu had said, would rise from a fallen position and travel with a host toward the columned entrance of the hospital on the right. The medical building into which the two entered she identified as *St. Philip.* Inside, all were mysteriously both dead and alive.

Standing amid the small crowd, Zatorah shifted her gaze among three sites. She noted the man lying, unconscious, on the concourse bench. She viewed the circular pattern of pavement bricks stretching several square-yards, in area. She took in the stone entranceway, straight ahead, that stood alone, without an attached building. It appeared that an edifice had been meticulously removed, leaving only a portion of its front.

It seemed obvious that the entire concourse was a monument honoring a bygone medical facility.[2] Etched in the stone entrance-frame were the words "Dooley Hospital." But, nowhere among the group of memorial structures did Zatorah see the name mentioned by Madam Lu—that is, "St. Philip."

Before the Cambridge group's taxi had even made the turn onto Marshall Street, a part of Merquan's mind was on excursion. It had split off and was visiting a different "order" of time. With the latest onset of epileptic seizure, he made the crossover, breaching temporal barriers. In this altered state, Paler accomplished time-travel, *psychically.*

Ensconced in the new environment, his mind functioned as a monitor, only—within a *host* central nervous system. For the duration of the altered state, he was a mere passenger within the mental system of one who had functioned, in another time. Merquan's new awareness came without physical sensation, although he perceived all that his host perceived. The part of his mind undergoing time-travel also *recorded* the perceptions.

In Paler's experience, equal lengths of time, in different time references, typically do not match, on a minute by minute basis. Five minutes, in present time, for example, might translate to five hours or five months, in a past time—and vice versa. When Merquan lost consciousness, in present time, amid onlookers, equal intervals of time, present and past, were not in sync. Seconds passed for those watching him twitch occasionally atop the stone bench. In Merquan's *past* time state, he had been monitoring the experience of his host for several minutes.

Merquan was able to determine that his host, this time, was Beatrice Bennett. She sat on a bench in the manicured expanse that faced two adjoining hospitals. Just as Beatrice was employed as a nurse, so were the two ladies accompanying her. Unlike Beatrice, they worked at the Dooley Hospital which was positioned left of the one that employed Beatrice. Typically, at midday, at this location, the three took a short break from their clinical duties. Their conversation was monitored by Beatrice's psychic visitor:

Bennett: "I see things the two of you don't see. I've seen things the two of you *haven't* seen—and for that matter, that *most* ain't seen. We will never be truly free until we wake up to some truths."

O'Brien: "Bea, it don't happen overnight. Slavery didn't end over night, but it ended. Girl, we're a whole lot freer than we used to be."

Hughes: "If you're talking about prejudice, Bea—that may be something that never ends. I don't believe folks can ever be completely free of prejudice."

Bennett: "I'm not talking about prejudice. I'm not talking about slavery. I'm not talking about anything got to do with white people. You don't understand the setup of this world, for *colored* people."

O'Brien: "Bea, we live, we do the best we can while we're alive, and we die. And if we're *right* with Jesus, we spend the *next* life in *glory*. That's *real* freedom. What *else* is there, for anybody? If you're not talking about anything to do with white people, or *heaven*, when we die—what other kind of *freedom* is there?"

Bennett: "Before you went to Dooley, you two used to work right over there with me. You saw the children. You saw 'em when they were born, you saw the signs of how they lived, you saw 'em when, sometimes, they died. It never dawned on you what's goin' on?"

Hughes: "Bea, you got this way of talking *around* a point. What exactly are you saying?"

Bennett: "I'm trying to get you to think about what you saw and what you see. I can't tell you exactly what I see until you, at least, begin to see things yourselves.

"Look, the little ones we patched up and sent home—what happens to so many of 'em when they grow up? You won't see 'em over there at Dooley, by that time. But, that's when I'll see 'em, again, at St. Philip.

"Gunshot wounds, stab wounds, general deterioration, disease[3]—sure, we'll patch 'em up and send 'em back for more of what they came in here with, or send 'em to the morgue.

"A lot of 'em, once grown up, will get their only meals from the *colored* poorhouse,[4] up Fifth Street in the Ward. Some of those—and others—will end up in the city jail, down the road.[5] That big, red-brick Virginia *pen* will be the final home for another bunch."

O'Brien: "I thought you loved being a nurse at St. Philip. Now, it sounds like you're dissatisfied, or overwhelmed or something."

Hughes: "Maybe you just need a vacation, Bea."

Bennett: "Maybe I see what my mother saw after she had me, and what my grandma saw, after she had her. It's a *trap* for colored folks, Liz...Winnie. It's a *trap* and we don't even see it."

O'Brien: "God bless it, Bea, I'm gonna' pin you down, one way or another, and get to the bottom of what you're talking about. What in heaven's name is this *trap*, who set the *dad-bum* thing, and who's gettin' caught in it? ...And be *specific*."

Bennett: "The trap is *human nature*, Winnie. We set the trap ourselves through ignorance. Who gets caught in the trap? Colored folks who do a lot of *free livin'* and little *free thinkin'*. Livin' free— *doin'* and *not thinkin'*—gets us in a trap."

Noting the time, the women put their conversation "on hold," to pick up later. Nurses Hughes and O'Brien walked to the marble stairs of the Dooley Hospital entrance. It had opened in 1920 as a facility caring for children.[6] It was to St. Philip Hospital [7] that Nurse Bennett strode.

Beatrice made her way, within the immaculate hospital, to her work station. Through her eyes, Merquan Paler took note of the year printed on a newspaper, inside St. Philip. It was 1924.

Paler's experience of monitoring aspects of his hosts' world had no unpleasant side effects for him. It was similar to riding in a vehicle as a passenger, undetected, alongside a driver. In terms of duration, it had, to him, a timeless feel, like watching scenes of an all-absorbing cinematic film.

As usual, when the experience was coming to an end, Paler's sensation was that of disengaging from a vivid dream. In this last *past-time* reality, he had memory of accompanying Beatrice Bennett for nearly an hour's time. Returning now to *present* time, those reflections were starting gradually to disintegrate. Paler could actually feel himself mentally trying to hold on to the memory. But it was to no avail. The final images of it, in his mind, faded as the former *splitting*, of his *psychic* self, now underwent reversal.

Continuing at rest on that bench, within the concourse, halfway between College and 12th Streets, Paler slowly opened his eyes. His immediate realization was that he'd had another seizure and was being watched over by both his adopted family and some concerned strangers. Adjusting himself to sit upright without support of helpers, Paler glanced around at the onlookers. One he took special note of was a woman staring back at him with an odd look of perplexity.

In typical "hood" brashness, Paler was near to blurting out one of his stock inquiries to someone ogling him after a seizure: *What's the problem—you never seen a somma-bitch die and come back to life?* His delivery, however, was interrupted by Patrice's comment:

"See? It didn't last but a minute." She was assuring the onlookers. She continued, addressing Merquan. "I can see you're all right. We caught you...and didn't let you fall or anything. You dropped your sandwich, though. But look. Shar'dey's coming with another one, now, and a soda. You know we gonna' look out for you."

Paler started to smile and nod his head, as he spoke: "Yeah, y'all my *lookouts, f' sho'*. Shit, a nigga be lost without his three *lookouts*. Y'all know I appreciate all this—right Markee... Shar'dey?" Receiving the children's smiling nods, Paler continued, addressing the onlookers:

"All right the rest of y'all that's standin' 'round. The show's over. The *Merk* done rose from the grave, again, like the *beast that won't die*. All y'all are excused, now. Thanks for the...care and concern, but a nigga want to eat in peace."

As nearly all the smiling onlookers graciously dispersed, one, Zatorah, remained to venture a brief proposal:

"I apologize for staring earlier," she began, "but I get this odd feeling of knowing you from somewhere." It was untrue, but she couldn't tell Paler she believed he was a significant figure in a *psychic reading* she'd had.

"You don't look like somebody I might'a robbed, when I was younger."

"*Merk*, you're just a nut," Patrice interjected. "Don't pay him any mind. This man might say anything out his mouth."

"No, it's quite all right. I can see by his rapport with the children, he must be a special guy. Look, I know of people here who do research in treatment of seizures. Let me give each of you my card. I'm Zatorah Leeman, as it says there. If it strikes your interest sometime within the next few weeks that I'm in Richmond, give me a call. And—. Oh, there's the van coming back to retrieve me. Bye, now. Take care."

Zatorah could tell by Merquan's expression that he wasn't up for pleasant greetings and formal exchanges of names. When she was gone and Merquan had finished his sandwich and soda, he walked to the nearest waste can. Turning to Patrice, he gestured toward the hand in which she carried Zatorah's business card.

"I'll take that," he said. "You ain't the one with the *big ep*, so you don't need it." He gently removed the card from Patrice's hand. "Watch close, sweetheart," he continued, "and see where I put *dumb* shit, for safekeepin'." With that last remark he tossed his own, and her, card to the bottom of the deep waste basket.

"She did seem like a nice lady, though, *Merk*."

"Yeah, Treecie—a nice lady whose elevator don't go all the way to the top floor...if you know what I mean."

Zatorah returned to the company of her travel companions. In between exchanges, they all took in sights of the MCV-VCU complex of buildings, as the taxi maneuvered through traffic. Arriving at an MCV parking deck, the commuter van's passengers reanimated their focus on Zatorah's brief departure, earlier.

"Well," Zatorah commented lightly, "if it were anyone else but the three of you, I would be embarrassed to come out with it. But, if anyone can appreciate prognostication, it's you. So—yes, the whole, how shall I say, *aura* of the area matched the description Madam Lu gave in her reading. Taking in that scene—and the scenery—from the van window, I knew I had to get a closer look."

"Well, I certainly can see one-to-one relationships between Madam Lu's description and the sight there. Of course, we're missing the part about the man being escorted to the hospital. Or did that happen, too, when the rest of us were circling the block? Come to think of it, I recall some kind of medical building to the right of the paved area." It was Professor Price's comment.

"No. That aspect of the reading is still a mystery. The young man lying on the bench did not appear to be at the concourse for the purpose of visiting a hospital. The seizure he experienced was, sort of, coincidental to the setting. ...But, as you said, Madam Lu's description of the site was right on target.

"My guess is that the area did have adjoining hospital buildings, at some time. I'll have to research it, when I get a chance. For now, what I've seen is further evidence that my decision to participate in the work here, in Richmond, is justified."

At the meeting, the Richmond agency working collaboratively with the Cambridge professors made its announcements. Therein, the remaining facets of research design were hammered out. Earlier, there had been some question as to the study's permanent name. That matter was settled, also. The total of eight professors would be conducting *Extranormal-*

Incidence Research & Investigation (EIRI), Richmond-based, at present. That which remained on the day's agenda was taking the Cambridge group to the place chosen for conducting the planned research.

A site, privately owned, was negotiated for the team's use—one with a convenient, central location in the city. Operations were to be planned and monitored from a building, constructed for the researchers, near 2nd and Byrd Streets. Within a well-maintained expanse of grass, bordering 2nd Street and showing a meandering brick road, a facility had been erected. As soon as the research was completed, the building was to be dismantled and the expanse returned to its original state.

Situated just north of the James River, the rolling, hilly estate provided a pleasing view of surrounding areas. Southward, it looked out on the Robert E. Lee Bridge, stretching across the river. The view north and west showed a skyline below which could be seen some of Richmond's most attractive architecture. Southeast, in a steep decline of terrain, was a Richmond landmark, due to its antiquity, called Gamble's Hill Park.

Essential implements of research had been left in Richmond, by the Cambridge workers, from those earlier, preliminary investigations. Included were vans equipped with specialized *wave-emission* and *energy-detection* devices. By day, these would be parked on the grounds provided the researchers for their operations. At night, the vans would prowl designated areas of the city, stopping periodically to bathe a locale in streams of electromagnetic particle-waves. Earlier investigations had identified places in Richmond showing concentrations of *extra-normal* energy—those of interest to the researchers.

The EIRI team wasted no time getting the present phase of study underway. As a central figure in the research to be conducted, the *spiritual medium*, Evan Nesset, was made aware of developments, as they occurred. It was now time for the researchers to meet with Nesset as an intact group. In preliminary investigations with an earlier version of the team, he had employed his gift of "channeling." Members watched as he seemed to enter into communication with *spiritual* entities. These were, or appeared to be, "called forth" with the aid of devices that detected *spiritual energy*, during bombardment by particle-waves.

The task, now, was that of working out a schedule with Nesset that outlined of his availability. By design, three investigation vans would travel, simultaneously, at night to selected areas of the city. Within each, equipment was poised to detect *extra-normal* conditions present. Riding with researchers in one of the vans, Nesset would be at hand, if apparatuses of the vehicle indicated a finding. If, on the other hand, either of the other two vans seemed to strike "pay dirt," then he could easily be transported to the scene.

Chapter Three

MERQUAN PALER STEPPED outside the Hill Street apartment—
the one he cohabited with his girlfriend and her two kids,
in north Jackson Ward. Walking the short distance to the corner
of Saint John and Hill, he found himself staring northward.
His focus this balmy morning was a tangle of weeds and other
growth, just visible beyond the boundary of housing units a
brief block in the distance. That which preoccupied him was
a vague sense of recall having source in an earlier seizure
episode.

Dimly, behind the wire fence separating brush from housing
units, his mind saw the image of a street with houses. The
"ghost" street within the steep declension of woods coursed
parallel to Hill Street. In a flash of remembrance, Paler saw the
name *Orange Street* and then the faint outline of a bleak edifice
labeled *Richmond Incinerator and Crematorium*. It seemed to
occupy a good part of a block's distance on Merquan's ghostly
Orange Street, from Saint John westward to Saint Paul.

Gradually, the vision in Paler's mind vanished. He felt no
alarm at any aspect of the brief visitation. It was just a fact
of life for him that he experienced phantom recall episodes,
now and again. He took it in stride, just as he did the epileptic
seizures. For this latest one, he responded in typical fashion by

shaking his head and taking a long drag from his cigarette. To himself he thought: *I sure can daydream some crazy shit.*

There were only a handful of Merquan's tendencies that really irritated Patrice. One was his tendency to try to smooth over an act of his that had angered her. Another was his preference not to carry a cell phone, in his travels. It was a practice bordering on bizarre, for his generation. It irritated Patrice to no end.

Given her possessiveness, where he was concerned, Patrice found relief in a certain reality, in spite of Merquan's *no-cell-phone* policy. He had proven to be unwaveringly scrupulous in reporting his plan to go one place or another. Courtesy of such candidness, Patrice could, when she so desired, make a well-placed call, or series of them. Thereby, she confirmed his whereabouts and could usually gain speedy access of him at such time that, in her mind, a "need" had arisen.

On this morning, as Patrice had been made aware, Merquan was en route to his mother's housing unit, some blocks away. In addition to Bonita Paler, Patrice had some knowledge of most residing in that 1000 block of Hickory Street. Thus, she felt quite at peace, knowing that for the next hour or so, at least, Merquan was comfortably within reach.

Another source of her calm were the separate gifts of $500, $200 and $100 he recently contributed to the household, to offset monthly expenses. As she was aware, it was a lot more than other state-aid dependent young women in her situation could expect from their live-in love interest.

Arriving at the intended address, Merquan turned the handle on the screen-door and entered the unit. As usual, when she knew he was coming, Bonita Paler left the lock disengaged. Once inside, the twenty-two year old strode through his mother's residence, as if he lived there, himself.

"Hey, Ma," greeted Merquan, calling out, tersely, into the kitchen. Even though it had been a full day earlier that he last visited, Merquan acted as if it had been just a few hours. He passed right by the kitchen entrance, moving toward the back area. He hollered, again, toward the doorway of one of the two bedrooms, partly open:

"Where are the two *she-devils?* I know you two ain't still in bed, with Ma in there cookin' like a *Merry Maid*, for y'all. Get up, *zombie-girls*. Pretend you got some life in you!"

"Go away," called out a little voice.

"Yeah, go away. It's Sunday, *Merk*," another, slightly older, voice iterated. And don't you come in our room, or I'm tellin' Auntie Nita."

"This is the thanks I get for tryin' to help you girls grow into respectful and productive citizens. It's all right, though. If you want to be a couple'a six and eight year old bums, then *be* it."

"*Merk*, you gon' still get us a puppy, like you said?"

"As soon as I find one that's already housebroke. I ain't givin' you two no puppy and have him worry Ma to death, 'till y'all get him trained. …Which one of you can clean up dog pee and poop, until he gets housebroke?" Silence ensued.

Wryly, the girls' cousin commented: "Yeah, just like I thought."

Olivia and Raynell, Merquan's only two cousins, were in Bonita Paler's legal care. This was the arrangement since their mother's passing, five years prior. The girls had no recall of the woman who had given birth to them, that is, Bonita's sister. So, from ages three and eight months, respectively, "Auntie Nita" was the only mother they knew.

Presently, Merquan relocated to the kitchen, where he took a seat at the table. While his mother prepared, simultaneously, breakfast and the stew that would be evening dinner, he conversed with her lightly. At the same time, he reached into his pocket, unfolding five twenty-dollar bills. The discourse shifted to that of the money:

Merquan: "It ain't much to give every couple a' weeks. Anytime I got some extra *doves*, they yours."

Bonita:	"You know you don't have to do this, Quan. You go ahead and keep it for yourself. You're probably gonna' need it, later."
Merquan:	"No fussin' now, Ma. I give you part of any money I can get my hands on, when I can. You ain't had no easy life, Ma. You ain't got epilepsy like me, but you got some'em that's worse, in a way. Ain't much worse than feelin' *depressed* most of the time—and havin' to take them pills."
Bonita:	"It's not too bad. I make it. Well, if you're sure, it sure will help. It always helps—a whole lot. But I won't take it from Treecie and the kids. You got her squared-away, right?"
Merquan:	"No doubt. I take care of mine, you know that. These other monies I got here? I lend to *homies* I can trust, to set 'em up, for awhile, so they can *eat*, for awhile. Each *ball* I put out there, I get it back—*and* with a little interest.
	"But, you know how I do. I watch my *paper*. And when the money comes back, I share it with you and the little late-risers, back there."
Bonita:	"You're a good son, Quanie. I'd be lying if I said I don't worry about you, sometimes. I know it's my fault that you got that epilepsy. Something happened—something went wrong when I was pregnant. Your father…I shouldn't have…."
Merquan:	"Aw, Ma—don't bring that bastard up, again. Let him rot in whatever prison that's got him."

Whenever the topic of Marquan's father came up between them, Bonita Paler felt emotional pain. There were facts about the man who was only a blur in Merquan's memory that she had not revealed. Her discovery, after some years, of attempts by his biological father to contaminate her pregnancy, horrified her. In spite of the occasional inclinations to share with Merquan what she knew, in the end she was unable to do it.

Since the time that Merquan was six, she had told him only part of the story, as she knew it. While he was at school, the authorities came to their home, on a mission to take away, forever, the man who had sired her only child. Some sort of intuition had compelled Mercer Paler to circle around their residence that day, before entering. In doing so, he postponed, yet again, capture by authorities. Mercer callously absconded within the week.

For years afterward, young Merquan would study the name listed as "birthfather" on his birth certificate, "Mercer Quinn Paler." Witnessing her son's frequent study of his father's name and feeling the boy's longing for communication with his dad was traumatic for Bonita.

Now, several years later, it was Merquan who showed disinclination to have the topic of his father further explored. He supposed, from some of his mother's less guarded comments, that the senior Paler must have done some unspeakable thing to her. Monitoring his mother's emotional state over the years, he assumed that her bouts with severe depression might be traced to experiences with Mercer.

Merquan initiated an abrupt change of subject:

Merquan:	"I still miss Aunt Nea. She was *out there*, from what I remember, but more fun than three PlayStations."
Bonita:	"I thought *I* would die when she died. Tenea was my baby sister. The sun rose and set on that girl, as far as I was concerned."
Merquan:	"It was always, to me, so *crazy* how different the two of you were. *Auntie* was a *firecracker*. Seems like she just had to be everywhere, and know everybody, and do everything she found excitin'. And then, finally, even drugs—that's

what brought her down, ain't it? She couldn't *roll* with it, like that.

"But, you, Ma—I'd bet a box of *hot wings* you ain't so much as ever *touched* a *doobie*. So how is that...?"

Bonita: "I never told you? Your Aunt Tenea was adopted. Your grandma and grandpa only had me. They adopted Tenea as a baby when I was five...almost six. So, you know, I guess it's *genetics*. They say we can be...*predisposed* to things through genetics."

Merquan: "That's *crazy*, Ma! It ain't never crossed my mind, she might'a been adopted. That's *crazy*."

Bonita: "But, that didn't mean anything to me. She was always my *Sister Nee-nee*, from the very beginnin', to the very end. Yeah, we were very different, though—night and day, but inseparable.

"When do you think you and Treecie might start expecting?"

Merquan: "Ma, I'm *scared* of babies. You know that. Any that's mine, I mean. I ain't tryin' to have no babies, Ma. I ain't for the hassle. Plus, Treecie's already got two. I don't even know why she wants another one."

Bonita: "I doubt that she *just* wants to have another baby. She wants another baby—with *you*. That girl's ridin' the *love-train*, at top speed."

Merquan: "Right now, Ma, I don't mean no harm, but if she come up pregnant—it ain't mine. 'Cause I do what I have to, to avoid that mess. I ain't *goin' there*, Ma—not no time soon. I'm just not feelin' that *baby* stuff. ...Nope—don't even want to talk about it."

Bonita: [chuckling] "Well, what if—?"

Merquan: "Aaahhh! *No*. ...No, Ma. No way."

Bonita: [still chuckling] "But suppose—."
Merquan: "Aaaahhh!"

Soon, Bonita Paler was reflecting on her own sentiment before she met Merquan's father. Regarding the prospect of having a baby, it had matched Merquan's exactly. But a whirlwind romance, and marriage, changed that.

In the next two hours, Merquan made his way to 1st Street and across the street-bridge that allowed travel over Interstate 95. His locale, at this point, was central Jackson Ward, and he continued to his destination. In the 200 block, west, of Jackson Street he was admitted into the residence of a long time acquaintance. There, a business transaction, of sorts, was made, involving a loan of $100. Merquan expected a return of $115 by the following Friday.

By 3:00 p.m. that Sunday, Merquan had completed two additional negotiations of the sort. One was transacted at a favored loitering spot in a 300 block of Leigh Street. The other deal "went down" in a small woodsy area between 5th Street and 4th Street, near Shockoe Hill Cemetery. All his business he tended to conduct within the historic boundaries of Jackson Ward.

Having covered over a mile distance, in all, Merquan was now walking along Bates Street, at the south wall of Shockoe Hill Cemetery. At the 2nd Street intersection with Bates Street, Merquan came upon Neil Twine. The twenty-year-old talked leisurely with four other Gilpin Court dwellers. As had been the case throughout Merquan's travel, free discourse sprang up between the encountered group and him.

Among the group of idlers, however, only Twine felt a genuine sense of deference, with regard to Paler. Merquan had engineered both Neil's and his cousin's employment as limousine cleaners at the downtown *Omega Hotel*. And he had accomplished it at a time when finding legitimate work was a big challenge.

After a time, Merquan began a departure from the social circle. Having discovered Paler's intended destination, Twine gave his own "so-longs" to the group. Talk between the two resumed, as they ambled northward on 2nd Street, toward the historic northern edge of Jackson Ward.

Neil:	"Damn, man, that fuckin' Joe, back there, done hit *bottom*, ain't he? One more nigga *whacked out* on *crack*."
Merquan:	"Bruh-man let it take him over. But, then, Joe been shootin' up as long as I can remember. Him and my aunt used to get high together. That shit goes back to when I was about... twelve—damn, *ten years*."
Neil:	"I'm glad you got me and *Cuz* that job with Priola. *Sellin'* to make a livin', like we was— shit, most niggas wind up *usin'* with the ones they sellin' to. That's how you get all fucked up, ain't it, man?"
Merquan:	"Homies got to know what they doin', Neil. Gots to keep your head, when you dealin' that *shit*. If not, the *stash* takes charge. Next thing you know, *crack* is dealin' the dealer."
Neil:	"You got a *sweet* hustle, f'sho, *Merk*—lendin' that *ball*. That and your hustle at *Omega* look like enough to hold you over good. I don't think a lot'a the homies could pull it off, though. If I tried it, *snakes* would be out the woodwork to *stiff me over*. Then, I'd wind up in jail for havin' to *spark* some niggas.
	"But you *do* that shit. How you know who to trust, like that? I bet a nigga ain't never tried to *roll over* you, after a loan. That's *crazy* how you do that shit."
Merquan:	"*Chillers* say I got *luck*. Maybe that's what it *is*. Some in the hood got that *insight* goin', so

maybe they're right. But, *luck* or not, I go by one rule: I never deal with niggas I don't know on the *up close*.

"Take, like, you and Tray—I been knowin' that nigga since we was runnin' through Baker Street School. Then, when you got old enough to *roll out* with him, I figured *like cuz, like cuz*. If I could trust him, I could trust you.

"So, when y'all were down, no money, and goin' to the *Moriah Church*, up there, for food, I staked y'all that first *ball*. And y'all niggas ain't never let me down once."

Neil: "*F'sho*. And now, workin' for Priola, we don't have to stay a step ahead of RPD and some jail time. You know what? *Cuz* and me—we thinkin' 'bout tryin' to do some classes at *Tech*, over there on Westwood."

Merquan: "No shit! That's what's up! What y'all niggas gon' be studyin'?"

Neil: "We'll figure out some'em. First, we got to get the shit set up. ...Man, you know what, *Merk*? You ought to try to get over there with us. Shiiiiit, smart as your ass is, you could become a goddamn...*engineer*, or some'em."

Merquan: "I don't know. I just ain't never liked school— sittin' up in class, bored as hell. GED classes almost put my ass to sleep."

Neil: "It ain't like *school*-school, where you in there with a bunch a niggas what come to class to play and shit."

Merquan: "I don't know. I might give it a shot, down the road. Right now, a lot'a niggas in the hood need that stake *e'ry* now and then. School would knock a hole in my game plan. What I do in the streets, and at *Omega*, takes *mad* focus—just ain't no room for more school-type studyin'."

Neil: "I bet Priola could get you some'em else, if you couldn't do that *lunch* thing—whatever it is. Hey, with your GED paper, you might can find a job in the *p.m.* You got brains, my nigga."

Merquan: "With my epilepsy, I don't trust workin' the kind'a job I'd be able to get, right now. But, maybe, later. Who knows?"

Neil: "It ain't none of my business, *Merk.* But, you know you could probably get a SSI check to live off, while takin' some classes."

Merquan: "I don't want that shit. Free checks don't do nothin' but make a nigga lazy. I do my hustle by studyin' the streets and people. If I can't make it with that, then fuck it. Bury my ass over there in *Shockoe.* Then come by and smoke a little *weed* over my grave, to show *mad respect.* You *feel* me, my nigga?"

Neil: "I'm feelin' you, *chiller.* Shit...you *da' man.* You *know your shit...f'sho'.*"

The two began walking westward on Hill Street, from 2nd Street, the surrounding area alive with the chatter of residents enjoying the outdoors. Reaching Saint James Street, they came upon Neil's cousin, Trayon, and two friends. One of the two young women present was talking on her "cell." Astoria had, in fact, spotted Merquan and Neil a minute before they were in speaking range. Immediately, she had called Patrice with an update:

"He's right here on Hill, Treecie, walking with Neil. Looks like he's probably on his way home. You want me to tell him anything?"

"No, if he's this close," sounded Patrice's voice, "he's probably on his way back. Thanks for the call, *Stori.* I can always count on you."

"It's what I *do,* girlfriend. Call me if you hear anything from De'Mon."

Chapter Four

B Y 11:30 P.M. the following Tuesday, a trio of EIRI vans cruised different areas of Richmond. The intent was that of detecting *paranormal* energy within selected environments. To drive the vans, the team had incorporated assistant psychology staff, from the college. Back at the South 2nd Street operations center, two members of the team monitored data sent electronically from the research vehicles. They also acted as coordinators of activities engaged in by members in the field.

The remaining six researchers were divided evenly among the three vans, accompanied by an equipment technician. Randomly, it was chosen within which vehicle the *psychic* "channeler" would travel. On this night Evan Nesset rode in the van labeled *EIRI-2*.

The focus-area of EIRI-2 was Richmond's historic *Tredegar Iron Works* site. Upon a visit there, in day hours, the EIRI team was thoroughly captivated by the panorama, in all directions. The façade that remains of the *Civil War* munitions foundry serves as the *open* part of the "Confederacy Museum," at that location.

Sitting on a north bank of the James River, *Tredegar* looks out on two equally stirring structures. One is the historic remnant of a Confederate bridge whose fiery last days[1] are recounted on plaques placed along it. The other is the base of the heavily travelled Robert E. Lee Bridge. As the researchers discovered, Tredegar Road forms a winding border between the Tredegar remnants and the river, and intersects with 5th Street at the latter's south-most end.

Typically off-limits to visitation, at sunset, the EIRI group received official permission to conduct investigations at the Tredegar site. Indeed, a major task of the Virginia school sponsoring the study was that of entering into agreements with city officials. Of necessity was gaining access to city locations of interest. Research planners had also to obtain approval to conduct the planned activities. Last, but not least, was the task of negotiating the cooperation of the Richmond Police Department.

In the preliminary study, the Tredegar site was thought to hold great promise, regarding detection of *extra-normal* energy. What needed to be seen, now, was whether or not Nesset could meaningfully "channel" those energy concentrations. Given the area's history, everyone expected that any *spiritual* auras found most likely remained from the highly "charged" last days of the Confederacy.

The locally renowned *spirit-channeler* had, in other investigative work, amazed collaborators with his interpretations of strange phenomena. His communications with "forces beyond" led to positive identification of individuals long buried, in anonymity. Other, equally daunting, mysteries were solved with his help—from missing items and pets to missing people. With that history, it was expected that Nesset's work with the EIRI team would prove to have forensic value.

The EIRI-2 van was allowed to park near the open-space, red brick ruins of the former *Tredegar* foundry. From the van's, open, slide-door streamed specialized electromagnetic radiation, produced by equipment in the vehicle. Watching the bluish glow of particle-wave bombardment within the open museum, the researchers thought the scene to be spectacularly eerie.

All around the "charged" expanse, Nesset executed erratic rambles, turns and sudden stops, following the ebb and flow of perceived energy concentrations. This, too, added to the scene's bizarre appearance.

A full fifteen minutes of such activity yielded disappointing results. In that time, Nesset received rich and varied "ghostly impressions." But his report was that the environment contained an *overabundance* of spiritual energy, such as to overwhelm the senses.

According to Nesset, *ghostly forces* churned and billowed and overspread the whole of the area and even spilled, at points, into the river. Such, he said, was the case all along the Tredegar roadway, wherever the EIRI van relocated, radiating its blue-hued emissions. In all, investigations were conducted for a quarter mile along the river bank.

Then a call from the 2nd Street operations center came. The EIRI-3 van was beaming *particle-waves* in an area of the city bordering a section called Oregon Hill. On the equipment's detection devices, the indicators were registering off the chart, virtually.

All team members had studied maps of Richmond, in order to have some familiarity with various locales. It registered to the Tredegar-location group that backtracking to the operations base would lead them to a roadway key to their new destination. The radio call indicated that EIRI-3 parked near the intersection of Belvidere and Spring Streets, accessible from 2nd Street. EIRI-2 raced to get Nesset to this new site that piqued the team's highest hopes for a significant finding.

In minutes, Nesset was, again, basking in the blue glow of waves, this time streaming in a grassy area at the western border of a large corporate building. It stretched nearly a block in four directions. Following the path of energy sensations he felt, Nesset moved along the edge of the great *Afton* edifice. His hands were partly outstretched as though he used them as antennas, to aid in perception.

Finally, Nesset stopped his ambling back and forth, and his face began to take on an expression indicating a mild trance. A signal was given, now, to turn on recording devices located inside the vans. In this way, within the small microphone Nesset wore were caught his low mutterings:

Nesset: "Sir, you're making me see that we're inside the Virginia State Penitentiary.[2] Is it so?" [A soft, mechanical sound followed briefly.]

Nesset: "Your name and a date, sir, if you can—I need them for our record. ...You're showing me what looks like C-E-L-A-P...R-I-L-8-1-9-2-1. ... You must move to another topic? Little time to spare. ...Yes, I feel your energy fading. Please, continue.

"There is another with you...who died days before you, at the penitentiary. I think I feel his *presence*. It's strong. ...It seems like you're showing me that he helped you die. ... But how—if he passed *before* you?

"The *other* wants to speak through you but needs to communicate with—. ...I lost your signal. Uh, what is this I see now? J-17...1-9-8-0-S-L-L? No? ...C-L-L? ...Z-L-L? Yes, I get it. That's the one.

"It's okay, I feel your energy fading. It's okay. Thank you, sir, for your presence. ...I...I...."

With that final utterance, team members saw that Nesset had become unsteady of foot, dropping to his knees. Full of both excitement and concern, the group rushed to tend to his condition. Each was, however, familiar with the usual conduct of Nesset's *channeling* exercises. Events, as vivid and intense as this one had been, always left him briefly languid.

Nesset's collaborators watched him gradually regain strength, with their aid. Each of the four EIRI workers on the scene marveled at the prospect of having made a "hit," on the very first night out. Back at the operations center, the two researchers manning equipment were equally thrilled. They had followed the course of events as it unfolded, with both audio and video devices recording Nesset's every move.

As everyone knew, a major task would be that of making intelligent sense of Nesset's vocalizations. In addition, it would be required that the interpretations be corroborated by factual information. That would all be accomplished in time. For now, nightly searches throughout the city would continue, with intent of gathering as much usable data as possible.

At noon the following Saturday, Merquan and Patrice exited a taxi sitting in front of Patrice's housing unit. The vehicle was filled with the couple's groceries. With all the friends and associates with cars they had in Gilpin Court, the pair preferred not to prevail upon any of them for travel around the city. It was that kind of like-mindedness that contributed to their closeness and comfort with one another.

The fact that they shared similar viewpoints, however, didn't mean they were immune to occasional discord. Patrice had a couple of issues on her mind that she intended to broach with her paramour. She felt she needed only to wait until the time was right. With her two children presently visiting family members, and the groceries all taken in and put away, Patrice thought the proper moment had arrived.

Patrice:	"I don't understand why you can't tell me what you do for Priola, to earn that kind'a money, when he calls for you."
Merquan:	"I don't want you mixed up in it, not even a little. The less you know, the better—that way, you can't slip up and say anything…."
Patrice:	"*The less I know, the better?* What am I—a little *child?* Don't talk *down* to me, *Merk*. That's not right."

Merquan: "Suppose I told you I meet him at the hotel, a hour so, to *kill somebody he don't like*. Then, what?"

Patrice: "Then, I'd know you were lying. And if you *weren't* lying we couldn't be together no more, after that. And that's something I would need to know. I couldn't be with no *killer*."

Merquan: "I let you in on what I do *with* the money—the part left over after I give you yours. I make more money off it. Then I give you and Ma part of that.

    "It's *good money*, so what's the problem, Treece? I don't kill nobody for it. I don't steal it. I don't sell drugs to get it. I use my *mind*. That's how I get the money. I use my *mind*. Can't you leave it at that?"

Patrice: "I just want to be...I just want to *know*. I should know, really, everything about you, I think. Two years we been together. We might get married, maybe. I'd like to have a son for you. Shouldn't I know...most everything—?"

Merquan: "*Married?* You want to be stuck the rest of your life with this *epilepsy* shit I got?"

Patrice: "I'm not having a problem with it, now. It's true that I can't get you to stop goin' out by yourself as much as you do and takin' unnecessary chances. But I deal with it.

    "That's the way it *is* in relationships. Some stuff you just got to put up with. I've made the decision to put up with that part, although I hate that you go around so much by yourself, and won't take any *medicine* for it. But the epilepsy, itself—you know that's never been a problem for me."

Merquan: "Hey, the *Merk* can't turn a corner without meetin' *chillers* that *got my back*. Any one of

	'em'll get word to you, if I have a spell and there's a problem."
Patrice:	"I don't want to get no 'word' like that! If you stop goin' around so much by yourself, there wouldn't be so much chance of things happenin'."
Merquan:	"Well, you know I'm'a be in the *tight* company of *my best homies*, at the club, tonight. But you still against that."
Patrice:	"You're actually going?! You acted like it was just some'em that crossed your mind, and you weren't sure! See how you do! You don't need to be goin' to no club, without me! You got a family here, at home! "And don't say it. Don't say *I can come with you*—'cause I don't want to go to *no club*. Nothin' but stupid thugs *up in* there."
Merquan:	"Treece, you know a nigga got to *hit* the club, *e're now and then*. That's been *me*, from word 'go.' You know this ain't no *new* thing. You gotta' admit, I don't *roll out* like I used to. And the reason is that the club can't compare with my *baby*."
Patrice:	"*Merk*, don't try to sweet-talk me. I'm serious and I'm mad."
Merquan:	"I don't see the problem. It's just *e're now and then*."
Patrice:	"And don't say '*e're*.' You didn't use to say that. But you get with those *wood-heads* and bring their talk back here with you."
Merquan:	"It's just *e're now and then*. Ain't no way I believe you want to deny a poor ol' epileptic nigga a little fun—*e're now and then*."
Patrice:	"Don't do that. You see how you are—?"
Merquan:	"And you know I ain't interested in them *weave-heads* that haunt the jaints *e're* weekend,

	down *the Bottom.* I know, and you know, and e'rebody know...a lot of 'em's packin' *fire,* 'down south'—that's on *the real."*
Patrice:	"I don't want to talk about *them.* ...So, you're going, anyway?"
Merquan:	"I got to stay...*informed,* Treece. I got to stay on top'a thangs, let niggas know *Merk* ain't 'left the buildin',' yet. You gotta realize: The way I *make it* right now—the money, the respect— is through *bein'* there, lookin', seein', hearin', knowin', bein' seen, bein' heard, takin' risks— all that! "When you look at me, you lookin' at a nigga who, his best *tool* in the bag for survivin', in the hood, is his *mind.* And that mean: I *gots* to *play the game.* I *gots* to show up at one of the clubs, at least...*e're now and then.* "You feelin' me, ain't ya? You know that a nigga with epilepsy and no SSI check and no people-skills is a nigga not worth your time, and Markee's time, and Shar'dey's time. "Now come here, with that moisture buildin' up in them pretty eyes, and give me a kiss and then try to tell me I'm wrong"
Patrice:	"You see how you do? That ain't right, *Merk.* You're always takin' advantage."
Merquan:	"The *Merk* don't take no *advantage.* I just tell the story the way it *is*—no frills. I'm all about the *true picture,* no dress-ups. I'm a...what do you call them types? ...A goddamn...*realist."*

Richmond's *Shockoe Bottom* stretches, generally, from 12th Street to 19th Street, west to east. North and south, it ranges from, about, Broad to Cary and bustles with human and vehicular traffic, from early evening. It is especially so on Fridays and weekends. It was the Friday night following

Merquan's talk with Patrice, that he and some friends visited a club near 18ᵗʰ Street. The night spot was equally close to both Main and Cary.

Club Celestine was popularly frequented by twenty- to thirty-some year olds attracted by its size and *charged* atmosphere. In the dance area, overhead lights spun a kaleidoscope of colors throughout the expanse. There, the spectacle of bobbing, bouncing, swaying and gyrating bodies elicited everyone's attention.

As hours advanced to, and beyond, midnight, patrons' social inhibitions gradually relaxed or faded. The process was fueled by a whole host of mood altering substances—everything from alcohol to hallucinogens. Dispositions, for the hordes of partiers, ranged from giddy and gregarious to sulky and sullen. Thumping of loud music actually gave the club goers a surreal feeling of freedom from the usual pressures for social conformity.

In time, some number of *Celestine's* patrons became gripped by a gnawing sense of mounting tension, in the air. The *feel* was that heightened emotions and lack of due caution, among the revelers, could lead to trouble.

Amid this "electrically" pulsating atmosphere, three events occurred almost simultaneously: First, someone bopping wildly on the dance floor elbowed another. In the second, a drinker at the bar stared a little too long at a guzzler, who, himself, leered at other patrons, from a few seats down. Next, two people began arguing over seats at a table. Very soon, the club erupted in wild, unrestrained violence.

In an alarming spectacle, the club's patrons fought from one end of the capacious ballroom to the other. Ultimately, the violence spilled out of the establishment's main exits. Within the minute there was even gunfire, and erstwhile clubbers ran in every direction. Vehicular traffic stalled as people ran up and down Cary Street, southward to Canal Street, and northward, over to Main.

Sure enough, Merquan and his troupe had been involved in the melee. While trying to maneuver away from the brawling, one of Merquan's associates was punched hard by an assailant. Seeing an opportunity, Merquan took it and executed a chokehold on the aggressor. With inhibitions severely dulled by drugs and alcohol, Merquan's intermittent acquaintance jabbed a knife into the subdued stranger's chest.

Merquan immediately released the man, who dropped slowly to the floor. Within the seconds of his descent, the stabbed man's blood transferred to Merquan's hands, arms, and shirt. Believing his condition unsuitable for police interrogation, Merquan got out of the club as quickly as he could. Through clusters of excited onlookers outside, he noted the arrival of police and took the same action as did his friends, making a solo run for it.

Sprinting across Main Street, at 17th Street, Merquan saw a police cruiser approaching, from west, on Main. It had pulled out of an area over which ran Interstate 95 and truss-bridges for locomotive—a locale directly across from *Main Street Station*. The blue strobe lights signaled emergency and for traffic ahead to avoid obstruction of its path. Out of all the people running and milling about, some inner instinct told Merquan that the officers inside had targeted him for pursuit.

Merquan decided to continue north, on 17th Street. He could see that traffic prevented the cruiser, pointed eastward on Main, from making the left onto 17th. With near reckless haste, Merquan ran through the wares-display sections of the 17th Street "outside" market. At Franklin Street, he turned left, westward, hoping to run the two blocks to Ambler Street, before being spotted by police.

Merquan was at something of a crossroads. An open field sat adjacent to this part of Franklin Street. In it was a hodgepodge of large vehicles, in temporary storage—the hulls of a bus, a freight car and some trucks. It seemed an attractive choice for someone engaged in "eluding." On the other hand, two brief blocks west of 17th Street, Franklin was interrupted by the long edifice of the *Main Street Station.*

Merquan knew there was an old, abandoned entrance to the train station, where it's side faced Franklin Street. He knew, also, that either side of the outside stairway could, in its present state, provide effective concealment. That was if it could be reached ahead of detection by police.

When police, in cruisers, arrived to survey the area, Merquan was crouched in the tight, unlit space he sought. It turned out to be a good place to hide. The downside of his gambit, though, was that epileptic seizure chose this time for an occurrence.

Chapter Five

F̲OR M̲ERQUAN, IT was like reentering a dream that had
earlier occurred. He knew the pattern of the *mind-transfer*
experience, as each was close to identical to all others. His
awareness was, again, placed within the mental functioning of
someone else, as a silent and passive passenger. But who was
the "driver" this time, he wondered, and into what year was he
thrust, now?

Tom McRoy sat on a curb at address 1540 East Franklin
Street.[1,2] It was mere feet from the place Merquan Paler would
crouch, hiding from police, more than one hundred twenty
years, in the future. Chatting with two others his age, McRoy
basked in what had evolved into a sunny, unseasonably mild
day in February, 1890. Although oblivious of it, all that he
experienced was being shared by a *third* attendant, but one of
no *physical* form.

Over their poorly tailored clothes, the three young men wore
patchwork jackets, donned earlier to ward off cool morning
breezes. Now, two hours later, in steadily warming afternoon
temperatures, the jackets were losing usefulness.

Each man haled from a tiny, oblong section of East Richmond
that evolved into a "colored" area,[3] after the Civil War. Those
crude structures the people called home sat within five one-
block segments, with Cary Street at one end and Canal at the

other. West to east, they covered the distance from Nineteenth[4] Street to Twenty Fourth Street.

So, just over half a mile the trio had trekked, before noon. Their destination had been East Richmond's "Seale" section.[5] 1540 East Franklin Street, where the trio sat, was only a block around the corner from an edifice called *Seale House*. For the last two hours, each had been entertained by some of the women who lived and "worked" there. At this time of 2:20 p.m., the three comrades' discourse focused on the young women who rented rooms in that building of dormitories at the corner of Franklin and Union Streets.[6]

S. Traler:	"Me—I don't think Jimmie know what he's gettin' into around here. This ain't Duval and Sixth,[7,8,9] where he's used to. This is *the Bottom*. You get your ass killed 'round here, if you don't know what ya' doin'."
T. McRoy:	"So far, he been *gettin' by*, just by keepin' that *easy* way he got. He don't rub nobody wrong, so the studs 'round here just let him be—so far. Ain't it right?"
S. Traler:	"Damned right, *fo' sho'*."
T. McRoy:	"Well, 'least he got sense enough not to *skip* through here, at night. That's when the *Bottom*'ll break you, if you don't know the corners. Ya'll know it like I know it"
L. Johns:	"Sommabitch, if it ain't the truth. But, like you say, he smart enough to be a *day man*, in these parts. He know that much."
S. Traler:	"Y'all seen how the *chickens* 'round here is startin' to look at 'im, like he *King Stud?*"
L. Johns:	"Oh, *hell* yeah. They crazy 'bout a light-skinned *stomper* with good hair, good threads, and a real job. I don't know 'bout Navy Hill, but the *chickens* on *this* side just about eat ol' Jimmie up."

S. Traler: "I tell y'all this: That ol' boy is beginnin' to see he might done bit off too much. He started with Annie Taylor, spendin' money with her, then goin' back to Navy Hill, where the *chickens* is a little harder to catch. Next, he back with Annie, again, for a little time, when he want her again.

    "But that ain't enough. He done started spreadin' the *corn* around *Seale*. So, now, even down here, it's more than just Annie *peckin'* at him."

T. McRoy: "The way I see it, Jimmie made two mistakes from *the go*. First—he ain't read Annie right, up front. She got a reputation.[10] Some things she don't handle too well. *E'rebody* 'round here know that. Two—a *rooster* got to let *chickens* know, up front, that it's *pay and go*—and *no mo'e*."

L. Johns: "Well, guess what. Annie know that Jimmie and Polly went out somewhere, earlier. She looked real funny when she got *that* news. And guess what else. Jim and Polly back, now. They up in her room."

L. Johns: "That boy better have his business right, when Annie see him again and want answers."

T. McRoy: "Damn! Speak of the devil—look up the street! Be damned if it ain't Annie, cuttin' through a side yard. She might be goin' to *Seale House*. Let's walk over and see if she's plannin' any mischief."

That Sunday afternoon chat among the trio of friends had occurred on the 23rd of February, 1890. On the morning of the 25th, Tuesday, the front page of the *Richmond Dispatch* displayed a shocking report. The events recounted, in print, occurred after the young men ended their talk and walked to the stated destination, on Union Street.

Richmonders who typically gave sole patronage to the city's one "colored" newspaper in 1890 made an exception this day. The reason: the *Richmond Planet* was a weekly publication, issuing copies only at week's end. Whenever a newsworthy event occurred, it was written up and featured the following Saturday. The incident involving Annie Taylor occurred Sunday, February 23. Not until March 1st would its most dedicated patrons be able to read the *Planet's* report on the events in question.

City wide, that which displayed in the first column of the *Richmond Dispatch* furrowed brows. In large print was the headline title, "A Cruel Revenge." An excerpt from the write-up follows:

Knife in the Hands of Annie Taylor
Ends the Life of James Bradley
—Inquest Yesterday

...The man was James Bradley, aged twenty-two. The woman is Annie Taylor, aged twenty-one. The neighborhood of the occurrence is Union or Sixteenth street [*sic*] near Franklin, and the two stabs were inflicted upon Bradley as he stood on the sidewalk near the blacksmith shop about 2:30 P.M. Sunday.

Annie was at once arrested by the police, and the wounded man was carried into Rachel Coleman's house near by, where he lay [*sic*] gasping for about twenty minutes, when death occurred. Deceased was a colored man.

His slayer is of the same race.

...The meeting between the man and woman took place at the house of Polly White (colored), No. 109 Union street, from which place Annie pulled Bradley into the street, where she proceeded to satisfy her vengeance.

Accused was present at the inquest with her counsel, Edgar Allen, Esq., but made no statement. She sat in the midst of the crowd, and laughed heartily at some of the witnesses of the occasion.[11]

That was the report of Tuesday, February 25th. On the day of the incident, McRoy, Johns and Traler actually watched the assault from a half block's distance. Repulsed by the spectacle, McRoy backed away from his place of observation. He did so after seeing the stabbed young man being pushed, by Annie Taylor, up the block, near Grace Street. At the time, McRoy had no idea that Jim Bradley would die from his wounds.

Unsettled by the attack he'd witnessed, McRoy foundered in deciding what to do, where to go, next. The final image of Jim Bradley coughing up blood prevented clarity of thought, for McRoy. In a sort of fog, he continued westward on Franklin Street. Looking northeastward, he saw individuals making animated gestures to policemen in a horse-drawn wagon, near Broad Street. No doubt, he thought, their intent was to report the stabbing.

McRoy thought about the people he knew to be Jim Bradley's adopted parents. He wondered if he should alert them that Jimmie had been stabbed and might be in dire condition. Most in the *Seale* area knew that Bradley still lived with them at 803 North Sixth Street.[12] At his present location, on the "hill" of Thirteenth and Franklin, McRoy estimated a travel time of less than half an hour. Indecision, again, kept him from carrying out a resolve to visit the Bradley home.

Maybe, thought McRoy, he should hurry down Thirteenth Street to Main. There, at one corner, stood the *Old Dominion Steamship Company*. At its front entrance was a basement barbershop, where Bradley had worked as "bootblack," or shoe shiner.[13,14] Within the clash of his myriad sentiments, he thought it might be helpful to alert Jimmie's employer of his trouble. It then dawned on McRoy that the shop was closed on Sundays.

After over half an hour of aimless journeying, McRoy found himself, again, in the area of Union and Grace. There, he spoke with people who still stood or milled about Union Street, discussing Annie Taylor's assault. From them, he learned that James Bradley had died before reaching a hospital. Of the two wounds Annie inflicted, the fatal one was that which punctured his lung.[15]

Later that afternoon, McRoy made his way to the home he shared with Donald Colver, his maternal grandfather. It sat within the five block "colored" section, between Cary and Canal Streets. Soon after, sixty-seven year old Colver returned from the little odd jobs he continued to do for pay, in the surrounding white sections.

It had usually annoyed McRoy when his "gramps" fell into a mood for sharing his bleak outlook on life. The older man was full of warnings of the superficialities of human existence. In his admonishments, Colver often put forth the view that man and beast are on this earth for one overriding purpose: to reproduce. Life, he said, is a *trap*, and the body is in collusion with the trap. Having and making babies is part of an evil scheme to keep human beings, "*'specially us coloreds*," he would add, symbolically chained.

This time around, Tom was shaken in a way he couldn't remember having been jolted before. Somehow, now, he felt a good deal more receptive to the kind of uttering that so characterized his gramps. Given what he'd seen this day, maybe his elder might offer something that could put him more at ease, Tom thought. He began telling Colver of the incident that occurred on Union Street.

Colver:	"Terrible! Ain't nothin' but terrible. A damned shame—a young man like that. And it's terrible for that gal, too. She likely get twenty years."
Tom:	"Why you feelin' sorry for *Annie*, Gramps?! She ain't had no right—!
Colver:	"Tom, she a victim, too. That ain't natural, what she did. Some'em *wrong* with her. That's clear to me. How much you know about her, Tom?"
Tom:	"She *ain't* no *good* girl, Gramps, that's sure. Annie *stayed* in *some* trouble. I mean, she's all

Colver: "Probably had a bad life. You say she 'bout your age? So, she 'bout born in'69. That was a worse time than now for coloreds. A lot'a whites *won't* generous like they is now. I ain't got to know her ma to know she musta' had a bad life, too. And probably, no fault her own, she passed it to Annie.

"Makin' a way was hard after we got free, Tom—hard, hard, hard—worse than now. If a chile ain't had no good protection, *a lot'a bad* could happen. There ain't no tellin' what that gal been through in her life."

Tom: "I hope they *hang* her, Gramps. Jimmy never even fought her back. And after she stabbed him, she pushed him on up Union, even while he was coughin' up his blood."

Colver: "Maybe she jes' *shouldn't'a been born*, Tom. You ever think of that? Maybe that Jimmie fella' shouldn't'a been born, either. Think of his pain, and his daddy's and momma's pain... and Annie's pain, and her momma and daddy's pain.

"Maybe none'a us should'a been born. I know *I* shouldn't'a been. I done seen some pain. You cain't 'magine what the times was like, before you. I was born 1823. Lord, the things I've seen, Tom...the things I've seen."

Tom: "I know, Gramps. You told me a lot of it. I still cain't see why you say nobody should'a been born. Gramps, if nobody was born, there wouldn't be no people, after awhile."

Colver: "This world belongs to plants and animals, Tom. This ain't no place for a *human being*, unless he choose to act like a animal. We all choose to act like animals, one way or 'nother. And then we do a big *pre-tend* game, that we *better* than animals.

"Tom, I always tell you: Be careful out there. Don't help bring no mo'e babies in this world, to suffer. I didn't learn it fast enough. Me and your grandma made your ma, before we knew any better. Then, your ma had you 'cause your grandma and me waited too late to let her know the truth about the world."

Tom:

"You never said before that you wish I wasn't born."

Colver:

"Now that you is here, Tom, I'd give my life to *keep* you here. You know that. But, this world is *full of pain*, Tom. You jes' saw some of it, today. This world is *full of pain*—around every corner, down every street, up every alley, in every house.

"You know your daddy ran off, Tom. Then, your ma died and, later, after that, your grandma died. And I tried to keep pain away from you, by myself. But it's out there, Tom. I'm jes' tellin' you the facts. It's out there. And it's a whole lot of it.

"Think about that when you out there with them young gals. You could bring into the world a *Annie*. You don't know. You could bring into this world a Jim Bradley, what grows up jes' to get killed, when it *won't* no need. You jes' don't know."

As weeks passed, the shock and horror felt by Richmonders over the murder in the 100 block of Union Street receded. For those who witnessed the crime, the unease was slower to dissipate. Everyone, however, seemed to wait with the same eagerness to know what would be the jury's verdict at

Annie Taylor's upcoming trial. On April 19, 1890, in a literal "eleventh hour" verdict, the wait was over. The following day, the *Richmond Dispatch* recorded the court decision:

TRIED FOR MURDER
Annie Taylor Convicted of
Killing James Bradley

...At 11:30 o'clock last night Annie Taylor was found guilty of murder in the second degree for killing James Bradley and her punishment was fixed at eighteen years in the penitentiary.

The jury were [*sic*] out only fifteen minutes. When they rendered their verdict the counsel for the prisoner said he desired to make no motion, and court passed sentence.[16]

On the evening of April 20, Tom McRoy paid his respects to the memory of Jim Bradley, visiting the area where he saw him stabbed. On Union Street, before midpoint, he could see and hear Shockoe Creek, at shallow stage, draining to underground.[17] He thought he could almost hear Jim Bradley's voice amid the falling creek water. Near Grace Street, he took note of Rachel Coleman's residence. It was there, as given in the newspaper reports, that Jim had died awaiting medical attention.[18]

At the corner of Union and Grace Streets, McRoy turned westward. After crossing tracks of the C&O Railroad, he found a makeshift bridge over Shockoe Creek, and crossed. Ten years later, *Union Station*[19] would be built, its north-most structures standing, and extending pass, where McRoy now crossed. Regarding the creek Tom had just crossed, he could see that it ran a diagonal course, to Union, from Sixteenth Street. For nearly two city blocks, from Marshall to Grace Streets, Shockoe Creek and Sixteenth Street followed a parallel path, yards apart.

Continuing westward, Tom passed a string of buildings converted to a training, or trade, school mostly attended by black folks. He, and most everyone else in Richmond, knew the facility was originally established to educate newly freed slaves. Named to accord with the "Union" area, a group of those structures became known as the *Union School*.[20] Some years later, its relocation to an expanse at Lombardy Street and Brook Road would be negotiated, but the name would remain in use. In time, it would bear the name, Virginia Union University.

For Tom McRoy, now trekking just north of the *Union School* line of buildings, the row had a special significance. His Gramps had relayed it, just as he had kept Tom aware of other relics of slavery. The grim and austere series of buildings once included the infamous *Lumpkin Slave Jail*.

Continuing in a southwest direction, Tom found Ross Street,[21] along which was one of Richmond's steepest inclines. Situated between Broad and Franklin, poorly paved Ross Street ascended, westward, and ultimately led Tom to Governor Street. There, Ross terminated, the street less than a mile in length from end to end. On errand, Tom made his appointed delivery, within a complex of establishments near the intersection of Ross and Governor.

Tom never imagined that, over half a century later, Ross Street, would undergo complete change. For two blocks leading to Governor Street, it would later be the site of looming state government buildings and paved grounds. That brief distance of Ross, before the sharp downward turn into Shockoe Bottom, would later be renamed. The name chosen was logical, given the lane's location between Broad and Franklin. Two blocks of Ross terminating at Governor Street became a section of Grace Street.[22]

Glancing at Ross Street's steep decline, east of Governor Street, Tom would have been amazed at the same view, nearly a century later. Looking from that later time, he would see a walkway bridge leading to a great edifice rising from Fourteenth Street. It would be named the Monroe Building.[23] From Tom's view in 1890, no great buildings overshadowed Ross Street's diagonal northeast course, downward. From his elevated position, he saw that it terminated south of Broad Street, prior to merging with flood-prone *Shokoe Creek* and Sixteenth Street.

Having completed his mission, Tom began walking the declension along Governor Street, southward. At Franklin Street, Tom's itinerary took him eastward. Treading down this steep decline, he was obliged to dodge horse drawn carriages and an electric trolley.[24] At the point where he crossed Fourteenth Street on Franklin, traffic of the sort was heavy and posed a constant threat to pedestrians and stray animals not fleet of foot.

The intersection of Franklin and Fourteenth was where Tom passed under an enclosed walkway, renown among Richmonders of the day. It connected two of the city's finest hotels. Called a pedestrian bridge, the structure allowed travel from the *Ballard Hotel* to the *Exchange Hotel*, and vice versa.[25] Visitors were spared the necessity of braving the elements and crossing busy Franklin Street, when necessity required back and forth treks between hotels.

For McRoy, the walk along Franklin, pass Fourteenth Street, put him at Mayo Street, on his left, and at Locust Alley, on his right. If he were looking seventy-five to one hundred years into the future, Mayo (now Ballard Street) would be discharging traffic from Interstate 95, toward Franklin. To his right, Locust Alley, rather than a lair for 19th century prostitutes, [26] would be the site of a large parking lot. Just ahead, the north end of *Main Street* (*Union*) *Station* would sprawl, preventing movement straight forward.

But no such obstacle stood in McRoy's path, in February of 1890. Still moving along Franklin, toward Fifteenth Street, he trekked along a road sprinkled with houses and small business on both sides. He ambled pass a livery and factories producing such commodities as soaps and brooms.[27] When his view, rightward, was not obstructed by something in the landscape, Tom peered at the 1500 block of Main Street [28] with all its bustle and commercial activity.

Onward, Tom plodded to the northwest corner of Franklin and Union Streets, where he often idled time with friends. From a 21st century perspective, the place was the east wall of *Main Street Station*, at the stairway of an out-of-use entrance. At that locale, McRoy sat, again, as he had on many earlier occasions. He used the time, now, to collect his thoughts about Annie Taylor, Jim Bradley and his grandfather's dark perspectives. It was at this time, beyond McRoy's awareness, that Merquan's *psyche* began to disengage from that of his host.

In search of Merquan, the driver of a midsized, black sedan cruised about Shockoe Bottom. But it did so in a wide perimeter, around points where police conducted investigations and took witnesses' statements. Inside, were the vehicle owner, Mario Mayfield, and two passengers: Trayon and Neil Twine. It was half an hour since the nightclub patrons had charged outside and scattered in all directions, after the disturbance. Using Mayfield's car as an impromptu meeting place after separating, the three friends reunited. Now, they scoured about, looking for the fourth member of their entourage this evening: "*Merk.*"

A site of focus for the three was the back end of *Main Street Station*, running the length of two city blocks. Looking south from Broad Street, however, they could see that police still showed intense interest in that area. Cruising eastward, from Broad near 16th Street, Mayfield slowed to a near stop, looking across the VCU parking lot expanse. But to avoid special notice of the police, he felt obliged to move on, eventually ascending Broad Street's eastbound incline.

After some time, and against the Twines' better judgment, Mayfield gave in to the urge to call Patrice. His hope was that Merquan had caught a fast-moving night bus home and was "chilling" there, waiting for his friends' call. As they feared, he had not; nor had he called Patrice. Now, to make matters worse, she was beside herself with worry, as was clear through her communication. It was pass two a.m. now. Merquan's friends felt it was time to expand their search strategy.

As the group knew, there were always homeless people and errant nightwalkers straggling about Richmond's "Bottom." The plan devised was for two of the trio to scout parts of the area, on foot. If they split up, each affecting the manner of a night person harmlessly wandering through, they might avoid suspicion. In that case, a policeman catching sight of one or the other of them may feel compelled to give only cursory attention.

Mayfield discharged Trayon in the 2000 block of East Franklin Street and Neil in the 2000 block of East Grace. The plan was for them to walk parallel routes, westward, keeping an eye on one another a block's distance away, at the numbered streets, 19th, 18th, 17th, and so on. If one of them spotted Merquan, the space to be covered by the other, to link up, would be small. Mayfield, for his part, would park, discretely, in various places nearby, his cell phone ready to receive a call.

At length, the cousins reached Ambler Street. Now, their search pattern would have to change. At Ambler, they were both blocked, particularly Trayon, by that long, back extension of the train station. Momentarily, Trayon paused before changing directions, prompted by intuition. After some seconds he heard a rustling at the station's abandoned entrance. Upon cautious investigation, he found that it was Merquan, still wearing the beige and bloodstained shirt.

From a block north—on Grace Street—Neil saw his cousin's signal. He, in turn, cell-phoned Mayfield and directed his navigation to Ambler and Franklin. Before any patrolling officers appeared, the cousins hustled Merquan into the black sedan. All except the driver laid low until the four friends were a good distance from Shockoe Bottom.

Chapter Six

For the EIRI researchers, it didn't take long to "conjure" a meaning to associate with Evan Nesset's utterances at the Afton Building. They agreed that "C-E-L-A-P...R-I-L-8-1-9-2-1," as played back from the recording, possibly signified a person's initials and also a date. If they were correct, they surmised, the *specter*, or whatever it was, had been rather direct. The team thought the voice in Nesset's head may once have had the initials, CEL. The date he gave as significant was likely that of April 8, 1921.

But Nesset had relayed a second cryptic offering from his *spirit* correspondent. In deciphering it, the researchers sought to use the same mode of interpretation, as with the first. Rewinding and playing the segment over and over, the group members thought they might, again, be hearing a date and initials. But did the "J-17" indicate January, June or July? In the tape, Nesset's voice was heard to say:

"J-17...1-9-8-0-S-L-L? No? ...C-L-L? ...Z-L-L? Yes, that's the one."

Given what they had so far, the team decided to test their theory. The course taken was to conduct research, during day hours, of the supposed dates and initials, within newspaper archives.

As it turned out, nothing appearing even remotely relevant was discovered for initials ZLL. Painstakingly, the researchers had scoured through records for each month beginning with "J," for the year 1980.

Possibly more than her colleagues, Zatorah had hoped the archives *would* have suggested a significance for "ZLL." The finding would spare her the awkward task of revealing that the mysterious "codes" actually spelled out her *own* initials and birthday. It made her appear a bit vain, she thought, suggesting that the Afton "ghost" might be making reference to her.

While the search for significance in "J-17...1-9-8-0-Z-L-L" was a bust, not so for April 8, 1921 date. What was uncovered riveted the team. The archival newspaper source was the Richmond *News Leader.* On the front page of an issue made available the following day, April 9, there appeared the report: PRISONER AT PEN ENDS HIS LIFE [1] At the center of the dark event was the penitentiary inmate, Claude E. Legge.

Barring occurrence of mocking, misleading coincidence, there, believed the EIRI team, was confirmation of their hypothesis. To their thinking, Nesset had, indeed, had a *spiritual* encounter. Belief in their success at the initial stages of investigation infused the group with added resolve. They felt certain that *paranormal* phenomena in Richmond could not only be found but also confirmed by factual record.

All agreed that similarly compelling findings would have to be made to strengthen their case. To substantiate their contention that *extra-normal* forces exist alongside *objective* reality would require multiple examples of the sort. It was especially true, they agreed, for the plethora of skeptics who would review the results of their work.

When no reasonable connection could be made to newspaper, or other, reports for Nesset's second offering, Zatorah came forward. Taking in the possible relation between the date and initials to her name and birth date, the other members were intrigued. As explorers of the *psychic* world, they kept open minds for plausible associations between objective and *psychic* realities. The group agreed simply to wait to see if further findings might shed light on the matter.

The very next night, after their celebration of the archival discovery, the team rode out, again, within the energy detection vans. It was alongside researchers in the EIRI-3 vehicle that Nesset rode. After visiting a number of locations that yielded no reward, it was time to visit the next scheduled one. In trial runs a year earlier, a small paved lot at a fire station in the 300 block of West Leigh Street had shown some *energy clustering.*

Moving westward to the site of interest, EIRI-3 crossed a wide intersection on Leigh Street, where a number of streets converged. There, the researchers took in the spectacle of the Bill "Bojangles" Robinson statue and memorial.[2,3] The vehicle was, now, within three blocks of its destination. At two hours past midnight, there were still a few Richmond nightwalkers to be seen. As with the earlier excursions, a police presence was secured as evidence that conduct associated with the van had official approval. An assigned patrol car was kept notified, this night, of the team's destinations.

Near the end of the 300 block, west, of Leigh, the van parked. There, its detection equipment began to activate. When the blue *particle-waves* targeted a location between address 316 and the fire station next door, on the left, the machines went wild. It was time for Nesset to put into play his *channeling* efforts, but with caution. The fire station presented no problem. But, to the station's right, buildings standing in sequence to the start of the block were private property. Within, people could not be expected to feel comfortable with strange goings-on outside their homes or businesses.

There were no concerns regarding the other side of Leigh Street. What had been the 300 block, odd, of Leigh was now a grassy field. Notably, it bore one of the city's many *historic-site* plaques. Before Nesset got underway with his channeling, one member of the investigators walked over for a closer look. He saw that it honored the initial cadre of black police officers in Richmond allowed, in 1946, to serve in the former *First*

Precinct.[4] The historic station, according to the plaque, sat at Smith and Marshall Streets, very near Belvidere and Marshall Streets, today.[5,6]

Aware of the EIRI team's procedures, the patrol car officer took measures to give the upcoming events the look of police business. First, she parked in front of the van. After radioing the fire station of no cause for alarm, the officer activated her car's blue strobes. This partly masked the blue glow of the van's electromagnetic emission waves, aimed at a space to the left of address 316.

At that space was an iron fence and gate behind which firehouse personnel parked. Nesset and the researchers hoped that whatever *entity* might be encountered there did not require entry into the gate, in order for manifestation to occur. The reason was that no such accommodation by the fire department had been requested or approved.

Standing at the curb, arms partly outstretched, steeped in the emitting blue waves, Nesset began to perceive a *spirit*. But it did, in fact, seem to him to have location *inside* the firehouse gate. To Nesset's surprise, even in his "spirit channeling" state, the energy he perceived had the "feel" of a child's *aura*. He began low murmurings and gestures as if to coax the *entity* outside the gate and closer to his field of perception. But the small, yet potent, force resisted Nesset's imploration.

Suddenly, the van's machinery, and Nesset, detected the presence of another *energy composition*. To Nesset, this new spirit seemed that of a young woman, perhaps a teenaged girl. From this particular paranormal "force," he detected what he later described as an amazing clarity of communication. In his mind, Nesset began to hear a slow, sketchy, ghostly dialogue coming from the spirit. Discourse, however, was directed not to him, but to the *child-force*, behind the stationhouse gate. The utterances were broken, at times barely decipherable. Phonemes Nesset heard, *spiritually*, he repeated verbatim, in a low murmur, for reception by the sensitive recording devices:

L-A-J:	"Co...out, lit'l one. Y...r'mem.... We pass on same.... You have some...to tell. Stand w... me. Not be afrai. Same day we pa.... And buried...."
A-T-B:	"Ann—?"
L-A-J:	"Yes. You...ha...thing t'...tell. You know...."
A-T-B:	"Friend...sit on step...good. He tell ev'b'dy one day. Truth! In jail...die. Have....leave...jail. ... Ann?"
L-A-J:	"Yes, Tre...I'm here."
A-T-B:	"Lady find...my frien'."
L-A-J:	"Who, Tre...who?"
A-T-B:	"Her...her...her...out...there."
L-A-J:	"Have...go, Tre. Did good. Good boy. See... soon."
A-T-B:	"Bye...Ann."

Nesset could feel the growing tenuousness of both "forces." Quickly, he beseeched the one nearest him for a significant date by which she and the boy might be identified in records. His impression was that they'd both died and were buried on the same day, although not necessarily with any connection.

Nesset:	"I read your initials, Ann, LAJ, but can you tell me your birthday, or when you passed? It is so important to have a way of identifying you, in life."
L-A-J:	"We...die...4...2-3...18-9...."

As soon as his "sensation" of the spirits had passed completely, Nesset, as typical, slumped to his knees.

The three-minute interlude, enhanced by the spin and stream of blue lights, was starting to garner attention within the block. From their windows, people watched with mounting curiosity. In order, quickly, to allay concerns, Nesset was helped back inside the van, and the EIRI crew anticlimactically pulled off.

Attention was drawn from the research vehicle by the fact that the police escort stayed on the scene. She now stilled her strobe lights and remained calmly parked for minutes, after the van's departure. If anyone cared to inquire about the episode, the officer would say it was just a test of some new equipment.

When the EIRI team analyzed the latest recording of Nesset's *spiritual* encounter, they reached a consensus. Most likely, the *spirit* with initials LAJ gave Nesset the date April 23, eighteen ninety-something. The next assignment, then, for student archive-specialists, would be to pore through a decade of Richmond death registries. Starting with April, 1890, the search would cover that month, alone, through 1899. The exercise was made a little more daunting by the fact it would involve no names, just initials.

Then, there was the ghostly reference made to "steps," a "friend," and a "lady out there." At the, earlier, Afton site a set of initials were, seemingly, a part of the otherworldly report, and no association with archival record was found. The team, upon Zatorah's alert, considered an intriguing possibility: Spirits of the past may reference factors, not only related to the past, but also related to the present, *real* world.

On the night of the Leigh Street "channeling," that hypothesis was revisited by Zatorah's research mate. Among the five who rode in the EIRI van that night, the only *women* present were project researchers. These were Zatorah and her Richmond-based counterpart. To Zatorah, her colleague mused:

"If the little ghost at the firehouse gate was referring to *one of us* as 'that lady out there,' my guess is that *it's you.*"

The study group had been provided college students to aid in archival searches. Those working, at present, with the researchers proved to be thorough in their efforts. One of them located an 1890s death registry having remarkable relevance to the search. Not to be outdone, the other uncovered an equally astonishing newspaper report.

The *Richmond Planet*, founded in 1883, was the first publication of its kind owned and operated by blacks in the South.[7] Circulated weekly, as noted earlier, its report of events was often several days after the occurrence. In the May 10th issue, 1890, notices appeared in tandem, which, when read by the EIRI investigators, mesmerized them. Rather than having location in a section *within* the paper, the report featured on the front page, as follows:

Passed Away

Brown—Died at the residence of parents, 318 W. Leigh St. April 23d at 6:30 o'clock [*sic*] p.m. Alphonso Trevilian, youngest son of George O. and Bettie M. Brown; aged 3 years, 9 months and 18 days....

The funeral took place from the residence Friday afternoon, April 25th at 4:30 o'clock....

Johnson—The funeral of Miss Lydia Ann Johnson took place at the Mt. Cavalry Baptist Church, Friday, ult. April 25th at 11 A.M....She was sick three weeks, and died on the 23d ult. in full triumph of faith. Age, 17 years, 8 months, and 23 days....[8]

Although the report did not address the *child-spirit's* uttering, it had every appearance of validating issues of the name-initials and date. Other aspects of the older *spirit's* uttering the team felt to be chillingly on target. For the team, the most stunning example was the "LAJ" relay that the two *spirits* expired and were buried on the same days, respectively.

For the following week, Nesset was scheduled for only one night of investigation with the EIRI team. Having no need to plan and prepare for post-midnight explorations left team members with free time, during the day. On one such early afternoon, Zatorah took occasion to carry out an intention she made weeks earlier.

In a rental sedan, she drove about the area wherein, reportedly, her parents lived, at the time she was born. Vaguely, her mother had described it as situated between the 2000 and 2200 blocks of Monument Avenue. For the most part, the blocks sit undistinguishable, amid the scores that make up Richmond's West End.

As it was a warm and pleasant day in early July, Zatorah decided to park and stroll through the indicated blocks. Whimsically, she fantasized about the arrival of insight, suddenly indicating to her the exact location of her family's old address. No doubt, she thought, the idea was a side-effect of witnessing Nesset's "sensations" of *extra-normal energy.*

Though imprecise about their former home's location, Zatorah's mother did indicate which side of Richmond's "street of Monuments" to focus on. Ambling along the even numbered side of the 2200 block, she took in the quaintness of the surrounding view. She admired the stately residences and smiled at the ample number of street joggers going one way and another.

Retracing her steps in the opposite direction, Zatorah stopped at the street that crossed Monument, at the east end of the 2200 block. Looking diagonally, across Monument, she took in the sight of a tan-beige colored building with beige stone steps. Sitting stoically at the southeast corner of Monument Avenue and Allison Street, the edifice seemed to have a serene character. Nevertheless, to Zatorah, there was something curiously compelling about the structure.

In a state of mild intrigue, she walked over to get a closer look. There, she saw nothing to indicate that the building had special significance. No signs or plagues told of business that might be conducted within, or whether it was simply a quietly elegant residence. Something about the building's side elicited her attention, also. Nearly a block long, it had a side entrance requiring a walk along stairs that ascended parallel to the building. These outside steps were behind a short wall also situated parallel to the building's western side. She thought the design suitable for discreet coming and going.

Couples strolling little ones along Monument made Zatorah think of her family, in the year she was born. They also elicited thoughts of her husband, Peter. She had spoken with him earlier in the day and planned to phone, again, at 2:00 p.m., one of his usual break-times. The twenty minutes leading to that hour, though, seemed the perfect interim to fill, chatting with her mother.

Torasine managed a moderately successful internet business from her home, and was almost always available. Speed-dialing her cell phone, Zatorah anticipated the lively communication that typified their mother-daughter talks.

Zatorah:	"Guess where I am, Mother! I'm on Monument Avenue! As we speak, I stand on a corner between the, even-numbered, twenty-one and twenty-two hundred blocks. And one of them includes the house you brought me back to, when I was born. Isn't that exciting? Don't you wish you were here?"
Torasine:	"Only so that I could whisk you away, back here to Cambridge. When I think of all the mall-stalking and other fun stuff we could be doing over your summer break, I just see *red*. And you've traded all that, to watch...*that Evan Nesset guy* pretend to hobnob with ghosts."
Zatorah:	"Oh, Mother, I've told you all the astounding discoveries we've made. You have to admit, our finds have been absolutely, out-of-this-world astounding."
Torasine;	"I don't *have* to admit it, but I will—being the model of graciousness that I am. Nevertheless, it seems to me you could let *the team* investigate all those *hauntings*, by themselves. But, I

know——. You-all believe that each member adds an important *ghost-finding* ingredient.

"For now, Peter and I are just waiting for these next two weeks to pass, when you get your two-week break from *waking* Richmond's *dead*. And, speaking of Peter—he's like a little lost lamb, here, not knowing what to do with himself, while you're away."

Zatorah: "As much as I enjoy the investigations, I am quite looking forward to being back home. Peter's my *real* soul mate, and you...well, you're *my mother*, although, *how* you can deny me knowledge of my *first* home——.

"Oh, Mother...isn't this a wonderful name for a street? I've walked up a block and I'm right here at the street sign. *Strawberry.* You're not going to tell me you don't remember Strawberry Street."

Torasine: "*Strawberry Street.* My God, I haven't thought about *Strawberry Street,* in years. That was the block at the corner from where we lived— going, I think, west."

Zatorah: "At last—more details about the location! So, that means we lived in the 2200 block. Does that jog a memory of the exact address?"

Torasine: "Nope—can't say that it does. Sorry. I remember that we lived, sort of, at the center of the block. And there was a brick or stone porch, before the entranceway. Anything helpful there?"

Zotorah: "Oh, I wish you could see it again, Mother. All the buildings have these wonderful pillared front porches—so stately and quaint."

Torasine: "That was Monument Avenue, alright—stately and quaint. But, ol' *Strawberry*——. I used to take you in a stroller all along Strawberry, south, I think it would be, to this little block of

	shops and then farther to the elementary school, and around, and back home. That brings back memories."
Zatorah:	"You see? *Memories*…it's good to have memories."
Torasine:	"It's good to have *some* memories."
Zatorah:	"There's another street here, Mother, that gets my attention, for some reason. It's *Allison.* There's this building on the corner of Monument and Allison.
	"In fact, as I think about it, I get the same feeling at that corner as one I described to you, earlier. Remember? I said I felt something odd at a set of outside spiral stairs and at an alleyway, near the corner of Fifth and Main. Both locations—the other and this—seem… how can I say...*relevant*, in some way."
	"Right here, across from me, at Allison…a big, stately edifice, kind of tan-nish, in color. Do you remember Allison Street? It's the block down from Strawberry."
Torasine:	"No, dear, I'm sorry. I don't remember any Allison Street or any big, tan building. Monument Avenue is a blur to me…the whole West End is a blur. Sorry.
	"Not to change the subject, dear, but guess who Mrs. Bergmier is seeing now. …Good ol' Mr. Glockespiel! …A cute couple, indeed. I call them The Willow and the Cactus. Need I say which is the Cactus?"
Zatorah:	"Mother, you are so bad."

The following night Zatorah was designated to do explorations with the group traveling within EIRI-2. Evan Nesset rode with the EIRI-1 group. But it would be the EIRI-

3 van encountering an energy-rich environment, such as to compel Nesset's *spirit channeling* efforts.

At Zatorah's special request, the EIRI-2 driver made a slight deviation from his intended course. Coming north on 4th Street from Canal Street, he parked in front of a hotel and adjoining café, after crossing Main. The driver paused there a few minutes. At the hotel's left side, an alleyway stretched, eastward, to 5th Street. EIRI-2 made the right turn through the path and parked, anew, on 5th Street. The van was now in front of a building with a two-sided, arching, outside stairway.

Zatorah had hoped the van's energy detection machines would show activity, while in the area. Even the slightest response would seem to corroborate her feeling that the locale between 4th and 5th Streets had a mysterious quality. As it turned out, in the brief trial that was made, nothing showed on the detector graphs.

There on 5th Street, EIRI-2 sat still a moment, while Zatorah tried to sort through the sensations *she* felt. That was when the call came from EIRI-3. The request was urgent, signaling that potent *paranormal energy* was detected at the odd-numbered side of Broad Street, near Adams Street. Given the nearness of EIRI-2 to the new destination, it arrived ahead of EIRI-1 and Nesset.

As they awaited arrival of Nesset and his attendants, the researchers at Broad and Adams positioned the two vans strategically. In minutes, they pinpointed areas in the 00-hundred block, west, of Broad Street that emanated maximum *extra-normal* energy. When, finally, Nesset was on the scene, with the police escort, the optimal spot for his "channeling" was known. The group gathered near the corner of Broad and Adams, at this time of 1:48 a.m. In the prevailing darkness of night, they took in the streetlamp-lit surroundings.

At two corners of odd-numbered Broad Street, at Adams, the researchers saw red-brick edifices, appearing as large converted warehouses. The site of interest, however, was the building on the southeast corner. As the teams took note, it rose only four stories, but each floor seemed, itself, two stories tall. Occupying much of its space at ground level, café "*27*," closed for the night, was a popular venue during operating hours. With name displaying prominently on the front window, a team member guessed it derived from the street address.

It was the eastern border of café "*27*," along Broad Street, upon which the EIRI vans' energy detection devices focused. Nesset, then, headed straight for that location, steeped in rays of blue light. Within seconds, his voice began to cut through the nighttime silence and calm. Whereas in previous occasions, he spoke of his *spiritual* perceptions in low murmurs, now his vocalizations were loud and clear:

Nesset: "Oh, God…it's on fire! The building is on fire! The east wall—it's collapsing in the flames! Officers, firemen all around! Oh, no…it's falling on them.

"Oh, no! Firemen, officers down, beneath the burning bricks! Bricks, burning wood, glass, all falling, spreading out, all over the street, in a great wave of flaming debris and embers!

"I see the rescue…the heroic rescue! The men are taken away. Fire trucks and equipment and hoses! Streams of water pour into the building, everywhere that there are flames!

"But now the scene changes. The fire is out. The building, the *Jurgens Building*, is a shell. And now the voices of the dead speak.

"I am listening. Please make your report known to me. I will repeat what I hear from you, so that those who work with me can also know your concerns.

"You say, *'The others want to speak.'* Who?

"You say, *'The woman.'* But, who—?

"You say, *'She is us.'* Who is…she?

"You say, *'They have message.'*

"You say, *'Message for woman, here.'* ... Here? Do you mean: where *you* are, or where *I* am. I can't get your precise meaning of 'here.'

"You say, *'With you.'* A woman who is with *us?* There's a *message* for her?"

"You say, *'Locate their man.'* What man? Who is he?

"You say, *'He is George. Will die eight years, ten months, twenty days.'*

"You say, *'First, get one from jail.'* Who?

"You say, *'Take man from jail...to George. ...He will speak for the others...and to the woman, who is there...and who is us.'* Please...I don't understand.

"I hear you say: *'She is our kind, and she is with you.'* Do you mean: 'She' is *your* kind, but she is with *us?* Or 'she' is *our* kind...and with us? Who *is* she...please...it seems so important to know, exactly. What do you mean when you say, 'our kind?'

"All right...I hear. I hear that you can say no more—except, *'The door closes, for now.'* I hear. I do hear. Goodbye. Thank you for communicating."

The police officer watching over the EIRI team's endeavors that night was glad that Nesset's "channeling" had been brief. Accordingly, he urged the group to wrap up as quickly as their concluding mission would allow. Nesset's yelling "fire" outside of a building converted to apartments was not something he had anticipated. Fortunately, no one had been aroused by Nesset's vocalizations.

Sensing the officer's mood, the researchers prepared, hurriedly, for departure. For a few blocks, the vans moved eastward on Broad, then turned south onto 1st Street, headed for their base of operations. Watching the "spiriting away" of the research vehicles, the officer, as prescribed, remained to preside over the prevailing calm.

Chapter Seven

AFTER NARROWLY ESCAPING big trouble with the police the night of the Shockoe Bottom club incident, Merquan settled into a compliant mode. Patrice had nearly begged him not to go out that evening with his "crew." But he did, and by all appearances, it could have resulted in catastrophe. Given an unlucky turn of events, Merquan might have been charged as an accessory to *malicious wounding* or even *attempted murder*. For now, he resigned himself to spend as much time as Patrice desired, at home with his *de facto* family.

The last job Merquan did for Priola was in early June. As the days approached mid July, both Merquan and Patrice knew to expect a call from him at any time. When it came, by means of the house phone, Patrice answered and handed the call over to Merquan. With mixed feelings, she listened to one side of the two-way conversation. She was disturbed by the mysteriousness of Merquan's relation to Priola, but welcomed, totally, the monetary benefit associated.

When talk between the two men ended, Patrice gave in to an urge to reanimate an old plea to Merquan.

Patrice: "It sounded like it's gonna' be Thursday—
              around eleven-thirty, again. Can I go with you
              this time, *Merk*? You know I'll stay out of the

	way. I can ride the bus down with you and just walk around downtown until you're finished."
Merquan:	"You don't know how long I'm gonna' be."
Patrice:	"You're always finished at the same time—like, at one. That's what you tell me."
Merquan:	"Suppose it runs longer, or shorter. It ain't like no clock-punch job. I mean, it could run longer or shorter. Ain't no way to really tell."
Patrice:	"I'll wait around for you at Kanawha or at Brown's Island.[1] Shar`dey and Markee love to go there."
Merquan:	"So, y'all gon' walk around down there, for a hour or two, waitin' for me to show up. That ain't one of your best plans, girly-girl."
Patrice:	"It's for our family, *Merk*. I want to be there— you know, just in case. You might, you know, have one of those *spells* downtown, again. You never know.
	"Can't we all ride down together, and then if you don't see us when you walk out of the *Omega*, you can catch the bus back, by yourself."
Merquan:	"It ain't like I have a seizure every day—or even every week, Treece. Sometimes months can go by—."
Patrice:	"You won't take any medicine for it, *Merk*. I've *begged* you to. At least you can let us ride down with you. No one where you work will know we came down together.
	"The kids and me, we'll stay on the bus and get off at another stop. Then, after you finish, if you don't see us right down at Kanawha, you just go on by yourself.
	"That's not asking too much. I don't ask that much of you, *Merk*—just to be a family."
Merquan:	"Well…I guess it's all right. Who knows? I might need a back-up today. It would be some

	wrong shit if I got run over by a bus with a *G* in my pocket. Then, at the hospital, with nobody lookin', the workers rob me. That'd be *fucked up*, wouldn't it?"
Patrice:	"I'm not gonna' let a bus run over *my man*, with or without money in your pocket."

In the two days leading to Thursday, Patrice resisted recurrent urges to ask Merquan, again, about the nature of his work with Priola. He had agreed to "family" travel to the *Omega Suites Hotel.* She reasoned that she'd better quit with that concession, especially considering a precedent would be set. If he allowed her and the kids to travel with him "to work" this time, it might likely become a trend.

As planned, the four rode a late-morning bus downtown, which, as usual, stopped in the block pass the *Omega Suites.* There, Merquan and Patrice parted ways, with intentions to reunite in an hour or so. Nonchalantly, Merquan proceeded to the hotel's revolving-door front entrance. He walked over to the elegant, arching counter behind which the pretty receptionist stood, stating his business.

In due course, a phone call was made and, in minutes, Priola entered the lobby from a wide hallway. After greetings, the two men made discourse, as they walked together, back in the direction from which the older man had come.

Priola:	"Well, bud, we got six this time. You think you can check six at once, or should we break them into smaller groups?"
Merquan:	"We can see how it works out. I don't think it should be a problem."
Priola:	"All right. Well, you'll let me know if it ain't comin' through, like it's supposed to. These things have to be right on the money—no mistakes."

Merquan: "I know. Like you say—there's a lot on the line."

Priola: "Not just a lot, *Merk*y—tons! Money, national prestige, avoidance of jail time…all that and more. But, so far, you've been *dead-on*. And, you know we test you, *Merkson*. We let you know that, up front. We set up duds in the groups, but you never get taken off track."

Merquan: "What you pay me tells me that."

Priola: "Oh, and that reminds me: For your work the last time, I got an extra couple of hundred. The whole *twelve* I got right here, in an envelope, in my jacket pocket. I pay *extra* when I think you had a greater challenge. But you did it. You *saw through* 'Ajax' Agikaelus."

Merquan: "So, he was clean, like I said. How did you get sure of it? You had him followed?"

Priola: "Didn't have to. *Ajax* is a confirmed 'ballplayer.' I threw him in, last time, to test your instincts. Remember, I told you I *suspected* him of being an undercover informant. That was to throw you off, see if you'd be influenced by suggestion.

"But, goddamn-it, you gave that son-of-a-bitch a *clean bill*, in spite of the doubt I pretended. So, *Merkson*, you're the *real* fuckin' *Wizard of Oz*, as far as I'm concerned."

Merquan: "I just call 'em like I see 'em."

Priola: "And you see the *hell out of 'em*, too, *Merk*s. You *see* 'em and see *through* 'em. What a fuckin' gift! And bud, I don't intend to be a fuckin' cheapskate about this, either. As, more and more, I see the evidence of your accuracy, I'm increasing your *take*. As you know, I make some serious *bananas* in my racket. Everybody I keep loyal, by peeling 'em off their fair share."

"And there's one very important thing I take note of about you that's not the case for most of my other important 'employees.' You're not committin' any crime, so you can't be blackmailed by the cops. You have nothin' to gain by *turnin' on* me, and everything to gain by workin' *with* me. It's a sweet deal, for sure."

Merquan: "No doubt. But so you know—I ain't the *turnin'* kind, no way."

Priola: "I sense that you ain't, Merks, and that's good—real good."

For the service he provided Priola, Merquan was always compensated four to six weeks *after* the fact. It allowed Priola and his "investigators" an interim within which to determine if Merquan's evaluations bore out. Priola always recalled that, from the beginning, he'd developed a special regard for Paler. That dated back to when Merquan was a part-time kitchen aid in the *Omega's* restaurant.

By his own report, Priola appreciated "brains," and he sensed that Merquan had his share. The older man set a pattern of initiating conversations with the younger. It was Priola's method of getting to know someone who interested him. Always, he was on the lookout for talent to incorporate into his network. By means of those talks and results from an unplanned sequence of events, he discovered Merquan's unique ability. Paler could detect individuals with motives to spy on, or be disloyal to, Priola's private affairs.

Made a *believer* in Merquan's special gift, Priola arranged for a more direct encounter among parties of interest. Instead of merely visiting the table of *Priola-and-guests*, as a server, Merquan would sit *as a guest*, himself. Typically, he was introduced by Priola as a smalltime recruiter of prostitutes for Priola's "operation." In addition, the others were made to believe Merquan supplied loyal *clients*, from among Richmond's residents-of-lesser-means. These, latter, according to Priola, were his "minority" patrons.

Priola, an inveterate planner of details, worked out a nickname for Merquan, to be used in the company of prospective employees. Always, he used the name "Impy," when addressing or referring to Merquan. It was both simple and logical, in that it was derived from Merquan's initials, MP.

To Priola's delight, "Impy," at the luncheon table, played his part to perfection. He had the "hood" manner, the inner city slang, the often deadpan and soulless facial expression that gave him an air of authenticity. In fact, none of Priola's guests ever imagined that "Impy" might serve a function in life beyond that which he role-played—and, ironically, did so for the purpose of furtively "reading" *them.*

The business luncheon ran to 1:20, a testament to the relaxed, unhurried atmosphere created. When it was over, the diners all parted ways, each receiving Priola's apparent seal-of-approval. As usual, Merquan exited stoically, giving the appearance of lacking social graces. In his pocket, he toted the envelope full of crisp "twenties" and "fifties" that Priola handed him across the lunch table.

All had gone well. To Priola, Merquan secretly pointed out the single diner among them in whom he detected a spying agenda. As he had been informed earlier, such individuals would subsequently undergo Priola's special surveillance. If they aroused suspicion of the least sort, they were denied farther interaction with Priola's darkly entrepreneurial network.

A block north of the *Omega Suite's* Cary Street entrance, Patrice stood with Markee and Shar'dey. She positioned herself at a corner that facilitated subtle watch of the hotel's double doors. Finally, her vigilance paid off.

From the hotel, Merquan turned, southward, heading in the direction of the historic remnants of Kanawha Basin. Scouring around for the three Keepers, Merquan's quest didn't take long, since they were a block behind, moving toward him.

In the bus ride home, Merquan proudly pulled a sum of eight hundred dollars, in fifties and twenties, from his bulging envelope. With the same ease he typically showed in purchasing his favorite street-vender sandwich, he handed the bills over to Patrice. He watched her beam as she spoke:

"Oh, *Merk*...thank you! Did you get a raise, *baby?"*

Merquan replied easily: "Damn if I know. I just do *my do* and step."

"All that money for a hour and half, at lunch!"

"I *do* this. What can I say? But, ain't nothin' but *paper,* though—paper I like to turn over to my sweet girly-girl."

"I just can't believe this, *Merk*—all this for just sitting and having lunch!"

In a voice, audible to Shar`dey and Markee, who occupied joined seats in front of the couple, Merquan added dryly:

"I swear I'm takin' me a nap, when we get home. Long, hard work like that make a nigga' as slow and sleepy as a two-toed... what's that creature called again, Shar'dey?"

As he expected, snickering laughter could be heard coming from the young Keepers. Then, they both answered: "A two-toed sloth!"

Laughing, Patrice added: "I told you watching *Jack Hannah* with the kids is good. He's *'into the wild'* and we're in *big paper.* Like those 'homies' of yours say: You're 'the man,' *Merk*—the *easy-money* man."

After the first half of Zatorah's two weeks of summer break expired, she became more and more conscious of the days remaining. Now, with only three days left, each group of hours seemed more precious than the last, in Cambridge. On this Friday before her early Monday morning flight back to Virginia, she set a full itinerary. Looking over her plan, she noted a two-hour gap between three and five p.m.

Zatorah arrived at Madam Lu's *House of Readings* at 3:10. It was the time she'd managed to schedule, earlier that morning. As she recounted, from earliest to latest, her experiences in

Richmond, Madam Lu's interest was on clear display. The session came with a fee, but it was of no regard to Zatorah. She took as much pleasure in sharing her accounts as she did in getting Madam Lu's responses.

With animation, Zatorah described Evan Nesset's *channeling* experience on Broad Street, near Adams. Enjoying Madam Lu's full attention, she also described research *findings* related to Nesset's encounters. In a friendly gesture, she was given permission to address the older woman as "Ma Lu."

Zatorah: "We found the report in a Richmond newspaper called the *News Leader*. It was dated Monday, March 14, 1921. On a later page, there were even pictures showing firefighters spraying the burning building. We, all of us, were just awestruck."

Madam Lu: "Most fascinating! Your *channeler*, Nesset, saw the fire as it had happened—ninety-one years prior."

Zatorah: "Yes. He saw the east wall of what used to be the Jurgens Building[2] crumble from the heat and fall to the ground. Four firefighters and a civilian died at the scene, on that terrible Sunday. Many others were seriously injured by the falling swell of burning debris. Nesset saw it all and described it, as though it was happening currently."

Madam Lu: "What a tragedy—and what a scene to witness, even after, nearly, a hundred years of its passing. I am always intrigued by surviving pictures taken of sites, years past. I have to know: How did the newspaper picture match the look of the site, today?"

Zatorah: "My God, I almost forgot! We made photocopies of the newspaper pages! I have them in my purse. ...Look at this, Ma Lu. In this top picture, you can see the south side of Broad Street, where Adams intersects—right there. That's the Jurgens Building, there on the left, on fire.

"On the other side of Adams, on Broad, that building, there, with the spires on top, looks exactly, now, as it does in the picture. It wasn't damaged at all. In the paper it's referred to as the *Masonic Temple.*

"The Jurgens Building was rebuilt and, apparently, on the same model as you see in both the bottom and top pictures. The only difference is: it's a floor or two shorter today."

Madam Lu: "This is so fascinating! So, these areas shown look almost exactly the same, today. I find it amazing that those two Adams Street-corner buildings are still there. They look old, even in the picture."

Zatorah: "Yeah, they do. Both have been converted to apartments and other businesses. The lower level of the old Jurgens Building is a café. Now look, here, just to the left of Jurgens, this used to be the Hopkins Furniture Company. It says it in the newspaper write-up. It was also damaged by the fire."

Madam Lu: "Breathtaking. Now, you said Nesset repeated communication he received from *spirits* of the dead. He did it so everyone near could know what was said."

Zatorah: "Oh, yes, Ma Lu, and it was chilling. Before the team left for our two-week break, we set about deciphering meaning from Mr. Nesset's uttering."

Madam Lu: "Thoroughly fascinating! Can you recall what was said? And what did your group come up with?"

Zatorah: "Take a deep breath, Ma Lu. It's about to get…
            pardon my slang…*really crazy.*"
Madam Lu: "I'm ready!"
Zatorah: "The group thinks some of the *spirits* have, on
            occasion, been referencing *me!*"
Madam Lu: [Stunned]
Zatorah: "Yes! …Okay, here it is. On that last event, we
            identified four *points of interest*, each worth
            analyzing in its own right. Each was given in a
            single word and then partly elaborated on later.

            "First, was the word, 'others.' Taken in
            context with all that was said, it suggests that the
            spirit world has or recognizes *separate groups*
            within its, uh, how shall I call it—sphere. The
            spirit relaying to Mr. Nesset used the words 'us'
            and 'others.'

            "Second was 'the woman.' When Nesset
            asked for clarity, the *spirit* seemed to say '*She
            is with you.*' And Ma Lu, you may remember I
            said the other *spirit*, the little boy who died in
            1890, spoke of 'a lady.' When pressed for further
            identification, he said 'her, her, her, out there.'
            Just like that.

            "There were two women in our group
            present. When we considered that the *spirit*
            might be referencing one of us, something said
            on a previous event of Nesset's channeling made
            me the more likely candidate."
Madam Lu: "You're talking about Nesset's contact with the
            prison inmate—the one that gave your initials
            and birth date."
Zatorah: "Correct. Now, that takes us to the third and
            fourth points of concern, in Nesset's Broad
            Street *channeling*. In each, reference is made to
            'a man.' *One* has connection to a jail. The *other*
            was said—or so it seemed—to be scheduled

for demise in eight years, ten months, and twenty days. But there's a problem with the interpretation."

Madam Lu: "I think I see it. Given that the reference is to passage of time, what is the start point to count from? Were you able to make clear sense of it?"

Zatorah: "It took some thought, and we tried different things. At a point, we researched newspaper archives for early in the year, 1930. That put us in the ballpark, counting time from March 13, 1921, the day of the fire. Specifically, we searched for reports on the death of someone named George, since that was the name Nesset quoted."

Madam Lu: "Oh, my stars, Zatorah! I'm actually starting to get a vision. It's a date, and I think it's related to your present topic. You just said early in the year, 1930. In my mind, I'm seeing the date, February 2. Did I just do a super fast, savant-like calculation, or is my spontaneous vision significant, regarding what you found?"

Zatorah: "Totally amazing, Ma Lu! I'm going to read you the newspaper headlines and following report, from the *Richmond Planet* newspaper, I photocopied. It's dated Saturday, February 8, 1930:

"*'Julia Frayser Cuts George Nelson To Death In Domestic Row...Killed in Self Defense*

"*'On the night of February 2, George Nelson, of 105 Coutts Street, was found dying of knife wounds on the corner of Second and Federal Streets. He died before reaching St. Philips Hospital.'*

"*...Julia Frayser, 27-years-old, was arrested the next morning for the murder.*' This next part, Ma Lu, is a quote from the woman, Julia:

"*'I had to cut him to keep him from beating me to death,*' she said. But, here—I'll give you the photocopy, so you can look at it for yourself. Now, is that fantastic, or what?"

Madam Lu: "Zatorah, I am more convinced than ever that your expedition in Richmond, Virginia has *spiritual* significance. I'm actually starting to get early signs of impressions I think could be related to your experiences. But they are weak and indistinct. My guess is that it is not for me, as yet, to know more, beyond what you tell me.

"But I certainly welcome any additional accounts you have. So, what about the second man that Nesset was told of? Were you able to discover anything about him?"

Zatorah: "Well, that's where we draw a blank. At the risk of sounding like *earthbound skeptics*, we can't be *totally* sure, as yet, that even the George Nelson *finding* is one-to-one with the message from Nesset's 'voices.' Regarding interpretations related to the *second* man—so far, we don't even have a guess."

Madam Lu: "Can we go over what you remember of what was said in reference to him?"

Zatorah: "Well, let's see. I recall Mr. Nesset relaying from his 'voices' that a man is in jail that must be taken to George. That's it—well, also that he must be gotten out of jail, first. So, there's some guy in jail, and there's a George, who has died. And some kind of meeting is to be arranged."

Madam Lu: "Zatorah, didn't you say that some mention of jail was made in the *channeling* event with the teenaged girl and the little three-year-old?"

Zatorah: "Yes, according to Mr. Nesset, the little boy told Lydia that someone died, or *would* die, in jail, if he didn't leave. That was the extent of it, as I recall. Of course, there was that mention of 'the lady' by the little one. But, not a lot was conveyed, there."

Madam Lu: "Zatorah, what a tantalizing set of events you have presented. I'd like to point out something I'm not sure you've given thought to. Have you noticed that 'jail' has been a feature of each *channeling* event Nesset did with your group?"

Zatorah: "You're right. The old Virginia State Penitentiary was the first—it being a sort of jail. And now that I think of it, so has the *possible* reference to *me* been a feature."

Madam Lu: "This is quite a twist: I'm always the one giving my *spiritual impressions* to others, in readings. But, in this case, *I* am the one being informed about *supernatural* occurrences.

"Well, now it's time I return to the usual course of my clients' visits. At this very moment, I receive *impressions* that I feel relate to you. Just like before, it concerns Richmond, Virginia locations.

"One is the area around the address given for that George Nelson fellow described in the newspaper. I'm seeing a name or a word...like 'award' or 'ward'...some kind of 'ward.' And a past president...the two are paired. It looks like *ward* and *Andrew Jackson*. Whoa—that can't be right. Now the words are transposing... *Jackson* and *ward*. Does it sound, in any way, familiar?"

Zatorah:	"…Yes. It's a section of Richmond described in various historic plaques around the city."
Madam Lu:	"I'm seeing the word 'north' in reference. So, if it has a northern part, that's where the significance lies.
	"The second of my two visions show the words *nine miles* or *nine mile*. I get the impression it's some long stretch of road. It seems there's someone there you should see. It is not clear who or why. But I see you driving along the road, next to a concourse, and some *thing* or place called…*Oakwood*.
	"Oh! It all just faded suddenly. But remember those names I gave you. They may be important when you return to Richmond."
Zatorah:	"I'll jot them down, right now. When I look at how that location you described, on my first visit, played out, I have no doubt that these place-names have meaning."

Chapter Eight

I<small>N</small> R<small>ICHMOND</small>, <small>AT</small> the next gathering of the EIRI team, members began planning activities for the remaining three weeks of research. Zatorah took this opportunity to suggest investigation of a Richmond area that had recently piqued her interest. The problem was that it was not one of the approved sites for study already mapped out and scheduled. Still, the group agreed to give old the northern Jackson Ward area a brief drive-through, in the one of the EIRI vans.

On the night selected, Zatorah and attendants within the EIRI-2 van cruised through two miles of Gilpin Court. From Federal and 2nd Streets to the corner of Hickory and Calhoun, and back, they rode, in an ovoid route. Quietly analyzing the environment for evidence of *extra-normal* energy, the van's equipment behaved erratically. In short, it did not show the type of sustained detection, set as a requirement for Nesset's work of *channeling*. Even with spectacular findings, there was warning by the police escort that Gilpin Court was not an advisable site for EIRI activity—day or night.

Zatorah was unwilling to abandon her interest in whatever *extra-normal* qualities the area might have. Thus, she determined to take up her own study of the former *northern* Jackson Ward. But why stop there, she privately wondered. She, then, added a plan to find the city jail, such as to do a visual analysis of it.

There seemed no question that the act was appropriate, given all the reference to a *jail* in Nesset's *channelings.*

There needed to be, at least, one more facet of her solo investigations, Zatorah thought. She felt it important to make drives along a road she found in a city map whose name uncannily matched the one Madam Lu gave. Getting to it in her rental car from the team's base of operations did not seem to present much of a challenge, she judged. According to the map, she'd have to drive to 25th Street, from downtown 2nd Street and Broad. There, she'd make a left turn, northward. Finally, near a termination of 25th Street, after about a mile, the map showed that Nine Mile Road began.

In every available hour that Zatorah was not working with the EIRI team, she drove through selected areas of Richmond. For the most part, she chose the stretch of Broad Street as the site by which, and from which, to judge all distances in Richmond. It became her favored locale for starting, in earnest, her many explorations.

She was particularly fond of Broad Street's intersection with 1st Street and with 2nd Street. For most of 2nd Street, she noted, traffic runs northbound only. On it she could drive from EIRI central operations to central Jackson Ward. Conversely, 1st Street traffic moves southbound, coming *from* the old northernmost Jackson Ward. In her mind, the latter's importance had been confirmed by Madam Lu. To Zatorah, Broad Street at those two numbered streets provided a good, central location of the city, north of the river.

Following her street map, this particular day, Zatorah took a turn, north, on 18th Street, from Broad. It was how, finally, she located the Richmond city jail. She found a place to park that was across from the largely red-brick structure. Next, she walked pavement along its front and around the long extent of its western side. Unsure whether or not she was imagining it, Zatorah thought she sensed a significant presence, or something, within the walls.

Her next destination took her to the end of the street on which she had parked. It "dead-ended" a distance of two blocks northward, where, now, she turned, left, onto a grossly rugged road labeled Hospital Street. Moving cautiously over train rails, Zatorah tried to reproduce, mentally, her street map's road design. If she recalled it correctly, the drive toward the steep hill in the distance should lead, again, to numbered streets.

Noting the environment, Zatorah could tell that this section of Hospital Street was a lowland area. Just ahead, another unrefined, nonresidential street "bottomed out" at Hospital Street. It was 7th Street, terminating at its north-most end, in a steep decline. Navigating Hospital Street's radical incline, westward, Zatorah saw that 5th Street was at the top. 5th was followed by 4th which was followed by 2nd Street. A large cemetery interrupted the path of 3rd Street.

When Zatorah had navigated the steep incline from 7th Street to 5th Street, on Hospital, she'd taken note of the raised highway under which she passed. It would have amazed her to know that the highway towered above what had once been Sixth Street. She would discover, later, that the looming overpass was part of a highway project, from half a century earlier, that radically disfigured the Jackson Ward of old.

Owing to previous drives to and through Gilpin Court, Zatorah felt a serene familiarity with the area, in bright daylight. It was this sense of calm that compelled her to park on Hill Street. As she had before, she thought it interesting that Hospital Street ended at one corner of 2nd Street, and at the other corner, Hill Street began.

Noting the time of 2:17, Zatorah's mood was upbeat, as she walked along Hill and adjoining streets. The area was animated with the sight and sounds of children and adults visibly enjoying the beautiful day. Not at all did she get the sense that a stroll around the blocks, alone, at this hour, might be unwise. By now, Zatorah had heard of Gilpin Court's evening-hour reputation.

Walking along Hill Street's 100 block, east, she knew that Coutts Street had once been situated a block north. She knew, also, that Coutts, at present, was a single block and no longer ran a half mile to 2nd Street, as in earlier times.[1] Therefore the "105" address given for George Nelson in the February 1930 *Richmond Planet*, was no more. Zatorah thought it would have been fascinating to stand at a dwelling on Coutts that signified where Nelson had once lived.

Zatorah continued along Hill Street, between St. James and St. John. Engrossed in thought, she was totally unaware of the person peering with curiosity at her, through living room curtains. It would have totally amazed her to know she had met the young woman previously.

For Patrice's part, she thought that the woman passing by the front of her housing unit seemed oddly familiar. She strained for complete recall, while following Zatorah's movement, until she turned south on St. John. Other matters vying for her attention, however, did not allow Patrice to give further thought to pinpointing just where she may have seen that face before.

Nesset's next *channeling* effort took place in a woodsy area of a park, sitting just north of the intersection of Williamsburg Road and Nicholson Street.[2] The site rested within the historic "Fulton district" of Richmond. In the *vision* he held, Nesset saw rows of streets crisscrossing the area, streets that no longer exist. From Wharf Street, near the river, to National Street, some blocks north, homes, long vanished, dotted the landscape. It was all in Nesset's retro-view, to the year 1921.

Nesset found himself witness to the *aftermath* of a deplorable crime committed in the area, rather the crime, itself. Oddly, the *spirits* entering into communication with him during his peer into the past were not the *victims* of the crime committed. They claimed to be, to *have been*, neighbors in the Fulton community, at the time of the heinous act. This was a *first*, for Nesset. He had witnessed past crimes being committed, via his *channeling* activities. He'd had communication with victims of such crimes. But never before did he experience overshadowing of victims' voices by those of the victims' *neighbors,* in the community.

That constituted only one deviation from Nesset's norm. It was communicated to him that he must *terminate* his collaborative work with the researchers. He was actually being advised that some type of *intra-spiritual conflict* was making the rest of his work with them untenable. He did not fit the bill, as it were, for receiving *new voices* that needed to be heard. From his report, the team was forced to conclude that a certain "class" of *spirits* was forcing alteration of their plans.

The new development sent the team into a tailspin. They felt it must be important, to their overall interpretation of Nesset's *channeling* efforts, to identity those "others." However, at present, they totally lacked definitive data and resources for accomplishing that feat. And, now, Nesset made it clear he had no intention of defying the *spiritual* request made to him. This latest course of events seemed to spell early termination of the project.

For now, the team placed their focus on Nesset's obscure "others," on a back burner. Following their usual pattern, they began attempts to validate the more substantial aspects of his final communication with the *spirit* world. Once again, the researchers turned to newspaper archives. Reward for expenditure of their time came from separate reports, within two archival newspapers.

Each newspaper recounted the story in gripping detail. But, it was the *Richmond Planet* that added an intriguing twist to interpretation of the event. As it was, the EIRI team came upon the account offered by the Richmond *News Leader,* first. That order of discovery is reflected in the presentation to follow. On its front page, column one, the *News Leader,* for the issue of March 12, 1921 gave this report:

GROSS CRIME IN FULTON
SHOCK TO RICHMOND
Two Negro Burglars Commit Capital
Offense on Woman as Ill Husband
Lies Helpless in Bed

Two armed negroes, who afterwards made their escape, entered the dwelling of Mr. and Mrs. John Edward Heisler, at 305 ½ Nicholson street, shortly before 5 o'clock this morning, and assaulted the young wife, each in turn presenting a revolver at the head of the husband, who is of slight build and in ill health, while the other committed a capital crime. The circumstances are almost unbelievably atrocious. Separating the husband and wife as they lay [*sic*] in bed was their six-months old infant. None were [*sic*] allowed to move.[3]

As the researchers discovered, the *Richmond Planet*, that Saturday-only publication, gave its report of the incident in its March 19 issue:

CRIME IN FULTON
MUCH EXCITEMENT HERE.
MEN NOT APPREHENDED.

Police Active Trying to Find the Guilty Parties

White and Colored People
Aroused

It is alleged that early Saturday morning, March 12, 1921, two men reported to be colored, entered the house of John E. Heisler, a white man residing at 305 ½ Nicholson Street, Fulton, which is in the neighborhood of the waterfront, extreme eastern part of the city and in the lowlands of this community, and after demanding money and securing only fifty-cents proceeded to criminally assault Heisler's wife in his presence. Both were threatened with a revolver and the husband was made to turn his face to the wall while both men in turn assaulted his wife. These white people are said to be of humble origin. Heisler is from Ohio.

...All this week white people have been filing into the city hall to secure pistol permits to purchase firearms. The rigid rules prescribed here against the possession of deadly weapons have kept defensive weapons out of the hands of law-abiding citizens and enabled the crooks to obtain by "the underground route" an unlimited supply. No colored people were seen in the line applying for these weapons. The excitement has now abated and the indications are that normal conditions will continue to prevail. There are many people, both white and colored, who doubt if any colored men committed this crime.

BLACKEND FACES

The ability of white men to black their faces makes it possible that this was done; as two men who would commit such a crime and then leave alive two living witnesses to possibly identify them, is highly improbable. They evidently consider that the deception has thrown the detectives off the scent and that they are safe from captures. Just why the bloodhounds were not used in trying to track the criminals is also subject for discussion. Colored people are as anxious for the capture of the guilty parties as are the white people and banding their efforts to accomplish this result.[4]

EIRI members tried to maintain the model of researchers' objectivity, but winced, nevertheless, upon reading the account. On the other hand, the report reanimated suspicions that there may be *wild* and *otherworldly* meanings to consider. Together, the total of eight wondered if they dared suppose existence of a *racial* factor embedded within the *spiritual* conveyances to Nesset. Even more, was there some astonishing connection between the *racial* aspects of the newspaper accounts and Nesset's *spiritual* "suspension" from further investigations? It seemed too bizarre to be true, even for investigators of the *paranormal*.

Until and unless the team could coax Nesset back to his work with the team, the project was stalled. Each EIRI member was forced, now, to find an interim activity by which to occupy her- and himself. For Zatorah, who was developing her own private mission, the next course was clear.

The following day, Zatorah drove along a planned route that took her to a set of traffic lights controlling an uneven, four way intersection. Just ahead was the corner of 25th Street and Nine Mile Road. She made the right turn and began traveling the road's length, east, to traffic-busy Airport Drive. The long drive she treated as a journey, of both a leisurely and exploratory nature. Among the sites noted along the way were *Oak Hill Cemetery* and a prominently displayed establishment offering *psychic readings.*

Near the wide intersection of Nine Mile Road at Airport Drive, Zatorah maneuvered to head back, in the opposite direction. After driving some distance, she decided to act on an impulse that tugged at her. It regarded Madam Lu's expression of an insight, during that last talk with the seer. At a roadside establishment promising *clairvoyant* analyses, for patrons, Zatorah found that "walk-ins," as well as appointments, were welcome.

After Zatorah explained the circumstances leading to her visit, the *reader* prepared herself to receive impressions. Within the minute, she began sketching on a drawing pad. Next, she asked Zatorah if the sketch of houses within a setting looked familiar. It didn't take Zatorah long to match the sketch with one of the housing models featured in Gilpin Court. The reader then put in an arrow, pointing to one of the units in the drawing. She spoke to Zatorah, succinctly:

"If you know a place that shows this arrangement of houses, go to this one. I have no address to give, only a picture in my mind of the setting. But this is the unit…where to make your inquiries."

Zatorah thought the best way to get from her location on Nine Mile Road to Gilpin Court was to backtrack to Broad Street. At that point she would make the turn, northward, onto 18th Street, as she had before. Driving along 18th Street, Zatorah approached the southern end of the Richmond city jail. As she knew, the road took a sharp bend, to merge with old 17th Street, presently, Oliver Hill Parkway.

Zatorah recalled that sensation she had gotten before, upon walking the stretch of white concrete wall, bordering the jail. Briefly she entertained the idea of parking inside the lot, at the front of the city jail, and repeating the former trek. In the end, she opted to continue motoring to the northern end of Oliver Hill Parkway.

Turning left at the street's terminus, Zatorah took note of a young woman and two children. They were walking, making the turn opposite of Zatorah's, *from* Hospital Street *onto* Oliver Hill Parkway. In a flash of recall, Zatorah realized it was the same trio who attended the young man who had the seizure within the MCV memorial concourse.

The sighting was undoubtedly *a sign*, in Zatorah's thinking. She felt her pulse quicken as she drove the bumpy stretch along Hospital Street. To her left, she marveled at the view of the MCV/VCU complex of buildings looming high above a declension of brush, in the distance. Within the minute she ascended the steep incline to 5th Street, a route with which she was now familiar.

The *psychic's* sketch bore a striking likeness to the block of Hill Street, between St. James and St. John Streets. Peering at a unit from her car window, Zatorah was certain it was the one to which the arrow pointed in the sketch. Inexplicably, she got the sense that this was not the day to execute the bold knock at the door she'd planned. Besides, drawn curtains gave the unit an appearance of being currently unoccupied by residents.

Chapter Nine

THE FOLLOWING WEEK, Patrice made the mile-long walk, from Hill Street to the Richmond city jail, without her kids. Standing alongside women of similar age and purpose, she talked to Merquan through the jail's visitation-room glass. She held for a moment the good news she bore, while looking him over, critically assessing his overall condition. As she noted, the color of his attire was still that of a suspected felon currently housed in *general* population.

She would have preferred to see Merquan in clothes indicating *isolated housing* due to a medical condition. But, then, from a positive viewpoint, his clothes signaled that he had, as yet, *not* had a seizure, during three weeks at the jail. Finally, she let her excitement and optimism pour forth, in her carefully modulated exclamation.

Patrice: "Baby, it's a miracle! We're gonna' get you out. We're gonna' get the bond money!"

Merquan: "Five *Gs?!* What the hell you and Ma gon' *do*—rob a bank?"

Patrice: "Listen, *Merk*, listen! Do you remember that lady, the one that was staring, when you came out of the seizure? It was in the MCV lot, down

	from Social Services, where we get those good subs."
Merquan:	"Yeah, I know where you're talkin' about."
Patrice:	"Well, remember that lady—the one you were gettin' ready to cuss her out, for staring? It's the one that gave us the business cards!"
Merquan:	"Oh, yeah. …I wasn't gon' cuss her out—just ask what the hell was her problem."
Patrice:	"*Merk*, you said she was crazy, but *she is not crazy!* She's gonna' help us! She's puttin' up the money!"
Merquan:	"What?! You serious? What the fuck…? Why in the *hell*…? *How* in *all* the hell—?"
Patrice:	"She's putting up the money, *Merk*. You're getting bonded out!"
Merquan:	"Naw! Some'em ain't right. How, in all the hell, did you meet up with *her* again? She must be a goddamn investigator or some'em. Tell her that's all right. I'll handle my own shit."
Patrice:	"Why are you acting like this? You need to be back home, while we work on your case, with your lawyer. What is the problem?"
Merquan:	"Naw, see—this shit sounds crazy."
Patrice:	"You want to stay in jail? You don't want to be home with us?"
Merquan:	"Damn right, I want to be home. …Shiiit. A nigga can't get no sleep in this j'aint. Niggas up and talkin' you to death *all-night-long!* Seem like half the hood is in this *mah-fuck*, for one thing or another—DUIs, trespassin', suspects of murder-in-the-first, like me; *e'rethang*.
	"Niggas is *off the chain*, up in this bitch, too, Treecie. A sommabitch ain't got no connection? That nigga gon' be fightin' day and night over goddamn…*anything*, 'specially shit like canteen!

	I'm talkin' 'bout his *own* shit, he paid for out his *own* account. It's crazy!"
Patrice:	"It should be either tomorrow or Wednesday, *Merk*. Now, until we get you out, why won't you tell those medical people about your seizures? I don't want you having one, in here—not in *general* population."
Merquan:	"Look, I *got* this. I *do* this. I been a on a *cloud* with half the niggas on my tier, at one time or another. ...Hold up! How the hell did that lady get back with you? You ain't never told me that. ...Or did you find a way to contact her?
	"And why is she puttin' up five *Gs—for me?* Find out who she's gonna' want me to kill, before you show her to the bondsman."
Patrice:	"Stop talking silly and be as happy and thankful as I am that you are getting out of this jail."
Merquan:	*"F'sho, f'sho*. But, this shit is crazy!"
Patrice:	"We got a lot to tell you about, when you get out, *Merk*. Ms. Leeman's involved with stuff that's gon' have you *buggin'*, when we tell you about it."
Merquan:	"Damn. She ain't no *Martian* or nothin' I hope. Next time, check and see if she got fingerprints. It's a known fact: *Martians* roll up in your crib, steal all your shit and don't leave one fingerprint for *the jake squad* to find."
Patrice:	"There's a time for jokes, Merk, and a time to be serious."
Merquan:	"I take all my jokes serious. Hey...how come *Markee-Mark* and *Shar`dey-dey* ain't wit' you?"
Patrice:	"They're at your mom's. They're all helping Bonita prepare for Olivia's birthday tomorrow. ...Look, try to get some rest and some sleep. You don't look like you've been sleeping. I hate

	seeing you in here. But, we're gonna' have you out of here in a day or two. Okay, baby?"
Merquan:	"Shiiit. Niggas be talkin' you to *death*, up in this bitch—*all-night-long!* That's when they ain't fightin' and tryin' to steal other niggas' shit. But, it's all right. The goddamn chaos is under control. I see that look on your face. You don't need to worry. I been handlin' this shit for three weeks."
Patrice:	"Do I need to try to talk with the sheriff or somebody?"
Merquan:	"No. You don't need to do nothin' but what you're doin'. It's like the TV news be sayin': 'CT' and the jail's *jakes* know how to keep shit in order, in here. ...Look, I'm good, so *chill*. ...But you know. ...Ain't no *picnic* up in this *bitch. Belie'e dat!*"

Twenty-five year old Ma'Sahn Dixon lay in a Richmond hospital bed clinging to life, courtesy of artificial breathing apparatuses. For three weeks to the present, he kept a comatose state, interspersed with moments of faint consciousness. Richmond sheriff's deputies were assigned to guard his hospital room around the clock. The reason was that, when, and if, Dixon recovered, he was to be escorted to face arraignment for second-degree murder.

Five weeks earlier he had accepted a loan of one hundred dollars to make a wholesale purchase of his illegal substance of choice. According to plan, he sold the pills he bought at "retail" price and made a profit. Dixon's lender allowed two weeks to pass. As a bad omen for keeping peace "in the hood," Dixon put word out that he had no intention of repaying the loan.

Evidently, it was Dixon's intention to destroy his lender's business. Among those versed in the *drug culture*, it is known that the allowance of a single unpaid illicit loan was the precursor of many more to come. The lender is driven out of business, unless an example is made of the defaulter. Thus, two outcomes were imminent. Either Dixon had to be duly punished, or his unremunerated lender lost all the respect he enjoyed, locally.

The whole matter culminated at the corner of Charity and 2nd Streets, in Gilpin Court. Standing with Merquan Paler were the cousins, Travon and Neil. They were there to see that the confrontation between Merquan and Ma'Sahn did not step far beyond the boundaries of a semblance of fair. As it was, nothing less than a literal knock-down, drag-out bloody fight was expected. It was known throughout Gilpin Court that Merquan had never pulled a gun or a blade, in a brawl.

Dixon, emboldened by the presence of three attendants, did not feel compelled to act in accord with what little moral code he embraced. He took the challenge to meet his adversary at the designated corner. His game plan, however, was to use a nine millimeter weapon to dominate the convention. It was legend that Dixon had, on numerous occasions, shot wildly, at individuals before. For that reason, he assumed no one would do anything provocative, when he showed his arm.

As he'd planned to, Dixon brandished the "nine" and started firing without troubling to take clear aim. Trayon and Neil both executed an automatic duck and roll maneuver and reached for their own weapons. But before they even had arms in place, an innocent bystander, several yards across the street had fallen. The man bled profusely from a gunshot wound caused by Dixon's wild spray. Surprised and relieved at not having been "hit," both Twines reciprocated gunfire.

As was known by all participants, it was Neil Twine who had persuaded Merquan to take Dixon as customer. Exploiting his friendship with Merquan, Neil overrode "Merk's" business instinct. Now Neil stood ready to punish Dixon for his betrayal of trust. His was the gun whose bullet pierced Dixon's temple. Afterward, Neil stood motionless, in shock, until Merquan took the revolver from his hand and pushed him to run.

The single eyewitness to give statements to the police was not a Gilpin Court resident, but someone passing through. From a block's distance, he saw Dixon firing his weapon and saw a man standing on outside steps fall during Dixon's barrage. Clearly, the witness informed police, that man was hit by a round from Dixon's gun.

The same eyewitness saw Dixon fall, after return fire from men who were apparent adversaries. According to all reports, it all happened fast and amid the scattering of several people at the scene. Unlike others who saw, or partially saw, the incident, the witness considered most reliable, watched from his vehicle. There, he made assessments from a position of relative safety.

When the shooting was over, the witness followed the path of a man he could tell was a main participant in the melee. Driving north, along 2nd Street, he headed for Bates Street. There, after a right turn, he cruised along the south wall of Shockoe Hill cemetery. In seconds, he passed the man he saw running along Bates. Later, the driver would say it was the sprinter who fired the shot that put Dixon in the hospital.

Bonded out of jail and back home with the Keepers, on Hill Street, Merquan had many issues to think through. One concerned his upcoming court case. For his court-appointed attorney, he needed to construct a convincing story. At their one meeting, at the jail, Merquan conveyed to her this: Dixon was shot by someone he'd never seen before.

Continuing, Merquan said he saw the shooter drop the gun and take off running. Desiring to have it for himself, he picked up the pistol from where it had lain. At the time, it seemed a good idea to hide the weapon and come back for it later. What better place than a cemetery? Along Bates Street, at the place where a strip of 3rd Street terminates, northward, was an area sparse of houses and people. Merquan said it was there that he tossed the weapon over the wall, into Shockoe Hill Cemetery.

When he'd reached the end of his tale, he could see the attorney's skepticism. Nevertheless, she recognized it as a scenario so simple as to render the story difficult to disprove.

It would be particularly so, if the prosecution's case was weak, as she suspected it was.

In addition to his case, another matter vied for Merquan's attention. He, now, knew some particulars of Zatorah Leeman's agenda. As an investigator of the *supernatural* she had the crazy idea, as he termed it, that he could be of some assistance. *"She wants to turn me into a damned ghost-buster, along with her and her crew,"* he complained to Patrice. Still, as wild and strange as it all was, in his thinking, she had, sort of, *purchased* his cooperation. She not only "anteed up" five *Gs*, for his bond, but also expressed a willingness to help, in any way possible, with his case. *"She got my ass trapped,"* he lamented.

The EIRI team and universities cosponsoring investigations were very skeptical of Zatorah's proposal. Altering the essential conduct of research, midstream, was generally unacceptable. In an effort to balance professional misgivings with the desire to display professional courtesy, they acquiesced—with conditions. They would allow this most unconventional stand-in for Nesset a single trial. But it would occur only after the replacement had signed several statements of disclaimer. These absolved EIRI and all related parties of liability for a slew of possible occurrences.

It was the way Zatorah integrated the various elements of Nesset's conveyances during his "channelings" that had won over the team. In a meeting they held to discuss the prospect of bringing a new player into their activities, she made her case. She first cited the April 9 edition of the *News Leader*, 1921, which reported the following:

PRISONER AT PENITENTIARY ENDS HIS LIFE

...Harboring the idea that he was to be electrocuted when he had finished a term of ten years for malicious assault, Claude E. Legge, 30 years old, of Leesburg, committed suicide in the Virginia penitentiary early today by taking carbolic acid. He drained the contents of a small phial of the poison at 5:20 A.M. in the hospital section of the prison and died half an hour later....

Dementia Aggravated

The prison officials were of the opinion that the execution of a negro [*sic*] in the death chair yesterday had served to aggravate the dementia from which Legge suffered and doubtless hastened the suicidal act....[1]

Zatorah: "From this, I interpret that the inmate who was executed is the one described, by Mr. Nesset, as wanting to convey something. In a twist, though, he wanted to get his message, not to Nesset, but to someone identified as having my birthday and initials.

     "Mr. Nesset's next spiritual encounter involved the teenage girl, Lydia, and the child, Alphonso. From my view of Nesset's report, the boy made what I believe are four significant points. One, he referenced someone to whom he felt friendly. Two, he seemed to suggest that the friend was in a jail. Three, the person's release was a matter of life and death. And four, the boy spoke of a lady 'out there'—possibly me.

     "Then, there was the 1920s fire at the old Jurgens Building that Mr. Nesset witnessed. At that time, voices spoke disjointedly of 'a woman out there,' also—and spoke of 'others' who desired to make communication. These voices, too, referenced someone in a jail, and, of course, spoke of George Nelson.

     "At that point, it was relayed that someone in jail must, first, be released, and then, taken to Nelson. This Nelson fellow, the spirits seemed to say, would speak for that, heretofore uncommunicative, group. Or, at the very least,

	he'll somehow prove instrumental in shedding light on unclear aspects of the mystery."
EIRI staff:	"Okay. I see the consistent mention of someone in jail. Apparently, you believe that your Paler fellow is indicated. Now, how do you tie in Nesset's experience in that little park area that used to be an extension of Nicholson Street?"
Zatorah:	"If I wasn't addressing open-minded colleagues who have investment in the *unusual*, I wouldn't be willing to say what's next. But I'm actually coming to believe that the *spirit* world has *racial* divisions, of some sort."
EIRI staff:	"Yes, we very lightly broached the topic earlier. But I thought we'd all decided it was a tad *too far out*, even for us."
Zatorah:	"It was evident, by the *Richmond Planet* reports, that black people of Richmond were distraught over what they deemed an unfair identification of the assailants, in the crime described. From Nesset's report, those communicating with him that night showed an irritated disposition. I don't think it's stretching too far to believe they could be *spirits* of black people from that past Fulton community."
EIRI staff:	"As long, Zatorah, as you realize there's no way we would even *remotely* elude to such a condition in our description of the research—.
Zatorah:	"Oh, I know. Of course, such a thing could never be publicized. But to further our own understanding, I think it's worth exploring.

"So, I'll continue. Now, think about it: The executed man at the penitentiary was black; but he couldn't, or wouldn't, communicate with Nesset. The *spirits* relating to Nesset on Broad Street referred to a woman as being 'here' and

	'with you.' It was also said that she was 'one of us.'"
EIRI staff:	"And you're thinking they were likely the *spirits* of white people from the time of the Jurgens fire; so, whoever the woman is that they referred to, she, like them, is white."
Zatorah:	"It's what I'm thinking."
EIRI staff:	"So, these supposed *spirits* of black people, perhaps, have certain whites in whom they have a certain 'trust' or something. And, while they may not speak *directly* to these whites, they may still have a message for them.
	"And, finally, the one connected to some of the messages—the mysteriously referenced 'her' and 'she' serving as a link to it all—might just be...."
Zatorah:	"Yes—*might just be me*. It was hard saying it, but I got it out. So, have I stepped over the *paranormal* 'line' into that *other dimension* called the *Twilight Zone?*"
EIRI staff:	"If so, welcome to the club. From the late, great Rod Serling, we've taken *over* the *Twilight Zone*.
	"But seriously, neither of us is in any position, at this point, to say you're on the wrong track. Of course, in order for your theory to enjoy our group's full, and private, acceptance, there must be confirmation. It's clear you believe work with Paler will provide it."
Zatorah:	"I do believe it."

The project managers at both the Richmond and Cambridge schools were adamant. Zatorah would have a single chance to demonstrate the value of her essentially unknown, untried participant: Merquan Paler. For accomplishing that feat, Zatorah chose to follow directives of those *spirits* that spoke to Nesset in front of the former Jurgens Building.

According to Zatorah's understanding of the "Jurgens ghosts," a meeting, of sorts, needed to take place. The principals were a man freed from jail and the *spirit* of George Nelson. It seemed to Zatorah, also, that she may have some mysterious role to play, if the assembly was actually accomplished. In her understanding, those *spirits* felt it important that some message be relayed to *a woman*—possibly her.

Chapter Ten

THERE WERE PROBLEMS inherent, Zatorah discovered, in following the usual course of the team's research—in Gilpin Court. Illuminating an area of it with blue-hued radiation from one of the vans was inadvisable. Seemingly unwise, too, was the prospect of someone, there, openly communicating with supposed ghosts. Police had warned that Gilpin residents may not be receptive to such goings-on, especially at night. In addition, no police escort could be approved for this barely sanctioned, offshoot study.

Forced, by restrictions, to invent a new procedure, Zatorah grabbed, proverbially, for straws. She came up with this plan: Merquan would sit within an EIRI van parked at a strategic location. Out of sight of residents, blue radiations from the energy detection apparatuses would wash over him. It seemed the only discreet set-up for putting an EIRI van, the radiations, and Paler, together, in a Gilpin Court locale. Now, again, early morning hours were chosen as most suitable for undertaking the trial.

No members of the team disagreed with Patrice when she suggested that her presence, if not essential, was quite advisable. More than anyone, she was knowledgeable about Merquan's seizure episodes, if one were to occur. Also, if he was going to be communicating with unseen *entities*, she thought it best that she be at his side. It was thus determined, given limitations of space, that Merquan's attendants be limited to two researchers, the device technician, and Patrice.

With only one chance to make an impressive showing to the team, Zatorah placed all her hopes on the *spirit* of George Nelson. She believed, thus, that finding the optimal location within Gilpin Court for attracting his *energy* was crucial. Since visiting the place where he lived was not an option, the next best location seemed to be the place where he died. Zatorah requested that the EIRI van park at a corner of Federal and 2nd Streets, across from Shockoe Hill Cemetery's west wall.

At this hour of 3:00 a.m., the van's presence added nothing to the area that should elicit special attention. Parked at the corner of the odd numbered side of Federal, the van's headlights trained on an entrance to the cemetery. The view of it, before the driver killed the beams, seemed appropriate for any *ghostly* undertaking to follow. Just inside the locked entrance gate, through the spare mesh of iron, monuments of marble were seen towering above the cemetery walls.

Within the van, it wasn't long before Merquan began showing signs of the onset of seizure. Patrice made sure he remained secure in the seat provided him, believing it would pass, in due course. It was the one occurrence Zatorah and her teammate had hoped would not disrupt proceedings. No one knew how instrumental to their objectives Merquan's seizures would prove.

Padrik Mews was shaken awake by his wife, Deidra, in their home at 137 East Federal Street. She heard a noise outside that disturbed her, the sound of someone gasping loudly for breath. Peering out their second floor window, the couple saw a man reeling in the street at the corner. Padrik recognized the man as someone from the neighborhood and, in pajamas, went out to investigate.

At first, Mews was unsure of what to do. He stood partly in the street beyond his doorsteps, and watched the man he knew as George Nelson collapse at the corner. In that instant, Padrik Mews unknowingly underwent an obscure process that amounted to *psychic merging*. He, for lack of better terms, took "aboard" a silent "passenger," within the functioning of his own mind. From this time until the equally strange "psychic disjoining," each conscious experience of Mews would be known by his new "guest."

At present, Paler had awareness of what Mews knew, regarding the time of day and the date: It was late evening, February 2, 1930. Mews had, in fact, made a mental estimate of the hour, for use at such time that the police arrived, asking questions. By now, others were peering through windows and some had working telephones.

Cautiously, Mews walked over to see what might be done in George Nelson's behalf. It didn't look good. As was evident, Nelson bled profusely from his abdomen. Every minute that passed before George was taken to the "colored" hospital to receive aid, put him closer to death, in Padrik's estimation.

Someone among Padrik's neighbors, staring aghast through windows, from the time of hearing George Nelson's first moans, called for police. Considering the area from which the report was called and the fact that there would not be black officers on the force for another 16 years,[1] the feeling of urgency may not have been great for the responders. Whatever the case, as everyone found out later, Nelson did not last long enough to get lifesaving medical treatment. He died that night before reaching St. Philip's Hospital.[2]

The following day, reports of George Nelson's demise and circumstances precipitating it would spread widely through all of Jackson Ward. The medium would be word of mouth. None of the white newspapers carried the story. For blacks desiring accounts presented by the "colored" newspaper, a long wait until the following Saturday, February 8, was required. Regarding the *immediate* hours following the Sunday night incident, Padrik Mews slept little. He was haunted by the image of the dying man. Nevertheless, at four o'clock a.m. he was up and getting ready for his walk to work.

Though in decline at this particular time, the grocery store employing Padrik Mews had once been part of a black-owned franchise. Twenty years earlier, in its heyday, the *Reformers Mercantile and Industrial Association* operated stores of the kind in cities throughout the South.[3] But its diminished prestige had little effect on Mews. Each workday, he proudly walked the mile from his home to his workplace at Clay and Sixth Street.

Taking in a 1930's view of Richmond, through the eyes of his host, Merquan was amazed at its pre-Interstate 95 character. Most striking was the image of *Baker* and *Duval* Streets—which he knew as north and south borders of I-95, respectively. In his 21st century memory, he saw the altered, gouged-out versions of those two Streets. He contrasted it with the 1930's view. Then, Baker and Duval ran, undisturbed, from Brook Road, westward, to Eighth Street, eastward, and bore modest dwellings and storefront businesses, all along.

There was more 1930's Richmond topography to be amazed at. Like 7th Street of Merquan's time, old Eighth Street, too, continued pass Duval in a steep decline, terminating in the Hospital Street "valley."[4] Also, in 1930, Seventh and Eighth Streets intersected not only with Duval Street but also with Baker, Preston, Bates and Federal Streets.[5]

East of Eighth Street's northward path into the valley was vast lowland property belonging to the Catholic Church.[6] Mentally reconstructing the area from "future" recall, Merquan estimated that those grounds comprised much of the view, southward, from the Hospital Street *valley*.

Often, in his travel to work, Mews took Baker Street, from Second-, over to Sixth Street. At Baker and Fourth, 406 Baker, specifically, he admired the "colored" *Richmond Hospital* with 25 beds, initially.[7, 8] It was also the home of the two black physicians in charge of its operation.[9]

Farther east, on the northwest corner of Baker and Sixth, sat a handsome, white-painted hotel adorned with black-framed windows. It gave Mews a feeling of pride to know that it, too, was black-owned and operated. From the hotel's front at Baker Street, the three-tiered *True Reformers Hotel* stretched, northward, nearly to Preston Street.[10,11] In 1930, after 66 years of existence, it still struck an awe inspiring posture.

As Merquan became aware, his host also enjoyed a trek straight along Second Street on his way to and from Sixth and Clay. Like the other route described, this one also showed the progress of "colored" Richmonders of the day.[12] The view at Second and Baker Streets afforded the animated image of people strolling by numerous small storefronts and making visits as patrons.

In Mew's day, Baker Street featured a leviathan constructed of large, reddish-tan blocks, the capacious remnant of a black-owned bank's central office.[13, 14] For years, the edifice was a local landmark, at Baker and St. James Streets. By 1930, the grand structure was more a monument, honoring the entrepreneurial spirit of blacks a score or more years earlier, than the functioning business office it had once been.[15, 16]

The stateliness of the structure brought Merquan to a sudden reflection. A thousand times or more he had walked, or stood, by the abandoned building, at the corner of Baker and St. James. Not once had he given any thought, as to its history. Now, as a "visitor" in the year, 1930, he had knowledge of the pride *St. Luke's Penny Savings Bank* and *St. Luke's Bank and Trust* inspired in black Richmonders of a past era. Those were names the large business office held.

South of Baker Street, businesses, both prominent and small, lined Second Street from Duval to Clay Streets. All were black enterprises—a real estate and investment company, three banks, two insurance companies, furniture and household appliance stores, a movie theater, an elks lodge built originally as a minister's mansion.[17] Farther south on Second Street, from Clay to Broad, could be seen a plethora of small and medium-sized enterprises: stores, barber shops, and restaurants.[18]

The district of Jackson Ward, almost exclusively black by 1934, was not limited to the central and northern boundaries described.[19] It, in fact, stretched nearly a half mile along Brook Road, westward. There, too, black-owned businesses were in evidence.[20] Many, like Padrik Mews, were aware of the semblance of an independent "black economy," [21] developed by the Ward's black entrepreneurs.

Jackson Ward residents took pride in the guarantee of representation, in Richmond's city council, by their district's own elected officials. The guarantee, however, was a two-edged sword. Those with political insight, were dismayed at the reality of blacks having virtually no political voice in the city's five other wards, due to gerrymandering.[22] The reality was that the *Jackson* ward, as a makeshift voting district, was designed to contain the majority of black votes within that one ward.

The Thursday following George Nelson's death, Padrik Mews met Deidra at her place of employment, in the 700 block of East Franklin Street. It was across from the Civil War residence of Confederate General Robert E. Lee.[23] Unlike her husband, she commuted to and from work via the trolley. On First Street, down the block from their home, she boarded it on the way to work. At various stops along Broad Street she could catch it, at workday end, before it turned on Second, headed to north-most Jackson Ward.

Every now and again, when it could be arranged Padrik walked from his workplace to meet Deidra at the corner of Seventh Street and Broad. There, at the southwest corner, she stood at the edge of *Thalhimer's* department store.[24] As it was for many Richmonders sauntering along the 600 block, odd, of Broad, ogling the store's window displays was a pastime to enjoy. The pair continued westward, which allowed Deidra to browse the wares at *Miller & Rhodes*.[25] In early 1930, it expanded most of the block between Sixth and Fifth Streets.

Conversing and sauntering toward Second Street, the Mewses knew well the sequence of stores west of Miller &

Rhodes. Also occupying that 500 block, odd, of Broad, the row of them extended to Fifth Street. Awnings that stretched out from the wall of a popular jewelry store provided shade, in summer, for passersby gawking at the finery. Next to it was *F. W. Woolworth's 5 And 10 Cent Store*.[26] Finally, at the corner of Fifth Street and Broad sat *McCrory's* "discount emporium."[27]

By five-thirty this Thursday, the Mewses were at home, setting the dinner table. As the couple's unseen "guest" had deduced, in many ways, the two shared similar perspectives. Merquan monitored their discourse:

Deidra:	"Paddy, our section back here is just goin' downhill. It's sure worse than it was when I used to visit up here from the *front* end of the Ward."
Padrik:	"You know what it is: We got some who just won't keep the neighborhood up. But, then, Dee, there's still a lot of us that do."
Deidra:	"Yeah, Jackson Ward's got extremes. Some live in…almost mansions—like, in the 900 blocks of Fourth, Third, and St. James. And Baker, *east* of Fourth Street—nice, big houses, almost no crime…."
Padrik:	"Don't leave out the big, fine homes in the *central* Ward.[28] But, we'll get there, Dee. We keep savin' like we're doin', we'll be buyin' a house in one of those areas, right along with the *money* people."
Deidra:	"Well, right now, we're just one block up from the *trouble* people. Coutts down to Orange and all the way over to Hickory—they're not trying to do anything."
Padrik:	"They ain't gettin' it Dee. They can't see what's keepin' 'em down."
Deidra:	"Yeah, too much liquor and too many babies. Babies cost money. If they can't afford to raise

them right, they shouldn't have 'em. Some in this back section of the Ward don't see the connection."

Padrik: "It ain't just *this* side. *That* kind of life is bringing the Ward down in a lot of areas, really. A neighborhood is all about the people that settles into it. Everybody got to feel that they got a stake in the community."

Deidra: "Back here, there's a whole lot of 'em with no stake in *nothin'*. Ain't got nothin' and ain't got nothin' to lose. Momma always said: People with more to lose are more careful with their lives—*and* with their communities."

Padrik: "You and me, Dee—we're gonna' make it to one of the good sections. Look, here, at this bank statement, again. Our money's growing."

Deidra: "I know. I can hardly wait, Paddy. They're just fightin' and shootin' and stabbin' one another— right down the blocks and around the corner."

Padrik: "You know this whole area back here used to be all white. After they freed 'us,' it started to change. First, we took over the central part and then started movin' north of Duval. My great-granddad used to tell me all about the Ward."

Deidra: "All white, huh?

Padrik: "Well, mostly. I'm talkin' the far north parts. There were mixed poor and well-off whites livin' back here first, and maybe a few free colored folks. You know they wouldn't put the big poorhouse for whites[29, 30] back there on Hospital Street, if it was always mostly colored back here."

Deidra: "I heard the *White Poorhouse* used to be a hospital, during the war."[31]

Padrik: "Maybe that's how Hospital Street got its name, huh?"

Deidra:	"Paddy, did your family ever have to go the *Colored Poorhouse*, for food, when you were coming up?"
Padrik:	"A few times, as a boy, I went in there with a sad story, to get a plate of food. Somebody saw me and told my ma. She put a end to that real fast.
	"One of my favorite things was playing, 'til late, in Shockoe Hill Cemetery, then climbing over the Fourth Street side-wall and headin' straight for the *Colored Poorhouse*, across Fourth, to watch the colored homeless filin' in. It's a shame to admit it, but me and my friends were lookin' to see a relation of somebody we knew, so we could tease 'em, later."
Diedra:	"Sounds like you were a rascal. I always tried to keep as far away from there as I could. I guess I can be glad that, where we are, two whole blocks of cemetery separate us from that place."
Padrik:	"That and three hundred dollars saved up. ... For now, our block of Federal Street is still pretty quiet, most of the time. Another year or two, and we can be out of this part of the Ward. ...Can you believe that people around here are still askin' me when we're gonna' have *children*?"
Deidra:	"They just want to see us in the same condition they're in. Like the saying goes: *misery loves company*."
Padrik:	"Those that want to see us with children, before we're ready, are the same ones that's raisin' trouble-makers, to follow in the shoes of their mommas and daddies."

As the undetected "guest" from the future, monitored silently, the Mews couple completed dinner together. It was sometime during collection of the dinner dishes that the *psychic disengagement* occurred. As the past cannot be altered by the present, the host was not the least affected by Merquan's *psychic* presence or absence.

Paler had been merely an observer of scenes and events that were of a bygone time. Now, he was undergoing the sensation he knew so well: that of traveling a short distance at, dizzying speed. At his "return," Merquan felt as though his mind slammed back in place within his own nervous system.

Coming to consciousness, Merquan felt the familiar rub around his shoulders. He knew before he focused his eyes that it was Patrice's handiwork. After some seconds, he recognized the people kneeling in an arc around him—the crew of the EIRI van. Next, he heard the approving shouts that reflected everyone's relief. Just as Patrice had tried to assure them, nearly three minutes prior, Merquan was recovering, intact, from the seizure.

The next order of business, for the investigators, was to find out if Paler could report any *otherworldly* experiences—ones verifiable. As Zatorah and her research mate knew, the course of their remaining study in Richmond hinged on that report. As they had been for the past ten minutes, microphones were in place to record sounds and images in the van. Zatorah's research mate led the exchange that followed:

Researcher:	"Merquan, you look fit as a fiddle. How do you feel?"
Merquan:	"Maybe just a little headache. Other'n that, feels like I just sat through a whole bunch'a movies."
Researcher:	"Really? Is it safe to say you had dreams over the past minutes?"

Merquan: "Dreams? No, I wouldn't say dreams. It was more like bein' invisible and watchin' stuff happen."

Zatorah: "Can you explain what you mean?"

Merquan: "It must be that blue light. All them times before when I came out, I would forget what I saw... and what I knew. But, now, all them lives and all them people—I remember 'em. They're in my head like movie scenes.

"Let me look out the door. Yeah, slide it open. Let me stand around out here a minute. Yep. The *homeboy* lived right here—him and his wife. This open space is where the house was, address 'one-thirty-seven.'

"And the other, *player*, George...he fell down right in this spot, bleedin' and shit—bad. They say he died on the way to the hospital. *E'rebody* was talkin' 'bout it that next day, Monday. Damn. All that *wild shit* is comin' back to me.

"I got two *Jackson Wards* in my head. This is crazy! I know what all this area *used to be*."

Van driver: "You three probably should get back into the van, don't you think?"

Merquan: "...Yeah, I'll get back in the van. Why not? You-all want to know if I can tell you some'em new, about this *ghost thing* you been chasin'. Well, I got two *Jackson Wards* in my head—two Richmonds, really.

"Lady, I'm gonna' be *real* with you. I thought y'all were *buggin'*, at first—just tryin' to find some'em to write about, to make some money or some'em. But now, I see that this *ghost van* is the *real shit*."

Patrice: "I've been trying to get *Merk* to clean up his speech. *Merk*, can you leave the profanity out?

	These people want you to tell what you've experienced, without the cussin' and all."
Merquan:	"My *bad*. You been right, Treecie. There were always groups that wanted to do better, talk better, live better. They were like *you*: trying to get the others to show a better side. They could see what was happenin' in the *Ward*. Them ones that just wanted to *live loose* was keepin' it down...draggin' it down."
Zatorah:	"Merquan, you said something about 'George' falling to the street, bleeding. That obviously was part of the scenes you say you witnessed. It also coincides with something I didn't tell you, when I explained to you and Patrice my mission here in Richmond.
	"There was, in fact, a deadly stabbing or slashing that occurred down the block which resulted in a man named *George* collapsing at this intersection. In the vision you had, did you get a sense of the time-frame?"
Merquan:	"I don't really want to call it havin' a *vision*. I was, like, *there*. I was back there, in the time that the stuff happened. I know it sounds crazy as a *bi*—. I mean, crazy as *hell*, but...."
Zatorah:	"Do you recall the time-frame, the year, maybe, that it happened—the incident with *George* that you mentioned?"
Merquan:	"It was at night, a Sunday in February... February 2, 1930. This is the thing: Everything I saw—I saw through somebody else's eyes. I can't really explain it, but I know what I saw."
Zatorah:	[stunned, speechless]
Merquan:	"But that ain't all of it. I'm realizin' some'em that is totally kickin' my *as*...my pants! I can actually remember scenes and remember what

I knew, during other seizures! I'm rememberin'
all *kinds* of shit! *It's crazy.*"

Zatorah's research mate couldn't be totally sure whether
or not Zatorah had mentioned *George Nelson* to Merquan and
forgot it. But Zatorah was certain she hadn't. To her, all that
Merquan had said, thus far, provided justification enough, for
making a plea to let him continue. She had strong suspicions
that Merquan was right, in saying the van's energy detection
devices played a critical role. Those radiations designed to detect
spiritual energy were now, she believed, aiding in Merquan's
connection, and *recall* of connection, with the *spirit* world.

The question now was: Could she convince project managers
that Merquan had made a connection with George Nelson, on
his own? Before making that determination, Zatorah knew it
was crucial to find out if Merquan was willing to continue the
investigation. She began the inquiry:

Zatorah: "Merquan, I believe you do have knowledge
               of past events in Richmond—knowledge that
               is *paranormal*. But much proof, or verification,
               or…corroborating facts, are needed.
               "I don't even know if we'll be allowed another
               investigation after tonight. But, if we are, I would
               be grateful for your continued participation."

Merquan: "Hey, you're helpin' us with my court case.
               You bonded me out. Short of committin' any
               crimes, I'm with you…I'm with you a *hun'erd*
               percent. It would be good to know how *long*
               you're gonna' need me."

Zatorah: "Our original research concludes in the middle
               of this month. I go back to Cambridge, then, to
               prepare for the fall semester at the university."

Merquan: "Hell, that ain't but about two weeks. It's *on*."

Zatorah: "I can tell you that any and all upcoming
               experiences like the one you just related to us

would help me make a case for moving forward in this offshoot study. Your identifying, again, something from the past that can be validated in research is just what we need. As I think on it, maybe a recall from *any* of the previous times you were in the altered state might be useful."

Merquan: "I get it. You need, like, *real proof* that I been *back* there."

Patrice: "I have an idea, Zatorah. It sounds like *you* already believe. So, you need something that will convince your team. How about this:

"How about your coworker give *Merk* a date, like, *off the top*, and see if he can tell something he saw or knows, that nobody should know about…unless they were back in that time. You know what I'm saying? Then, you go and check the records, like you-all do, and see if it's there."

EIRI staff: "Hmm. That's an interesting idea. If Merquan gives us something to work with, we can all retire for the night with not one but two potential pieces of ammo. Tomorrow, bright and early, the team can start the work of verifying what we have. Merquan, are you *good* with me choosing a year, randomly?"

Merquan: "Put her in 'drive' and let's run her off the cliff."

EIRI staff: "Okay…I like this. So, let's see——. How about a nice, even year like 1920? To make a finding even more amazing, let's try for a specific month…January. What we'd like is some obscure detail to research later."

Merquan: "Here you go: I 'travelled'—that's probably the best word to use—I *travelled* with a lady who had lost everything and was homeless. She used to stay, at night, in the *Colored Poorhouse* building, on the grounds between Fourth and Fifth, across from Hospital Street.

"Agnes Dogget—that was her name. I can see the scenery from her walk down old *Fifth* Street, to Baker. Back then, *Fifth* Street didn't curve into *Fourth*, like today. It ran through what now is the I-64 off-ramp and continued over I-95, to Duval and the rest. There wasn't no highways there, then. In fact, there were houses all along the way, on the old *Fifth* Street. It's hard to relate it to the way it looks today.

"I'll give you an example: Bates Street is right up at the next corner. It starts at the edge of cemetery and runs like the street we're on— except, right out there, this street, Federal, is blocked at the cemetery. But Bates, up at the corner, runs along a couple of blocks, to 3rd and on to 4th Street. That's *near* where I threw that *nine* over the wall."

"Anyway, right now Bates is a little *shorty* street. Back then, though, it ran not just to *Third* and *Fourth*, but also to *Fifth*, *Sixth*, *Seventh,* and goddamn-it, *Eighth* Street! And the same for Preston and Baker! Even Federal, where we're at, picked up again at *Fifth* and ran to *Eighth*. That is some wild shit! If we ride up there, you wouldn't be able to imagine it."

Patrice: "Wow. That would blow me away to see the proof of that."

Merquan: "It's crazy, Treecie! ...But, back to that lady I was talkin' about—. In her walk, she would get to the 800 block of *Fifth* Street, right over where '95' is, now. I remember it. And right in that 800 block, near Duval, was this house with the sign. I can still see it. It said: 'For Sale: $5,500.'

"I think she had lived in it, once. It was red brick, and I'm rememberin' seven, eight…ten rooms, even though I never saw the inside. But *she* knew the inside, and I have a fuzzy picture of it, from *her* memory. Don't ask me how that works. I can't explain it."

Zatorah: "Was Ms. Dogget the owner? And do you have a specific address? If so, records may still exist."

Merquan: "Naw…I…think that lady, one time, rented a room in there. Yep, that's what it was. She lived all alone in that room, in that big house on *Fifth* Street. And none of her four children ever came to see her at that…'Lange House.'

"Dang! That's what she called it—*Lange House*. She had to leave, when it went up for sale. Three sons, and her youngest, a daughter—and none of 'em came to help, when she had to go to the poorhouse for shelter and to eat.

"Oh, man. I just found out some'em. Goin' back like that—rememberin'—it's makin' me dizzy as hell. Whew…my eyes—I'm gettin' a headache behind my eyes."

IERI staff: "Whoa…okay, we're not going to overdo this. You've been a real trooper, Merquan. We've gotten a lot done. We can pick it up again, when you've had some rest and time to think about everything."

Patrice: "Yeah, we definitely have to let you get some rest. You look tired, baby."

Merquan: "By tomorrow I'll be good as new. So, whenever y'all are ready for the next one, I'll be set to dig up some'em good for you."

Zatorah: "I won't be surprised if we find that you have, already."

Zatorah and her colleagues made quick decisions about sources to check for corroboration of Merquan's report. Since 5th Street, north of Clay, was largely black in the time of interest, ads in the one "colored" newspaper were checked. For January 17, 1920, the *Richmond Planet* recorded a list of properties for sale, on page two. The researchers perused the excerpt below, from the column of interest. It was the property entries for north central Jackson Ward upon which they focused most.

VALUABLE PROPERY FOR SALE
ON LONG TIME PAYMENTS
Two 6 Room Houses, Frame, on N. 7th
Street, near Baker Street, each.......$2,750
One 3 Room Frame House on Bates Street....$ 900
One Ten Room Brick *on N. 5th St., beyond*
Duval St. [italics added]................$5,500

...As we have plenty of money on deposit at this time, we are in a position to give exceptionally good terms to those desiring to purchase any of this property. Address

MECHANICS SAVINGS BANK
RICHMOND,   **VIRGINIA**
JOHN MITCHELL, JR., President
Call at the N. W. Corner of Third and Clay Streets or see the
President at 311 N. Fourth Street [32]

That which astonished the team, next, was the name recorded on a street map of Richmond, drawn in the last quarter of the 1800s. In this and later periods, next to hand-drawn building markers were written the name of home owners and business owners. The EIRI team took special note of a small, square marking, placed just north of Duval Street, on Fifth Street. Near it, the owner's name read "JG Lange." [33]

When presented with the findings, those corroborations did impress EIRI project managers. However, the medical condition accompanying, perhaps facilitating, Merquan's *extra-normal* experience worried them. In order to continue working with the researchers, they concluded, he would have to be attended by appropriate medical staff. The original plan made no such provisions, and it was thought to be too late in the study to alter it so radically.

In the end, it was decided that the present research must enter the conclusion stage. It was to do so without farther exploration of, and utilization of, Merquan Paler's "apparent gift."

Looming overhead was a matter that took precedence over any and all matters concerning Merquan. The following week, he was to go before a judge who would determine the merits of his malicious wounding charge. Moderate bond had been set at the initial arraignment, which seemed a good sign that the case against Merquan was less than ideal for prosecutors.

The next sign of weakness in the indictment was revealed in the decision for hearing in a lower court. At that time it was known that Paler's handprint was found only on the gun's barrel extension. It was consistent with his story of having picked the weapon up, *after* the deadly shot had been fired from it. Tips had led to Merquan's arrest, at home, the day of the shooting. The fact that no substantial residue of exploding gunpowder was found on his hands, at that time, also cramped the case against him.

Skilled courtroom arguing by Merquan's public defender led to the judge's ruling against the Commonwealth attorney, in Merquan's case. As part of the process, the tactic of discrediting the key eyewitness' account was also employed. The judge agreed that testimony given by a nearsighted observer, not wearing glasses at the time, lacked reliability from a block's distance.

With the court case behind him, Merquan thought more deeply about an idea vying for his full attention. Even without the blue-light radiation from the EIRI van, he had faint recall of his various *past-time* experiences during seizures. The reconstructions were fuzzy and disjointed, but, unlike before, he was in possession of them. But even more stirring, to him, was the gnawing feeling that an underlying *theme* bound those experiences together. More and more, it seemed that, by *design*, of some sort, he needed to grasp a central and core meaning of it all.

With the EIRI study in Richmond essentially concluded, Zatorah made a proposal to the research team. Just over a week remained for gathering data. As Zatorah knew, the team had elected to use it to write the study's preliminary description. She asked to be allowed a portion of that time to continue work, *informally*, with Paler and Patrice Keeper. Access to an EIRI van, a driver and a technician were needed. In addition, she required a team member as a crucial second witness and participant. As before, that person would help in all the recording activity.

When she received the team's cautious agreement to proceed, Zatorah sought an assembly of equal importance. It seemed clear to her that the two adult figures most prominent in Merquan's life were Patrice and his mother, Bonita Paler. He had already agreed to further work with the team. But, she thought, the prospect of having him undergo seizure, for research, must take into account several points of view.

Accompanied by her research colleague, Zatorah arrived at Patrice's housing unit on Hill Street. Waiting for them, as prearranged, was Patrice, Bonita and the central figure, Merquan. Very soon the anticipated discussion got underway:

Bonita:	"I can't really say if it's a good idea or not. I mean, it turned out all right that last time. And with Treecie right there—I guess it's good. But, you know, it's up to Merquan."
Patrice:	"Yeah, it's definitely up to you, *Merk*. You sound like you're all for it. …See, Zatorah, we really thank you for getting *Merk* out of jail. He wouldn't tell the medical staff over there about his condition, so they could put him where he'd

be watched over. For all we know, you may
have saved his life."

Zatorah: "I was more than glad to do it. In fact, one
could say it was *required* that I do it, according
to those *otherworldly* reports I told you about.
But, I have to say—. I can't help but feel self
serving, in asking you-all to do this.

"Our project managers considered it too
risky, and yet I have opted to continue, with the
agreement of all of you. Part of me feels like
I'm not being as concerned, Merquan, for your
welfare, as I should be."

Merquan: "You want just five days of work out'a me, for
just a couple'a hours a day. I even get to have
my *baby girl* ridin' wit' me. Now, if we hit 'dirt'
in just *one* hour, I still get paid for *two*.

"So look here. I done figured out the money
and it comes to a *ball*—a *hun'ed* dollars—every
half hour! Lady, I'm *in* like a *hairpin*."

Findings from Zatorah's new, unofficial, research could not
be added to the EIRI study description. Even so, the offshoot
team knew that methods they chose for conducting explorations
must be planned carefully. The goal, as usual, was to obtain
results compelling enough to report to an interested audience.
As usual, methods used to achieve those findings must appear
valid. Zatorah and her research colleague plotted the following
course:

The EIRI van's large "cargo" section was to be curtained
such as to make a view outside impossible. The van driver was
given a pre-devised itinerary known only to her and the two
researchers. For each day of trial, the driver chose two sites on
the list to visit, which she revealed to no one beforehand. In
this way, none of the van's cargo riders ever knew the locale in
which they were positioned at a given time.

On the first evening of Zatorah's resumed research, the van driver parked southbound on 17th Street, across from an Exxon filling station. Merquan sat in a corner of the van, purposely assuming a meditative state. Blue light radiations cascaded over him, from a source above. After a minute, he lost consciousness of the van's inside environment. Soon, his mind merged with that of a young fellow who walked through the van's exact location—263 years prior.

Chapter Eleven

"MASTER" (*MASSA,* IN the slave parlance of the day) Monahan sent the boy on an errand which required journey to the original city's northern boundary. Even considering Cro's rambling tendencies, Monahan Sr. expected him back to the main house in half an hour. On *Main Street,* four blocks east of flood-prone Shockoe Creek, sat the Monahan house. Forming the young city's northern border was a wide dirt road called *Broad Street.*[1] Cro's journey, then, comprised about half a mile, one way.

Few endeavors gave Cro greater pleasure than traipsing about the city's original *northwestern* boundary. He was, in fact, at that location when he unknowingly became host to the visitor from over two centuries in the future. In Cro's day, Richmond's western boundary was the street later named 17th Street.[2] To Cro and his contemporaries, it was known as "First Street." [3] Over many years, First Street would be "pushed" nearly a mile-and-a-half west of its original location.

Richmond's *original* First Street held a real fascination for Cro. It stood at the edge of a wide gorge in the earth ploughed by the ebb and flow of creek water. From a region north of the city, Shockoe Creek meandered its way, ultimately, to adopt a course parallel to original *First* Street. Near Broad Street, the creek flowed around great rocks that stood, from base to pinnacle, up to four feet in height.

At every opportunity, Cro played about the area, leaping from stone to stone. During flood stage, knowing the position of those rocks was crucial to crossing the creek's width, which had the potential of spanning a distance of two city blocks.[4] On this day of high tide, the creek's eastside waters tickled *First* Street's western side.

The other feature that lured Cro to the old *First & Broad* locale was the steep earthen incline that began just beyond the city's western border. To him, the landscape of trees and brush growing out of a slope provided innumerable opportunities for exploration. At the top of that incline towering over the creek, westward, the terrain leveled. But more unrefined land stretched for miles.

Land at the top of that incline was sprinkled here and there with self-built homes belonging to folks of the county surrounding early Richmond, that is, Henrico. As an unpaid courier for "massa" Monahan, Cro had some familiarity with a number of them—people who preferred a wide distance between themselves and neighbors. Upon making a delivery, atop "the hill," and returning to his town's western border, Cro typically indulged his favorite activity: It was walking precariously along the steep slope of land overlooking Shockoe Creek.

In every direction, the view from early *First & Broad* filled Cro with wonder. Northward, he saw a landscape that might have been the result of a powerful earthquake or land-altering fault. Or, perhaps, eons past, a meteor plowed through, radically splitting the terrain. Whatever the causal event, for Cro, the great expanse, northward, of gouged earth presented a spectacular vista. Later, at the valley's base, a mile-long stretch of road, northward, would be carved out, aptly named "Valley Street."[5] In the 20th century two more names would be applied: 17th Street and, finally, Oliver Hill Parkway.

Looking east from old *First* Street, Cro could actually see Richmond's eastern boundary, at that time. The distance was only three quarters of a mile along *Broad Street*—yet another steep incline. During and after a great rain, the surface of the dirt road was so treacherous that a trek downward required much caution. Even so, one thing was well known at the time. Traveling, on foot, from *original* Ninth Street (later, 26th Street), down to original *First* Street, was usually safer than a horse-drawn carriage ride along that route.

So, at the intersection of old *First & Broad*, Cro stood between two hills, east and west. The city proper sprawled a mere 36 blocks, square, east and south of that point.[6] Running errands for "massa" Monahan, Cro regularly sprinted along the nine blocks, east to west, and the four, north to south, effortlessly. The one area he was forbidden to explore was located south of Cary Street, a swampy location along the river. The area would later include a street called "Canal." The James River, and its swampy northern bank, marked the city's southern limit, in 1749, and remained so for the following 161 years, to 1910.[7]

For three years, Cro had belonged to the Monahans as human property. In that time, he earned the total trust of the family patriarch. In day hours, he travelled about the city on one mission or another with no more oversight than that provided by townsfolk going about their usual affairs. No one suspected for an instant that he may harbor feelings of ill will about his station in life. Cro's dream of rafting southeast, on the James, toward the town of Williamsburg, where he was born, was the last thing Richmond's *master* class suspected.

Cro wasn't sure, himself, why he chose this day as the one on which to attempt his escape. For months, the raft he constructed and hid on a hillside above *First* Street showed no sign of having been discovered by others. In that interval, the creek ultimately flowing to the James had swelled numerous times. But not often had its width and depth matched the dimensions it took, this day that Cro gazed upon it.

From a tangle of brush on the incline towering westward, above old *First* Street, Cro freed his raft. Down the steep hill he pushed it, until the makeshift vessel was buoyant in the creek water. He covered himself as best he could with leafy branches and other shrubbery and let the creek's slow current compel him southward. Cro lie flat and still on the raft. As he did, he wondered if anyone who saw the anomaly in the creek would care to investigate. The answer came quickly.

Along a route which would later include part of Sixteenth Street, Cro's craft drifted. Ever so slowly it moved southward, toward Grace Street. There, at the creek's bank, onlookers ogled the strange site. Very soon, they determined that beneath the branches and twigs was someone who, very likely, attempted to conceal himself.

More enterprising spectators among them felt driven to wade out to the raft and try redirecting its course. But the creek's width stretched a distance of two city blocks, east to west—old *First* Street being the eastern boundary.[8] At Shockoe Creek's center this day, its maximum depth was about five feet and strewn with rocks of varying size.

By the time the raft and Cro reached *Franklin Street*, heading for Main, the group following its voyage continued to grow. Overcome with curiosity, some of the younger members of the monitors waded out close to the raft. One of them made the identification:

"It's Cro!" he began crying out. Soon, a chorus of the onlookers repeated the revelation: "It's Cro! It's Cro! Go get Mr. Monahan!"

Drifting ever so slowly, southward, pass Main Street, Cro perceived a most alarming site, through his cover. It was "massa" Monahan running, with rifle in hand. He saw the old man make the turn, southward, following the creek's flow, at its eastern bank. Next, he heard Monahan's angry shouts.

"Cro, you *black traitor*—get off that raft or I'll shoot!"

The area between Main and Cary Streets, east of Shockoe Creek, was a great expanse of flatland, a grassy field north of the river's swampy bank.[9] It was across the field that Monahan moved. Finally, he stopped, and with careful aim, he fired shots at the figure floating slowly and placidly on the creek, heading for the James.

Merquan's consciousness was obliged to disengage from the *psychic composition* of his host. One reason was that Cro was dying from shotgun blasts that struck his head.

Still awash in the shower of blue radiations, Merquan relayed his recent experience with crystal clarity. His audience, unfamiliar with Richmond City's early history, found the description of its original *scope* astonishing. East-west boundaries extending only from present 17th Street to 26th Street seemed unreal. Imagining political boundaries of Richmond ranging from Broad Street to the James River, north to south, was equally amazing. Regarding Shockoe Creek, there was no present-day sign of it to accord with Merquan's story.

During the EIRI team's obligatory research, however, it was discovered that each of Merquan's characterizations was valid. Richmond was described as encompassing only a fifth of square mile in the 1740s, with boundaries set as Merquan described. As for the visible and flowing Shockoe Creek of report, it, too, was found to have been a past reality.

It was discovered that the creek had flowed southward from a gorge alongside present Richmond-Henrico Turnpike. From there, it snaked behind Hospital Street, northeast of Jackson Ward. After coursing through the basin of Hospital Street, Shockoe Creek took a route along a section of present-day *I-95*. At a site that used to be Clay and 14th Streets, it ran eastward, near old 16th Street. Next, Shockoe Creek streamed, southward, to Marshall Street, then to Broad Street, and onward to the river.[10] The team also found early photographs of the creek's *flood waters*, stretching from 15th Street to 17th Street, at Main Street.

There was a one day reprieve following the test of Merquan's "past-time transport" ability, at the location of 17th and Broad Streets. Then work got underway, anew. The site chosen, next, was just south of the intersection of Main Street and Wharf, in the city's far East End.

With aid from the EIRI van's *extra-normal* energy detection radiation, Merquan, now, entered into *psychic merge* with "Tess." As he soon discovered, Tess was a 25 year old black woman who, the morning before, was imprisoned within the slave jail run by *Robert Lumpkin*.[11] As Merquan later recalled and relayed to the EIRI team, the date was April 4, 1865. It was a cool Tuesday morning, the smell of smoke still heavy in the air.[12]

All along the river bank, from *Eighteenth* Street, eastward, to *Rocketts Landing*, were groups of newly freed people.[13] Until the national government had its *Freedmen's Bureaus* up and running, former slaves had to make a way for themselves.[14] With nowhere else to go, they constructed makeshift shelters by the James River. Tess, having made impromptu friendships with other ex-slaves, joined them.

Like the others, Tess had heard, via a human communication chain, that new freedmen had found employment, farther south on the river.[15] As word had it, theirs was important work. From the bluffs of Chaffin and Drewry, northward, they helped clear the river of dangerous articles that could jeopardize President Abraham Lincoln's visit to Richmond, this day.[16]

Tess and her peers, waited patiently beyond the noon hour. For now, there was little else to do but wait. Their world was undergoing rapid and radical change. No one was sure how it would play out, in time. For now, however, the prospect of "ol' Abe Lincoln" coming to look over the newly Union-captured city seemed a good omen. Tess and the various groups seeking shelter quietly inhabited staked-out areas along the river. As they did, they kept a respectfully discreet watch-out, for the Union president.

Finally it came—the sight of a single, open boat, and rowmen, and two figures sitting beside one another at the front. These latter were Abraham Lincoln and his son Tad.[17]

On the morning of the previous day, April 3rd, black people held as slaves in Richmond had, more than ever, come to grips with a certain reality. It was that Confederate loss to Union troops would mean the end of slavery. Thus, the human masses aligned in clusters within Tess' field of vision viewed the Union president as a godsend. To them, he was second only to *Christ*, himself, as an instrument of their freedom from bondage.[18]

In a speaking style that was a mixture of spiritedness and cynicism Tess carried forth conversation with her attendants.

Tess: "If anybody told me last week I'd be *free* out here, watchin' the President ridin' down the river to take a look at *free* Richmond, I'd'a spit on they shoes."

Ginny: "*Lordy*, there he is! Our *savior*—it's like lookin' at *Jesus* hisself! Maybe he *is* Jesus! I prayed our Lord would set us free, *and we is!* The good Lord sent him, *f'sho!*

"Look at him—the man what done put a end to slavery! Lord, Jesus, in heaven! *Praise the Lord!*"

Tess: "Where was *the Lord, Jesus in heaven*, last week, when I was bein' beat, in Lumpkin, and taken the vantage of? I don't want to hear 'bout no white man's *Lord*—not all I been through in my life."

Louisiana: "Girl, you don't want to be sayin' that! The Lord'll curse you for sayin' stuff like that. Be thankful. Jes' look there. God done *sent* us our savior!

"You look real good and hard. That's *ol' Abe Lincoln* hisself. This is as fine a sight as I *ever* done behold. Ooooh, look at him! The Lord above sent him to answer our prayers."

Tess: "Yeah, I'm thankful. But I'm *mad*, too. I'm *real* hurt and I'm *real* mad. I ain't scared to say it:

I'm mad at any God what let happen to me, *what done happened to me.*

"So, you go on and praise that *slave massa's God*, all you want. And praise Abe Lincoln, too, if you want to, and call him *Jesus*, if you got a mind to. But don't 'spect me to sing wit' you."

Virgie: "I bet Abe Lincoln ain't never owned no slaves."

Tess: "Maybe. I ain't got nothin' 'gainst him. I'm glad he's here and I'm *damned* glad he and his Union soldiers done what they done—givin' us our freedom. But it was his *kind*...his *kind* what 'slaved me and beat me and used me for they pleasure, and I ain't never gon' forget it!"

Jinny: "I'm scared to ask what happened to you at *Lumpkin*, Tess. All I can say is no massa, or massa's family ever laid a hand on me."

Tess: "You right. Don't ask me 'bout *Lumpkin*. And it ain't jes' been *Lumpkin*. I done had me five massas in my life—been sold fo'e times, in Georgia. They cain't do nothin' wit' me—'cept beat me and try to make me give up. But I fight 'til I die. So they got to sell me or kill me. They kill me, they don't get no pay."

Ernis   "Well, you free now. You don't want to give the *Lord* no credit?"

Tess: "No. ...Took too damned long. My mammy didn't teach me to believe in no *massa's God*, anyway. She hated massa, and when he got word of it, he sold her. So, then, I hated him, too—and he sold me. And he was religioooous... kept a Bible with him...preached *the word* and *e're-thang*."

Louisiana: "Oooh, look! He's gettin' out down near *Eighteen* Street.[19] I wonder if they take him to see them two soldier prisons."

Ernis: "*Castle Thunder* and *Libby*—yeah, I heard me some bad talk 'bout them jails." [20, 21, 22]

Louisiana: "Yeah, them Union prisoners is free like us, now. The Union Army, what come in to put out them fires, done saw to that. I hope they take Abe Lincoln to what's left of that *Lumpkin*. Maybe the President make 'em pay for what happened to you, Tess."

Tess: "Maybe—but it cain't help me now. The pain won't go away, Lucy. It ain't never goin' away. I'll be mad about it 'til I die."

Ernis   "Nah, you'll get over it. You meet you a good nigga man and settle down and have babies and care f'yo' fam'ly and...."

Tess: "If your *Jesus* was standin' right here, Ernis T, I ask him why his Daddy make some niggas so messed up in the head. You think I ain't had some nigga men? They jes' as *messed up in the head*, as the white one is *mean*.

"Ain't none'a you 'round here never take a good look at this thang? We Africa. Mammy taught me good. Africa men don't respec' they womens. And they don't respec' no other Africans that ain't in they same tribe.

"So, now we here. It's the same goddamn thang! Nigga men don't respec' they womens and ev'y chance they get they tries to disrespec' otha' niggas, when they can get away wit' it. Tell me I ain't right! Y'all scared to look at the truth.

"This world full'a animals that get by—by eatin' otha' animals. The white man is a animal that feed off niggas, when he can. The nigga is a animal that come here with the same appetite as massa. And now he can *worship massa's God*, while he feed off otha' niggas. Too bad y'all

	ain't had Mammy to put y'all straight on this mess. Some'a y'all wouldn't know the truth if it leap up and bite off your nose."
Virgie:	"It's gon' be all right, Tess. You gon' get better. I'm gon' *pray* for you. I'm gon' pray *hard*—every night and every day—for you. God is gon' take care'a you and take that pain and hate out your heart. I know it in *my* heart.
	"You a good, sweet person, Tess—down inside. You jes' been hurt so bad. But God is gon' lighten your heart and make a way. 'Cause I'm gon' pray hard, like I did for the *end of slavery*. We all gon' pray for you, sista'. We love you out here.
	"I see that tear comin' in your eyes, sista'. But, it's gon' be all right. I'm gon' pray hard for you."
Tess:	"How 'bout pray for some food for us, out here, Virgie. But if it take a *hun'ed* and mo'e years to answer it—like it did slavery—all us is *up that river*, over there, without a row stick."

Once again, without knowing where, in the city, the van had stopped, Merquan reported a *past travel-experience* that matched the locale. After recounting the memory of it to his attendants and, simultaneously, in recording devices, Merquan made a request. He wanted the driver to take them all to the intersection of Cary and 19th Streets. Upon arrival there, he pointed at a lot stretching to a northwest corner of that intersection.

"That's where *Castle Thunder* was," he informed, "right where that parking lot is. All of us, we took a route to here, on the way to see Abraham Lincoln. I know it sounds crazy, but I saw all of it."

"And *Castle Thunder*, you say, was a prison for those who sympathized with the Union?" The question was that of Zatorah's research partner.

"Yeah, but not only them kind. It had some of the area's worse thugs and killers up in there, too.[23] That's what people around me said. According to report, that j'aint wasn't no country club. What little food there was was rotten. Conditions as bad as you can imagine, they said.

"And down the street, on 18th, on the left side, that little red building is where part of another big jail was. That one was for the Union Army *officers* that got captured—*Libby Prison* they called it. They also called it 'the dungeon.'[24]

"A whole bunch of us, in separate groups, walked to see the President, up close. The group I was in came down Canal, then we crossed and walked down Cary a ways. We didn't get to see Lincoln, sort'a, up close, until we were at *Fourteenth* and Main. Real tall, he was...worn-lookin', but at peace.

"You would have thought Richmond was almost all black, there were so many of us out there.[25] The white people seemed mostly to stay indoors. But blacks were out in streets, in every block you could see. If they caught a glimpse of Lincoln, they hollered and cheered and praised the Lord, like it was the end of the world, or some'em. All that excitement—I think most forgot they were hungry."

Chapter Twelve

T̲H̲E̲ EIRI RESEARCHERS found President Lincoln's visit to Richmond on Tuesday, April 4, 1865 a matter of historical record. The informal manner of his arrival is also documented. While the original plan had been for the steamer, *River Queen*, to carry the president to a docking point in Richmond, difficulties on the James thwarted that arrangement.

Indeed, every detail of Merquan's report amenable to verification was, in fact, corroborated by archival record. Within a book of Richmond historical photographs were pictures of *Libby Prison* and *Castle Thunder* at the locations Merquan cited.

Findings related to Merquan's most recent *extra-normal* work with the researchers had everyone excited about their next exploration. In the expedition to follow, the van was parked on 12th Street. It was just yards from the intersection with Leigh Street and yards from the west end of *Martin Luther King, Jr. Memorial Bridge*. Merquan's altered state lasted a total of four minutes this time. When he emerged from his "sleep," he recounted two days in the life of a drywall hanger in the year 1922.

The man, Curtis Skimmer, worked in building refurbishment. Presently, he was with a crew trying to renovate a building whose transfer of ownership was being negotiated. Since 1867, it had been designated, under federal mandate, for municipal use by the *Freedman's Bureau*, in Richmond. The city, later, utilized the structure as its first school for black students.[1, 2]

Extending half a block along 12th Street, between Clay and Leigh, the building had been known by three names. For a decade, to the year 1886, it was called the *Richmond Colored Normal and High School.* During ten subsequent years, the term "normal" was dropped. For 12 years, leading to 1908, it was given the name *Armstrong High School.* By 1908, however, the site was deemed unsuitable as a Richmond public school. Thus, this first version of *Armstrong High* was moved to a Jackson Ward location and the old structure designated for use by the city's building and grounds department.[3]

Working on the building's interior, Skimmer masked the mixed emotions he felt. He knew, from local legend, that the structure was built the year he was born. He had, in fact, attended the *Colored Normal School* in his latter teenage years, to 1885. Once he'd determined that a "normal," or teacher preparatory, school did not suit him, he opted to study a trade. Now, he was back at his *alma mater*, aiding in its alteration from a city warehouse to a structure within a medical school complex.

At the end of his "time-travel," Merquan Paler was, at first, groggy, but soon the memories of his experience crystallized. Piece by piece, he began relating aspects of them to his audience within the EIRI van. His excitement was evident, as he hinted at the identities of students, at the *Richmond Colored High and Normal School*, who had been classmates of his host.

Zatorah, with the others, listened raptly to Merquan's description of people, sights and sounds, in Richmond of 1922. Near the end of his talk, she recognized an opportunity to ask Merquan about the site where she'd first encountered him and Patrice. The locations—the present one, on 12th Street, and that at, former, 13th Street[4] and Marshall—had proximity.

She thought Merquan's most recent *past-time* host might have held information about the latter location. Perhaps Merquan had been, and was still, privy to it. If so, she dared hope some relevance could be found to that first reading she'd received from Madam Lu.

Intrigued by the research, the van's driver cordially began steering along a short route, to the end of Marshall Street's 1200 block. Her destination was the Dooley Hospital Memorial. Before the vehicle arrived at the site, Merquan offered his guess as to the lot's further significance.

Merquan: "I can tell you this, Z—in the year St. Philip was supposed to open, blacks in Richmond were on-edge. I heard my guide talkin' about it with some *chillers* in his day. And you know what? The way y'all researchers like to get that *verification* from archives and stuff? I think I got some'em for you.

"It was two years after the fact, Z, but this topic actually came up in a conversation. I can 'hear' 'em talkin' 'bout a newspaper article, came out *May 1920*. Blacks suspected whites were runnin' a *oky-doke* and then tryin' to backslide. See, the white city leaders approved building a all-black hospital downtown. This was gonna' add to the single other one, located in Jackson Ward.

"But it started goin' around that black people were about to get *shafted* out of what was promised to 'em. People just started thinkin' that, all of a sudden, whites makin' the deal possible were tryin' to renege."

"So, one of the white newspapers investigated and put it out, in a back page, one chiller said, that there would be no tricks. St. Philip was gon' be all black—staffed *and* served."

Parked near the MCV memorial concourse, all within the van listened to Merquan's report. Zatorah noted that the place where he pointed out St. Philip's former location seemed to match well Madam Lu's reading. At that juncture Zatorah was certain she would find the occasion to ask Merquan's aid in another matter. It was one with no relation, at all, to the EIRI study.

Other Richmond areas interested her, personally. Perhaps, later, he could try a *past-time* exploration of locales that had given her those odd sensations, when she visited them. Specifically, these were 4th and 5th Streets near Main, as well as the block of Monument Avenue, between Allison and Strawberry.

More so than the others listening to Merquan's accounts, Patrice took note of subtle changes in his dialogue. She thought his word usage and grammar showed the slightest signs of elevation. Some words she had never heard him use before, like "verification" and "renege." It was, to her, further confirmation that something real and influential was happening, as a result of the explorations.

Before the group wrapped up the evening's investigation, returning Merquan and Patrice to Gilpin Court, a request was honored. Merquan asked that they follow a westward route from the hospital complex, along Leigh Street to 4th Street. At that location, a right turn was made, going the block, north, to Jackson Street. The EIRI van was stopped, briefly, there on 4th Street.

Directly across the street, on Jackson, multiple highway signs were displayed, on a metal traffic signal post. They pointed the way to I-95, North and South, and I-64, East and West. Standing outside the van and taking in the view, northward, Merquan compared the site with the one in memory, ninety years past. To his attendants, he pointed out something he considered an anomaly.

As was plainly discernable, 4th Street, looking north from Jackson, made a sharp bend rightward. Oddly, it didn't extend in a straight line like 1st, 2nd, 5th, 6th, and onward. Merquan elucidated:

Merquan:	"It didn't curve around like that in the 1920s. I'm sure it wasn't like that in the thirties and forties, either. You see that big, grey building on the left, with the parking lot built into it? You can see it's fairly new. Guess what—. It's sittin' right on top of the old path of 4th Street."
Researcher:	"You're saying 4th Street used to extend straight ahead, instead of turning rightward, like now? ...Well, that's odd."
Merquan:	"You want to see odd? Let's get back in the truck and make a *left*, here on Jackson. There ain't no place to park right in this area. But you can park for just a couple of minutes in the *Bethel AME* lot. It's just right there on 3rd and Jackson."

Once parked, unauthorized, in the church lot, the group of five, minus the driver, crossed Jackson, still on 3rd Street. There, they faced north again, such as to get a view of the street's northern layout. They saw that, similar to 4th Street, 3rd Street made an abrupt rightward turn, beyond Jackson. Now, Merquan led his entourage, on foot, northward, on 3rd Street approaching its curve. As he did, he spoke from his recall of the street's early design.

| Merquan: | "Keep in mind that none of the numbered streets run *due* north. On a map, you would see that they all run, like, northeast. Only from 17th, on, do they run straight north, after a few blocks pass Broad. But you don't notice it at ground level. |
| | "So, here's the deal: 3rd Street didn't used to curve around like what you see, here. It went straight, over that hill, to the left. You know that on the other side of the hill is the 95 highway." |

Patrice: "I just never took special note, before, how 3rd Street curves around and runs into 4th Street, the way it does. That's 4th Street picking up on the other side of the building with the parking decks. That must be its *name*, up there, near the top."

Zatorah: "Yep...says *UNOS*—United Network for Organ Sharing."

Merquan: That's the one that sits on the route of old 4th Street. Let's walk down a little ways. I'm gonna' show you why I think it's important to be looking at all this. 4th Street had a special meaning for the *guide* I 'travelled' with last time.

"Now, let's cross over from this UNOS building. This dirt-lot, here, that we're on—this is part of the old route of 4th Street. I'm gonna' say it ran right through, where these two trees, here, stand. There're almost like a marker.

"That's the Interstate down there, on the other side of this wire fence. The side closest to us was the extension of Duval Street, runnin' east and west. On the other side of I-95 was Baker Street, also runnin' east and west. Now, you see those two trees on the side-hill, bordering the interstate? That was just about where 4th and Baker met." [5]

Patrice: "That *is* kind'a interesting, *Merk*, but why was it important to your 1920s guide?"

Merquan: "Let's move on from this lot and follow this *modern* path of 4th Street. ...Walking across this bridge, we can get a better look at those trees on that hillside. See—those trees mark the corner of what was Fourth and Baker. That was the intersection. Right there, the 400 block of Baker Street, east, began. Guess what—. My

153

guide came close to dying in a hospital that was at 406 East Baker Street.

"The year he got real sick, I think, was 1917. There was only one hospital for black people, then. It wasn't real big, not by today's standards—only had maybe thirty, forty, beds, tops. Today, it would be seen as, really, a big ol' clinic with beds. Back then, though, it was a major deal for blacks.

"Let me see. It was called...the *Richmond Hospital and Nurse Training School* [6] or some'em like that. Two doctors ran the hospital-clinic and helped train nurses there."

Zatorah: "Can you recall their names, Merquan?"

Merquan: "Well here's where I get to let you-all *in* on the significance of those students I said my guide went to school with. You remember me callin' the names, Miles Jones and Sarah Garland? Well, they both became doctors, got their training at *Howard U*, in D.C.[7]

"But, it was Miles and his wife, Mary Jane, also a doctor, who ran the hospital. *'Dr. M. Janie Jones'* is how her sign, outside her home office, read...and she went by her middle name, *Janie*, with friends.[8, 9]

"As I think on it...it seems like there was some hushed-up controversy with 'em. If you look this stuff up, try to find some'em on another doctor related to Miles and Mary. I think it was Mary's older sister. Yeah, that's right...it was Sarah Garland. Dr. Sarah Garland...*Jones*. Maybe I'm mistaken on it. If you-all look it up, maybe you'll find out what the real deal is with it.

"Anyway, in 1917 when he got sick, my *guide* had to wait until they got a bed free at the

Jones's *Richmond Hospital*, on Baker. I think he had pneumonia or some'em. He got lucky and they found a spot for him. They got him treated just in time to save his life.

"Man, I'm tellin' you—lookin' across at the Interstate, I can still see faint images of numbered streets, from Second to Seventh, crossing over, from Duval to Baker. If I concentrate, I can still see the houses, all along those blocks. Looking over there at that I-95 hillside, I'm actually seein' the 'ghost' of that hospital.

"Here's some'em else: The two doctors lived in a big 'ol house, a block down Baker and around the corner on 3rd Street. The address, I think, was...908." [10]

Patrice: "Merquan, you mentioned other students, besides the Joneses and Garland, your guide went to that *Richmond Colored School* with. You said they also became important in Richmond. I wrote down a *Margaret Mitchell* and a *John Mitchell Jr.* Were they related? And what became of them?"

Merquan: "I don't really think they were related. From what I remember, I'd say they weren't. John Mitchell Jr. was born on a slave plantation that is now Brian Park.[11]

"Uh-oh. The headache is startin' up. And it's messin' with my recall. Hold up...give me a few seconds."

Zatorah: "If you're not feeling well, we should stop. We can pick it all back up tomorrow, or later.

"Patrice: "Yeah, *Merk*. Are you all right?"

Merquan: "I think I can do a little more. It seems like it's important to get this out. Now, let me go back to Margaret. She...was...born in a abolitionist mansion, up there in Church Hill.

          "Oh, man…I'm losing it…the memory. I know she was important, though. …Yeah, it was in Church Hill that she was born, on Grace Street. I'm almost sure she was born a slave.

          "And John Jr. …became the editor! That black newspaper…he became the editor! [12] … Whoa, my head—."

Patrice: "That's enough, *Merk*. We can pick it up another time, like Zatorah said."

Through follow-up inquiries, the EIRI team found that Evan Nesset, their earlier *spiritual medium*, had moved on to other projects. By now, though, Zatorah and fellow investigators found themselves increasingly interested in Merquan Paler's reports. With diligence, the researchers organized their efforts to corroborate the tantalizing descriptions offered. The extent to which new findings might be integrated into conclusions drawn from the earlier ones was not known. But with a mere few days left in their scheduled time for research, they thought they should gather as much data as possible.

Now, to their archival search arsenal, the team added books describing Richmond history. In addition, *Google Maps* and other tools of internet investigation were employed. One of the first fruits of labor came from a newspaper alluded to by Paler. The *Richmond Times Dispatch* featured the article in its May 28, 1920 issue, page 12. Merquan had spoken of concerns Richmond blacks had about establishment of a new hospital, designed for "colored" operation. The discovered article read as follows:

OPERATE ST. PHILIP AS A STRICTLY NEGRO HOSPITAL
Authorities of Institute Deny Emphatically
Reports to the Contrary

Rumors current among the colored people of Richmond that St. Philip Hospital at Thirteenth and Marshall Streets, is not to open as a negro [sic] hospital, are emphatically denied by the hospital authorities. Not only is the hospital to be opened for colored patients, but it is to be run exclusively for colored patients, it is stated.

St. Philip is the new seven story brick, splendidly equipped hospital recently completed at a cost of more than $200,000 by the Medical College of Virginia, with funds contributed largely by the people of Richmond. It is the largest hospital of its kind, exclusively for negro patients, in the entire South.

It is thought that the rumor started through the announcement of the opening of the Dooley Hospital, adjoining St. Philip as a children's hospital. This, however, does not affect the original purpose of the erection of St. Philip, which, together with the Dooley Hospital, is being rapidly equipped, shipments having been held up in transit. Both hospitals will be ready to open in the near future.[13]

To the team, it was nearly indisputable confirmation that Paler had acquired knowledge of past events through *extra-normal* means.

Some of the researchers pored over pages of library books that address the history of blacks in Richmond. Within these sources, they found references to the Richmond hospital operated by Drs. Miles and M. "Janie" Jones. They also found that Janie was actually Miles' second wife.[14] He and his first met as teenagers at the *Richmond Colored High and Normal School*, formerly located on 12th Street between Clay and Leigh.

Dr. Miles Jones' first wife, the researchers uncovered, was born Sarah Garland, in Albemarle County, Virginia. The estimate of her birth year is 1866. Her parents had been plantation slaves until the end of the Civil War, in 1865. The researchers drew private speculations that both of Sarah's parents were of mixed racial heritage. Accounts in Richmond's single black newspaper described Sarah's appearance as essentially indistinguishable from Caucasian. "Her complexion was fair and no one would have presumed she was colored," [15] it was written of Dr. Sarah Jones. The report came in an issue of the *Richmond Planet,* reporting of her passing in May of 1905.

To the team, records suggested also that Sarah's parents had privileged status, as slaves. Her father, George W. Garland learned architecture before moving to Richmond a few years after Sarah was born. His betrothal to Emma Boyd[16] resulted in the birth of two daughters. The eldest, Sarah, would become the first woman doctor of African heritage to pass Virginia's Board of Medicine.[17]

It amazed the researchers to find that George Garland built a number of public buildings in Richmond in the latter 1800s.[18] Included among them was the Baker Street School in Gilpin Court, which Merquan had attended.

To test Merquan's report on the original route of Richmond's 4th Street, the team consulted two sources. Just as he described, archival maps of the city showed that numbered streets, 1st through 12th, ran parallel, without curvature, to the mid1950s. It was evident that construction of I-95, in the latter 1950s and early 1960s, altered the street map of Richmond in various ways.

First, the interstate cut a winding path from Lombardy Street, in the west, to the Leigh Street valley, beyond Twelfth Street, eastward. That aspect of its design essentially split Jackson Ward into halves, north and south.[19] Also, on-and-off-ramp connections between Interstates *64* and *95* made necessary the new curvatures of 3rd, 4th, and 5th Streets. Finally, three streets running east and west, in the northern Ward, underwent dramatic reductions in length. These were Bates, Preston and Baker Streets. Only Hospital kept its original path.

Essentially, Zatorah's colleagues were as impressed with Merquan's knowledge of Richmond's past as was she. However, they felt compelled to consider alternate possibilities to account for his historical insights. What if, they posited, he had acquired the information prior to his work with the team?

These researchers of the *paranormal* found it prudent to adopt a measure of skepticism in all of their analyses. It was especially the case for, theretofore, untried delvers into the *extra-normal*. As they knew all too well, the world was full of *pretend psychics* ready to perpetrate all manner of deceptions. After much thought and discussion, however, everyone, and particularly Zatorah, agreed that Paler did not, at all, fit the model of a "psychic prankster."

In fact, Zatorah was pass any state of doubt about Merquan's authenticity. She had been the one to initiate a meeting with him, from the beginning. That being the case, there was no basis for deception on his part. Rather than a devious, *undercover historian* of true Richmond stories, she saw Merquan as a smart, small-time, young hustler of the "projects." This and the otherworldly events that led her to him legitimized him in her view.

The one facet of his *extra-normal* experiences that gave her pause concerned the apparent underlying factor of *race*. There seemed every indication that Merquan's relation to the past included a dimension of ethnicity. She recalled that it coincided with Nesset's accounts, during his *channeling* on Broad Street and in that Fulton area of Richmond. It was the only factor of Merquan's *past-time connection* that gave her unease. She couldn't accept that issues of genetics could have meaning *after death*.

Two days remained before the scheduled time of Merquan's final work with the researchers. To preclude any uncertainties, both he and Patrice confirmed, to the investigators, the pair's earlier agreement to do the final exploration. In the interim, all parties were free to mull over Merquan's astonishing revelations and determine the proper meanings to attach.

At home, with the children asleep this late evening, Merquan and Patrice continued a talk they had started earlier.

Patrice:	"Like I said before, I *like* the new words that come out, now, when you talk. And there you are, straining to keep your *usual* way of talking."
Merquan:	"The *new* sounds funny, to me. I like my old way of sayin' what I need to say."
Patrice:	"I say let the *old* pass on and slip away. It must be *meant*, or it wouldn't be happening. If you find yourself about to speak more...*standard type* English, just go with it. I don't see a problem."
Merquan:	"I know *you* don't. You been tryin' to get me to talk like a *English* teacher, almost from the *jump*. But it *ain't me*, Treecie. What would I look like walkin' around Gilpin sayin' stuff like:

"'Look, people, we all have a past here that is trying to communicate with us. We're turning deaf ears to very important messages. It's time to wake up and reorder our lives.' ...Somebody would throw a rock at me."

Patrice:	"Then, we'll throw rocks back at 'em, *Merk*. You've never been afraid of anything before. Look, baby, something's happening. You're undergoing a change. And I think it must be good. I sense the change in you. You said, yourself, you feel that there's some *purpose* to visiting all those past places. Suppose when you find the purpose, you don't have to have those spells anymore. Wouldn't that be good?"
Merquan:	"It would be like a *Ferrari* out front and a lifetime supply of *Buffalo wings*. I've thought about that end-of-epilepsy thing, too. There's no tellin' what all this is leadin' to.

"I'll be honest with you, Treecie. I do feel myself on the verge of comin' up with some'em to speak to people about, to inform, to enlighten. I just haven't got the full meaning yet. I don't know exactly what I want to say."

Patrice: "It's probably on the way, baby. Just give it time and go with your *new vocabulary* flow. You know what I'm sayin'? I think a new day is coming, too—with *my man* at the center of it.

"*Merk*, you've actually been goin' back in the past, during your spells, and learning stuff—a whole lot of stuff. And just think: You're just starting to remember so much of it. All of what you told us, when you woke up—you know Zatorah's been callin' us and tellin' us it's all *on the real!*

"So, there's no telling where this thing is going. It gives me chills, when I think about all that stuff. ...Oh, *Merk*, do you still remember that flashback you had earlier today? You said there used to be a street behind Hill Street, where, over there *now*, is just trees and bushes growin' wild."

Merquan: "You're talkin' about *Orange Street*. Maybe I should tell Zatorah about it—see if she can look it up. The city put an incinerator and crematorium on Orange, between St. John and St. Paul.[20] And all the blacks back here in Jackson Ward were chokin' from smokestack ashes fallin' all over the place. And the people here complained and carried on but the city basically told 'em *'live with it'*—or, if it had to be, *'die with it.'*"

Patrice: "Maybe *I* can go over to that state library Zatorah talks about, and look it up. ...I'm going

161

to write this down. That incinerator was put there in the 1890s, you say?"

Merquan: "Hot damn! Look at *baby-girl* turning into a *researcher.*"

Chapter Thirteen

THE PRESENT THURSDAY marked the conclusion of the researchers' field work on the *Richmond Project*. For this final exploration, Zatorah was paired, deliberately, with a different willing member of the team. It was thought to be important that as many of the seven witness Merquan's experience, first hand.

As in the case of the earlier expeditions, the EIRI van driver did not inform her passengers of the evening's destination. However, from the exploration made two days prior, she had heard Merquan's reference to Richmond's *Church Hill* section. With three sites left on the list of possible places to visit, the driver, this evening, drove stealthily southward, along 23rd Street toward Broad.

In a block across from a Church Hill elementary school the van parked. As was typical, the block was quiet at this time, approaching dusk on a summer weekday evening. Totally unaware of his nearness to Bellevue Elementary, Merquan allowed the sensation of seizure to overtake him. By now, he was familiar with the way the van's blue light radiations facilitated the altered state into which he drifted.

By means of the *paranormal* process he'd undergone so many times before, Merquan now looked through the aged eyes of Pearly Minks. This day, in September, 1846, was thought to be her birthday. Whether off by a few days, weeks, or months, she was now one hundred years old by the count she had been taught to follow as a little girl.

With a memory stretching back to 1750, in sketches, and to 1752, with clarity, Ms. Minks was a fountain of wisdom. It was inarguably true for the *servant* class surrounding her and of which she was a member. Whites of the "big house" wherein servants, like Ms. Minks, were employed appreciated Ms. Minks' sharpness of mind, also. But it was to a lesser degree and to a much less obvious extent.

Through his eighteenth century host, Merquan came to a realization that brought mixed feelings. Blacks of 1846 Richmond, Virginia might have either of three statuses: legally free, owned as human property, or kept as paid and *non* owned servants. Fortunate to be ensconced in that latter station, Ms. Minks and her peers were disinclined to abandon it, to wander off into a hostile social system. Thus, the role they played within the mansion sitting high in Richmond's *Church Hill* section was far from unhappy for them.[1]

Although attended by, at least, one fellow servant when venturing outside of the *Van Lew* mansion, Ms. Minks still moved about with care. She braced herself, both hands gripping the cane that was a third leg steadying her gait. By now, her speech, too, came slowly forth, the southern drawl of an uneducated former slave. But she had long since mastered the art of marshalling and articulating her thoughts, even while laboriously getting from one place to another.

Upon stepping out of a side entrance of the mansion,[2,3] one facing Twenty-fourth Street, Ms. Minks was attended by Okey Lanson, 35 years her junior. She was on her way to take a seat in a side garden of the large home, this dusky evening. A second, very informal, celebration of her one hundredth year was to occur there. There would be exclusive participation by servants, neighboring slaves, and young children who sprang from three classes: servant, slave, and employer.

Essentially, the gala was to be a talk-fest, for the adults, and an opportunity to "feed" from Ms. Minks' articulations. Still and all, the Van Lews had provided refreshments to embellish the festivity. These included bacon biscuit sandwiches and lemonade, aplenty, to help wash down Ms. Minks' *food for thought*. The fact was, not everything Ms. Minks had to say was pleasant and easy to "digest."

In spite of that fact, her attendants seemed never to get enough from the woman they all came to address in a corrupted version of "Mother Dear." That term of endearment, properly pronounced, was commonly used by members of distinguished white families of the day.

Mel Orley:	"*Muh-Dee*, bless da *Lawd*, you done made it to a hun'ert."
Ms. Minks:	"How many times I got to tell, you, Mel. You cain't *bless da Lawd*, even if da *Lawd* you speaks of is real. Whatever *Lawd* they is in the heaven do the blessin'. People cain't bless nothin'."
Mel Orley:	"Now, *Muh-Dee*, you don't want to be sayin' '*maybe there ain't no Lawd*', again. You gon' be goin' to meet your Makuh' soon enough. You better be a'tryin' to patch things up with the Creatuh'.
Ms. Minks:	"There ain't no Creatuh' like what them white folks been tellin' you Mel, you fool. It's some'em else, but it ain't that. If they was a *Good Lawd in heaven*, like what *they* try to say, you wouldn't have that bad leg. You...."
Mel:	"Ain't no shame in havin' a bad leg."
Ms. Minks:	"It's a shame how it *got broke*. That ol' Carolina mastuh', a' yourn, years ago, did it. I swear, you ain't got the sense you was bo'n with—believin' in a *Good Lawd in heaven*, that that *devil slave*

	master taught you. …No, I ain't sayin' all white folks is devils—jes' the slaveholdin' kind."
Rose:	"*Muh-De-uh*, you don't believe the *Good Lawd* got you to a hundred?"
Ms. Minks:	"Rosie, chile, *I* got me to a hun'ert, by standin' up under all them whippin's put on me over the yea'uhs. *I* got me to a hun'er by preferrin' the whip, over evil hands grabbin' at me. I got me to a hun'ert by figurin' some'em out, after I had my son, Puggy.

"All the pain you set children up for comes back on you. Puggy suffered in this world, and it was my fault for bringin' him here. I did all I could, not to bring no mo'e, and so my own sufferin' went waaay less.

"Dat's how I got myself to a hun'ert, Rosie. And if you want to make a hun'ert, keep listenin' to *Muh-Dee-uh*." |
Benjamin:	"*Muh-Dee*, yo' prediction sh'o came out like you said."
Ms. Minks:	"How I'm s'pposed to cipher which one you talkin' 'bout, Big Ben? Some days, *Muh-Dee* make predictions all day, all night. Been a good week, since I seen you and your sweater you wears every Tuesday and Saa'day."
Benjamin:	"All right, *Muh-Dee*. I's talkin' 'bout the one you made 'bout that little Willie, what come 'round here sellin' them *loco-focos*[4] for his masta'. I hear the Van Lews is gon' be tryin' to buy freedom for that boy's ma and pa."
Kasper:	"Lawd, I thought *fo' sho'* *Muh-Dee* was wrong on that count. But I hears the same as you, Ben."
Ms. Minks:	"*Muh-De-uh* misses *e'ry* now-and-then, but most of the time what I sees is right. And I still ain't told all I sees 'bout that li'l fella'. I had a

dream—*and* a vision—that he's all growed up, see. And he comes to work for the Van Lews.

"Now, it's who I sees him marryin' that could put a part in all yo' nappy haids."

Louise: "*Muh-Dee*, you so funny! Who you see marryin' li'l Willie Mitchell? He don't look like he gon' even be strong enough to *jump* the *marryin' broom*. So, who is it? Is she even born yet?"

Ms. Minks: "Ain't been long is in this world. You-all know them Drapers down the hill?"

Ben: "The Drapers come in massas and slaves, *Muh-Dee*. Which is you talkin' 'bout?"

Ms. Minks: "Which ones jes' had a newbo'n, Ben? You know them white folks ain't had no chile recent. Who else am I talkin' 'bout but the Drapers' newest little *property* baby, born in them slave quarters in back'a da' house?"

Rose: "Oooh! You 'ferrin' to the baby, Lizzy! You see li'l Willie and that newborn—?"

Ms. Minks: "Jes' as clear as I sees li'l Frank, over there, tryin' to steal a biscuit. ...Get away from them biscuits, boy, 'til it's time to eat! I swear that boy is half *fox* and half *wolf*.

"Yas, I'm 'ferrin' to that poor, sweet, brand new li'l slave baby, Lizzy. ...Now, y'all close yo' mouths befo'e one of these gnats out here fly in. You think you surprised now? Well, you ain't heard the rest, yet. So, make sho' you sittin' snug in your place, befo'e you falls out yo' seats.

"Like I said, in my mind I done seen li'l Willie and Lizzy *married*—but what's mo'e, I sees the *chile* that stand in the middle of that union."

Ben: "Yo' visions is gettin' longer and longer, Muh-Dee. You sees that li'l baby, havin' *her own* baby."

Ms. Minks:	"I do—and bo'n right ov'a there in the Van Lew house. Oh, it's near twenty years away—I'm gon' say a couple'a years short of a sco'e—but I done seen it. So, you can believe it or not. I sho' ain't gon' be around to laugh at them what don't. Oh, but by that time, it's gon' be *plenty* changes in this world."
Sissy:	"What kinda' changes, Muh-Dee-uh? Is *Jesus* comin'? Is He comin' to carry home the faithful?"
Ms. Minks:	"Now, chile, you knows better than ask *Muh-Dee* a question like that. They ain't no Jesus *comin' for to carry you nowhere*, Sista'. The only place you goin' is where you carry yo'self.
	"You can learn a lota' thangs from that ol' slave-master a'yorn. But *religion* ain't one of 'em. He got his *God* and you got to find yo's, yo'self."
Sissy:	"Well, tell us 'bout the changes comin' that you see. It's good, right? Is it gon' help colored folks?"
Ms. Minks:	"It's wauhr, Sista'—big, bad, terrible wauhr. White folks fightin' each otha'—some colored folks fightin', too; but, mostly waitin' to see what's gon' be."
Sissy:	"Sound like *Armageddon* in the Bible, *Muh-Dee-uh*. We hears about that in sermons at the *African Church*. *Muh-Dee*, you ought to come back to visit the *African Church* sometime. The white minister tell us all kinds of good things about the *comin' of the Lord*.
	"I know you don't like carriage rides up and down the Broad Street hill, but it's just right beyond Fourteenth. Ain't nothin' gon' happen like you say it might—the carriage comin' loose

and rollin' backward, with you in it. ...*Muh-Dee-uh*, you say some funny things."

Ms. Minks: *"This-here* is what's funny: A white minister preachin' to a slave congregation 'bout *his* God. And he don't even believe *colored* folks got souls to make it to heaven, in the first place. What's funny, chile, is you sittin' up in there worshippin' the God of the mayne that's enslavin' yo' people.

"*Muh-Dee-uh* been tellin' you—*all'a ya'*—you better find your *own private* God to talk to, befo' it's too late. Me—I done found my *God*. And it ain't jes' in the sky, either. It's all around.

"It's them trees, that grass, that river down there, that Chimborazo Hill up yonder, it's you, and these sweet little white and colored chi'ren sittin' 'round, big-eyed, listenin' and waitin' for *Muh-De-uh* to say it's time to eat. These look like they think *Muh-Dee-uh* might be the *Second Comin'a Christ.* 'Peers dat *Muh-Dee-uh* got some'a dese little angels in a spooky way.

"Don't be scared'a *Muh-Dee-uh*, chi'ren. Ain't no *Judgment* in this ol' soul. I ain't 'gainst nuthin' but shams and hypocrites."

Joseph: *"Muh-Dee-uh*, you is soooo funny! I'm sho' the *Lawd* broke the clay-mold, after He made you. I won't be surprised to see you is *third in Command*, up in Heaven, when the time come."

Ms. Minks: "This boy heard, and yet, ain't *understood,* a word I said. Ain't no heaven like what you been taught, Jo-Jo!"

Sally: "So, *Muh-Dee*, that li'l teeny Mitchell boy gon' marry that little baby Lizzy, and she gon' have their chile in the mansion, you say?"

Ms. Minks:	"Exceptin' it ain't gon' be his baby, Sally. Lizzy's baby gon' be four, when they marry. You know Miss Beth knows a lot'a them *abolition* folks. It's gon' be one of them such friends what get Lizzy in the *fam'ly way*. And then, baby-Lizzy's baby gon' be bo'n right there in the mansion. … Yes. I sees it like that."
Missy:	"*Muh-Dee-uh*, you sure know how to tell a windin' story that's en'ertainin' as a carnival. Keep'a goin'. I bet you even know what Lizzy's daughter-by-the-*abolition*-man is gon' be named."
Ms. Minks:	"Sound like you ain't fo'sho' *Muh-Dee-uh* really got the *seein'* gift. It's all right, though. Hopefully, for all yo' sakes, you'll be around to see 'dese things come about.
	"The chile of the chile…her name? As a fact, I do see it. I sees the name…*Mag-da-lena*, like in your Bible. *Magdalena Draper*—part *colored*, part *abolition*. Far as my *vision* go, she gon' be a force to reckon with, in this town, too."
Calvin:	"Magdalena Draper?"
Ms. Minks:	"…Well, maybe it's *Magga Lena* …*Margie Lena*. Some kind'a Lena Draper! *Maggie Lena Draper*—how's 'zat? Look, *Muh-Dee-uh* ain't young as she used to be. Sometimes the pictures and words I sees runs into each other. But, its one of them ones—or real close."
	"And you can believe this, too. Miss Beth is gon' take Lizzy's chile under her wing jes' like as though she was her own great-niece. And you know Miss Beth Van Lew. She ain't gon' *care a lick* that the chile is mixed. And, I sees Miss Beth doin' her best to help the little one

	get a *legal* daddy, too. And that's were li'l Willie Mitchell come in."
Sissy:	"That sho' is a good story, *Muh-Dee-uh*. Ain't nobody, nowhere, can tell a tale like *Muh-Dee*. Oooh, and when I sees that li'l Willie again, I'm gon' tease him *black and blue*."
Ms. Minks:	"Not you, and *not no one else* out here, gon' tease li'l Willie. You gon' go 'bout your usu'l business, when you comes 'cross him, and act like you ain't heard a thang. And *all* you-all is gettin' that order—*straight* from *Muh-Dee-uh*."

Merquan's excursion with his "host," Ms. Minks, lasted through the celebration of her birthday. He continued to share the composition of her mental awareness, as she returned to the *Van Lew House*. There, she occupied her favorite rocking chair and drifted off into a serene sleep from which she did not awake. Before her demise, though, that otherworldly process of *psychic-disengagement* took place. A minute later Merquan was coming to consciousness within the EIRI van, having virtually traversed 166 years.

For Merquan, during his altered state, the *Van Lew Home* had a distinguishable aura about it. And although, in the present year, it had not existed for a century, its "ghost" emanated *waves* that Merquan felt he detected. Therefore, the first words he uttered upon regaining his senses were these:

"You don't even have to tell me this location. We're up on Grace Street, at 23rd or 24th. I can *feel* the *Van Lew Mansion,* outside."

No one except the van driver knew their group's location in the city. When all the occupants stepped out into the late afternoon, they saw before them the tan-bricked school. They also noticed the city's *historic-location* plaque nearby and went over to inspect it. The inscription they perused was as follows:

ADAMS–VAN LEW HOUSE

Richmond mayor Dr. John Adams built a mansion here in 1802. It became the residence of Elizabeth Van Lew (1818-1900) whose father obtained it in 1836. During the Civil War, Elizabeth Van Lew led a Union espionage operation. African Americans, such as Van Lew's associate Mary Jane Richards (whose story closely parallels that of legendary spy Mary Elizabeth Bowser), served in Richmond's Unionist underground. Van Lew served as postmaster of Richmond from 1869 to 1877. Maggie Lena Walker, nationally known African American businesswoman, banker, and leader of the Independent Order of St. Luke, was born here by 1867. The house was razed in 1911, and in 1912 the Bellevue School was erected in its place.[5]

"According to Muh-De-uh," Merquan muttered as much to himself as to his attendants, "Maggie Walker should have been born in 1864." Aware of the quizzical expressions of those around him, Merquan explained.

That which he began relating to the group tantalized them all. He had evidently visited, in a *past-time* experience, the old mansion that had stood there. He'd met the people who were alive at that time. To the man, and woman, they wanted to know if he'd met *Elizabeth Van Lew*, herself.[6]

"I remember a woman," Merquan began, "who was called different varieties of her name. She was 'Lizzy' to some, 'Beth' to others, and to a different group—usually children—she was 'Bet'. I'm guessing she was the woman whose name is mentioned there.

"But," Merquan continued, "if you want to *step* my recall *up* some notches, let's go back inside to the blue light. In that glow, a lot'a my memory comes back clear. Then, I should be able to tell you, maybe, a lot of what my guide knew. As you know, I lived in her mind for the time I was in the past."

Of all that Merquan was able to recall and relate about life in the *Van Lew* house, two facets were most notable to the group. One was Merquan's gallant portrayal of *Elizabeth Van Lew* as a crusader for the "Negro" cause, up to the time of his visit to the past. The year was 1846 and Merquan remembered that *Van Lew* turned twenty-eight in October that year. It was, in fact, the month after Ms. Minks celebrated her one hundredth birthday.

The other feature of Merquan's recall that amazed his attendants was his description of a slight and dapper man who mesmerized the *Van Lew* home, upon his visits there. As Paler recalled, the man was a writer, poet, and one-time editor of the *Southern Literary Messenger*, with offices at Fifteenth and Main Streets.[7, 8] In the struggle to name titles of works by the writer-poet, Merquan managed to produce a few. These gave his audience facile awareness of the man to whom he referred.

Ms. Minks had, if fact, found many of the poet's lines enthralling. She'd asked that they be read to her on many occasions by residents of the *Van Lew* mansion. Portions of "Muh-Dee-uh's" past knowledge of the poet's lines were, now, also in Merquan's memory. In his recounting of visits by the writer and poet, Merquan gave the following recitation:

> *"Much I marveled this ungainly*
> *"Fowl, to hear discourse so plainly.*
> *"Though its answer, little meaning,*
> *"Little relevancy bore...."*[9]

In Merquan's recall, the man never failed to thrill *Van Lew* house guests with his own recitation of his works, at dinner parties.[10] Even before Merquan recalled the man's name, it was known that he spoke of Edgar Allan Poe, whose life spanned the years 1809 to 1849.

The following day, Zatorah and her colleagues located and uncovered various materials that verified Merquan's stated recall. Archival accounts, biographical materials, books of Richmond history indexing the *Van Lews* and *Maggie Lena Walker*—it was all there to be found in local libraries. Indeed, *internet* searches of those names turned up much of the same information given in paper-medium texts.

To the researchers, it seemed, again, practically indisputable that Merquan Paler actually underwent *past-time* experiences. By means of them, he acquired obscure tidbits of information that could be verified by existing records. Again, it had to be considered what the likelihood was that Merquan had gathered his data, in advance. But, even if he had, the task of making his report match the group's un-foretold location would, itself, require a sort of *extra sensory perception.*

To facilitate the academic growth of her two nieces, Bonita Paler bought a desktop computer, primarily for their use. It supplemented *"i-books"* and other technologies supplied by their school. Bonita, herself, rarely explored *internet* capability. This day, however, at Merquan's request, she sat nearby, as he and Patrice searched *Web* information for the topic "Maggie Lena Walker."

At a site given as *encyclopediavirginia.org,* Merquan found what he sought. It was confirmation that Maggie Walker had, in fact, been born in the year projected by his *past-time* "guide." As he recalled, Ms. Minks had predicted the birth to occur "a couple'a years short" of twenty years, counting from 1846. The seminal part of the *Webpage* information, for Merquan, read as follows:

Early Years and Family
Maggie Lena Mitchell was born on July 15, 1864 (until 2009 most scholars thought that 1867 was her birth year), on the Van Lew Estate in Richmond. Mitchell's mother, Elizabeth Draper, was a former slave who worked as an assistant cook for Elizabeth Van Lew, a staunch abolitionist and spy for the Union during the American Civil War (1861–1865). [11]

While the four kids they oversaw played, within sight, outside the Hickory Street housing unit, the three adults resumed their conversation.

Bonita: "You two don't think it's *scary* that *Quan* was *back in time* visitin' with people who are dead and gone? And, it's got to be true. How in the world would you know there's been mistakes in Maggie Walker's birth year?"

Merquan: "Well, it's…it's wild, for sure. But, Ma, the thing is: It's been happenin' all the time. All those times I had the seizures, I was travelin' back. Some of it I can remember, like in sketches, even without the blue light in the van we told you about."

Patrice: "Bonny, *Merk* and me—we think he's on the verge of something. Ever since he's been working with Zatorah, he started gettin' feelings that he's about to start on some kind'a *mission*. I can tell it, too. I don't know if I like it, but I'm not gonna' try to stop him. I probably couldn't if I wanted to. You know how *Merk* is."

Bonita: "I've noticed a change in him. You know you *talk* different now, don't you, Quan? You talk like your thinking and your ideas have gotten bigger. It's all that goin' back in the past, ain't it?"

Merquan: "I don't see how it could be anything else."

Bonita: "So, what is it that you think is happenin'?"

Merquan: "Actually, Ma, I'm pretty sure of it, now. All those visits had a…a *theme*. They weren't just… random occurrences. All those people, Ma… all those people I got to know are together, and they got warnings. And they want *me* to *sound* the alarm. *That's* the *scary* part."

Bonita:	"They're together? And they got warnings…for who? What *kind* of warnings?"
Merquan:	"I think it's for us…all of us in the *race*. It could be for *all* black people—all over the world. Sometimes I hear the words *'original people'* in my head. By that, I'm pretty sure they mean people with closest ties to central and southern Africa.
	"Ma, I know it sounds crazy. But, what part of the whole thing *don't* sound crazy? It's *all* crazy. Going back *in the past* is crazy. So, if one part is true, then why wouldn't everything I'm seeing be true?"
Patrice:	"Bonny, I've seen it coming for a week, now. *Merk*'s gradually been getting ideas of what those…*ghosts of the past* want.
	"So, it finally all came together, *Merk*? You know what they want?"
Merquan:	"I don't even know how to get it out, without soundin' like somebody *gone over the edge*. And if I can barely tell my girl and my ma what this thing is, how the hell am I supposed to *preach* it?"
Bonita:	"A message for all *black* people. Quan, I got to tell you: I want to hear it…but, in some way, I'm not sure I'm *ready* to hear it. Why just *black* people? I don't think I like that."
Merquan:	"I'm just gonna' go on and try to say it. They say the *African* race began the *human* race. But where the *world* is goin' is not to the *benefit* of the African race. We have to make adjustments, for the good of future generations—that is, for descendants of the *original people*.
	"Now, just hear me out. We got to face some things, as a race. We have to look at the pattern of history, especially over the past five, six

hundred years. We look at *today* and say *'Oh, we've made great strides.'* But you got to look at what's happenin' from a *world view*, not just a local view. We have to look at what's been happenin' over some hundreds of years.

"Don't ask me how I know this history...I just know it. And it's in books, if you want to verify it. The *original people* started falling behind the later groups, as early as the 1400s. For six hundred years, *we*—as a world-group, not just in this country—haven't come close to catchin' up. And it's all related to the pattern of our *baby-makin'* and *baby-raisin'*.

"Treecie...Ma...it ain't due to nothin' else. There ain't no other factor that is more responsible for us lagging behind other groups. It's the pattern of our baby makin' and baby raisin'. Now, don't make the mistake of thinkin' about individuals and lookin' at particulars. You got to look *from space*...figuratively. You got to look at the worldwide picture."

Patrice: "Those ghosts, *Merk*, are telling you that we, with the closest ties to Africa, racially, aren't raisin' our kids right?"

Bonita: "Quan, I know that *you know* this is not something you want to be goin' around sayin'. Is it possible that the message is maybe something else?"

Merquan: "If it hadn't come in fragments that gradually collected into the big picture, I might have doubts. In other words, if I had gotten the whole vision, sort of, all at once, I might think it was some kind of *mental* issue. But, you would have to see what I've seen, all in a hundred segments, and see how it all pieces together, to know why I'm sure of what I see.

"Again, Treecie, don't look at individuals. I know you're raising Shar'dey and Markee perfectly. They couldn't be better. But you got to look at us, as a whole, from Africa to America. Why were Europeans—and on some occasions, with the aid of *North-Arab* helpers—able to get millions of Africans out of Africa, in order to enslave 'em?"

"Oh, sure, there was all kinds of trickery and deception and force. But that can't explain why it didn't happen on that scale to any other group. Having too many babies to raise properly, having a culture of little respect for members of your own kind—that's what tipped the scale, in the negative, for the 'original people.' That's what's tippin' it in the negative direction for us all, as a group, on the whole.

"Look outside that door. What's out there? We got our children out there playin' a block, some yards and feet, away from kids who have already started showin' signs that they gon' be thugs and criminals in a few years. Y'all know it as well as I do. We all grew up in *Gilpin*—it's basically all we know. It sure was all I knew before I started piecin' things together, with *their* help—that is, my *past-time* people.

"Ma, I remember how hard you tried to keep me in the house, to get me to come home from school and study. You tried to get me to spend time in libraries and stuff and not get too caught up *in the hood*. Well, I had my own ideas. I chose the hood over the books and school. What happened was you *lost out* to the pull on me from what was goin' on around me.

"Ma, what I'm tryin' to say is that if the culture around here wasn't what it was, you wouldn't have had such fierce competition. We're in the middle of a culture—actually, a *subculture*—that's failin' us. And it ain't just *Gilpin*. Gilpin is just a sample of what's goin' on, all over Richmond and all over the country.

"*Africans* are in the middle of a culture that's *their* making, that, now, is *part* of them. It's a pattern of havin' babies-upon-babies—without the *means* of raisin' them to respect themselves and their own kind. With that pattern, the 'original people' set themselves up for failure, hundreds of years ago.

"And the *descendants* of the *original people* are still following that pattern. Not all of us, obviously, but enough to see the negative effects in big way."

Patrice: [shaking her head] "*Merk*, anybody can see— you are... transformed! You have become a *messenger!* I mean...I see what you're sayin'. I see it. You've laid it out...I can't pretend not to *feel* what you're sayin'. You bring it *down front* and make it clear.

"Bonny, you see it, don't you? I mean, he took an idea that, at first, sounded...*crazy*. But he just laid it out. Is he wrong? Is what *Merk* is sayin', like, *out in the field*—or does he have a point?"

Bonita: "Treece...Quan—it's what I would call a hurtin' truth. It's a truth that's a cryin' shame, if it's *all the way* true. I get a picture of *ghosts of the past* as being very disappointed or very sad. Is that it, Quan? Are they sad over the way things are?"

Merquan: "They're sad like you were, when all your hopes for me fell in. They're sad like we will be if our hopes for 'Livvy' and 'Nell' and 'Shard'

179

and Markee get *smoked* by the pull of the worst Gilpin's got to offer, on its 'plate.'"

Patrice: "I'm, like, turning this thing around and around, in my head. It's so easy to see, now. I used to wonder why they treat us different, like when you go to the big malls and stores. Now, I bet it's because other people see our weakness.

"They see us as having babies we can't afford and raising them to be disrespectful of everything. That's it, ain't it, *Merk*? Other people see *in us* the same thing your past people are talking about, to you. But, why is everybody, everywhere, seeing it, except us? I can see people in countries over the world looking at Africa and shaking their heads. I see other groups looking at us, over here, and shaking their heads.

"I can see 'em talkin' about us: '*All they do is have a bunch of babies they can't afford and then raise 'em to be disrespectful of everything and everybody.*' Right now, I know that's what the other groups say about us. *Merk*, you're *on* it. You pinpointed it. But, what can we do?"

Merquan: "Treecie…Ma, they're telling me: *we better wake up.* What can we do? The answer is a very simple one. We got to stop treating *having babies* as though it was something as simple as blowing a bubble, or buying a plant, or a pet.

"As I said, that was the *original people's* early mistake. It was the thing that cost them their equal place in the world. Now, we, the descendants of the *original people*, are following the same pattern. That's what's got to stop.

"Babies not *raised right* are tomorrow's criminals. Remember that big *BP* oil spill in the Gulf back in 2010? Well, I'm here to tell you that babies not *raised right* are Africa's—and the United States'—oil spill, *on land.*"

Bonita: "Quanie! That's harsh...way too harsh!"

Merquan: "I know... I know. But, it's the truth. How do you think our dead foremothers and forefather's feel knowing they passed that *bad legacy* on to us, and we're passing it on to future generations? They see it now. And they can't do damned thing about it. It's too late.

"The *dead* try to communicate with us, Ma, all the time. We don't listen. We, who raise our children badly, here and in Africa, just keep spilling that *bad oil* all over the place. Here, trillions are spent dealing with the spillage, in all the various ways. There, in Africa, the devastating cost is in Africa's status in the world."

Bonita: "What about you, Quan? Do you think I made a mistake in having you?"

Merquan: "Well, think about it, Ma. I haven't been out there committin' no crimes. And when have you known me to just *out-and-out* disrespect people? I used to lend money to small *dealers.* That ain't no crime. That's called hustlin'. You ain't raised no thug and no criminal—just a chiller who knows how to find a hustle to *make it* on.

"And my baby, here, Treecie, ain't raisin' no thug and no *hood-heifer*, either. Markee and Shard' gon' make it out of Gilpin. Treecie and me—we already done talked about that.

"But, I said it before: don't look at, and think in, *particulars.* You need to get the *big* picture. We got an on-land *oil spill* here, and in Africa. We got to *stop the spill*—not just keep *treatin'* the spillage."

Patrice: "You said something about where the world is going, *Merk*, I think—and it not being good for descendants of Africa? Have those spirits told you something?"

Merquan: "Some parts of the world are heading for major catastrophe, Treecie. Somehow, it's going to affect the descendants of the *original people* more than anyone else. ...Yeah, yeah, I know it sounds crazy. But, like I said before, it *all* sounds crazy, depending on the place from where you view it.

"It's coming in the next fifty, sixty years. We descendants of the *original people* may have just enough time to avoid passing on a *holocaust*, en masse, to our descendants. See, it's about the numbers. The catastrophe, whether natural or manmade, is going to *target* a single group, more so than all others. And it's gonna' be the group with least status on the planet."

Bonita: "Quan...I don't like hearing this. It just don't *sound* right. Why just one group, like that? How can a catastrophe just pick on one group?"

Merquan: "Like I said, Ma, it could be either a *natural* or *manmade* holocaust. And the group with the greatest number of badly raised, idle, unproductive, members who have the least investment in society will suffer most. That *group* will suffer most. That's what they're tellin' me.

"They've already shown me it's comin', Ma. I know it don't sound good. But it's comin'. And they, *the spirits of the past*, want me to sound the warning. No one else has listened to them. It's the only part of this whole thing that really scares me. I don't know how to get it out there to people. I don't even know where to start.

"Ma, you brought into the world the only
one with the ability to receive *their* message.
Somehow, it was in the epilepsy. It must have
been. That's some wild shit, ain't it, Ma? Excuse
my lapse into my old style, but you got to admit:
It's some wild cat litter."

At Merquan's comment about his epilepsy, both he and
Patrice noticed the sullen and thoughtful expression Bonita
donned. He thought, maybe, he'd finally found a way to cast his
condition in a somewhat favorable light. As he knew, Bonita
always blamed herself for his malady. From what he could
gather, it had relation to some mysterious interaction between
Bonita and his father, during her pregnancy.

Always, Bonita had been vague about it. And that was all
right with Merquan, for he preferred being spared any new
information concerning his father. He was told that agents,
investigating Mercer for suspicion of distributing illegal
substances had, finally caught up with him. Merquan didn't
even care to know what prison he was in.

At length, he decided to try to lighten his mother's mood,
by revealing to her a suspicion he and Patrice had. Something
in the overall change Merquan was undergoing caused them to
hope that the spontaneous seizures might be in abatement. It
was a fact that, besides those promoted by the blue radiations
in research, no "spells" occurred since he'd begun working
with Zatorah. That sidelight of information produced the effect
Merquan desired. Bonita showed joy at imagining surcease of
his seizures.

Interrupting discourse among the trio, Patrice's cell phone
chimed musically. She recognized the number showing in the
phone's window and answered with a greeting to Zatorah. To
Zatorah's voice on the other end, Patrice listened intently.

Richmond-based work by the *Extranormal Incidence
Research & Investigation* team formally terminated at 6:00
p.m. Zatorah pointed out that that time was just four hours

away. She and her Cambridge colleagues would be catching their flight back to Massachusetts in two days, which was Sunday morning, upcoming. She went on to explain that for two weeks she had turned around in her mind an idea for which she could not reach a decision.

Now, in the final hours that remained, she opted to end the mental stalemate and take action. She was proposing a *spur of the moment* investigation, employing Merquan's *paranormal* abilities.

If she and Merquan were available, Zatorah resumed, she would like to pay Merquan to undertake a final exploration. It would be one not at all related to EIRI research. Earlier, Zatorah had been informed of Merquan's loss of his hotel job, during his incarceration. Zatorah said she thought the twenty-five hundred dollars she could pay Merquan for the added work might be helpful. It would be pay for work over the next two to three hours. On the other hand, she would quite understand if Patrice and Merquan had had enough.

While Zatorah waited "on hold," Patrice relayed the offer to Merquan. Following a brief discussion, Merquan took the phone. He told Zatorah that he and Patrice would await pick-up in front of the Baker Street School, at St. Paul and Charity Streets. He never even asked about the location to which they might be headed.

It was during the EIRI van's slow maneuver through an alleyway between 4th and 5th Streets that Merquan slipped into the altered state. The driver had come southward, down 5th, from Franklin Street and turned, right, into the pathway, just before Main Street. It was one of two Richmond locations where, months earlier, Zatorah had received odd sensations from the surroundings. She suspected a significance related to her past, for both this and the Monument, at Allison, location. She hoped against hope that Merquan could help her uncover that significance.

Chapter Fourteen

I N THE 00-HUNDRED block, odd, of 4ᵗʰ Street, across an alleyway adjacent to the hotel, was a large parking lot. That was the scenic layout this blistery cold day of January 4, 1981. The entire block was void of human traffic, with the exception of "Chappy" Wilson, who made his way from the lot to the hotel front.

Born in the first week of the year, 1900, Chappy could always relate a 20ᵗʰ century year-of-interest to his age at the time. This evening, as he hobbled, with walking cane, across the alleyway, he became host to a visitor from the future, *psychically*. The person whose mind would, for a time, be merged with his would not be born for nearly a decade.

Embraced in the warmth of the hotel lobby, Chappy greeted the staid but professional desk clerk. As he did, he took note of the young woman standing at the guest intake desk. With one arm she supported the weight of a cheerful, playful five-month-old. In the other hand, she grasped the handles of several large bags. Chappy greeted the young woman, too, as well as the baby, who acted as though he was part of the collection of people she knew and liked.

"I don't think I ever saw a prettier baby in all my life," Chappy commented sincerely.

"Say, 'hi' to the nice man, Zatorah. Ahhh, look at her. She likes you. This is my little *angel* baby. Aren't you my *angel* baby? Yes, you are.

"She has a gift for knowing nice people, when she sees them. She's Mommy's angel. That's right, sweetie—wave to the nice man."

It added warmth to Chappy's heart, this bitterly cold January day, to be in the company of the pretty and friendly mom and baby. From the lobby, he turned and entered an aisle of carpeted floor, showing all its intricate designs. It led to the room he rented monthly, #112.

Standing in front of his unit, searching pockets for his door key, Chappy took his usual assessment of the surroundings. The hallway was dimly lit and serene. It seemed that all the guests and tenants were of like mind, in that they treasured peace, quiet and civility. A gentle scent permeated the air: the light smell of aging foundation in potpourri with internal cleanliness and meticulous upkeep. Before he could get his key into the lock, he heard, then saw, the young woman making the turn into the hallway.

It was with much effort that she moved along, weighted with the baby and the bags. Finally, at room 109 she stopped, lowering the bags to the floor. In seconds, the young woman began a spate of dialogue. To Chappy, she seemed buoyant but infused with a nervous excitement. Her shoes, he noted, were thin and slight and far from suited for the outside cold. Instinct told him that she was in some, perhaps mild, crisis but was nonetheless quite valiant in the face of it. Over time, her words confirmed his guess.

Torasine:	"Looks like I'm going to be staying right across the hall from you. I'm Torasine and this is Zatorah."
Chappy:	"Well, 'hi' again. You're just here for a night or two, I guess?"

Torasine: "I think they have me scheduled until early Thursday—that's four nights, counting from this evening. I'm in the *WIC* program, at least for now. You ever heard of it? It stands for *Women, Infants and Children*?

"See, what they do, if you're having problems with, like, domestic violence or something, is this: Social Services partners with agencies to put you up, secretly, for a time. I say 'you' but obviously I'm talking about women."

Chappy: "Oh, I didn't know this hotel was engaged in a partnership of that sort."

Torasine: "Well, I don't think it is, really. It's really the YWCA. Did you know there is a 'Y' around the corner on 5th Street?"

Chappy: "Uh, yes…I think I've seen it. It's just through, and on the other side of, the alley on the left, isn't it?"

Torasine: "Um-hm, that's it. They provide, sort of, like, shelter for women. But, sometimes they get full and then arrangements are made with other facilities, I assume for pay by the city."

Chappy: "It's nice that they have these kinds of services."

Torasine: "Well, you're looking at someone who never dreamed she'd be a patron of Social Services. But, it just goes to show you. You never know when fate's going to deal you a rough hand. After a few days and nights here, they have me set up for what I hear is a couple of comfortable rooms and bath in a very discreet facility located in the West End.

"Oh, you know, I never did ask your name."

Chappy: "I'm sorry. Everybody calls me Chappy—young and old. The name's Charles Emit Wilson. I've

	been living here now for almost ten years. It's real nice and quiet. I've never had a bit of trouble. Everybody's friendly and respectful of everybody else. I enjoy living here."
Torasine:	"Well, that's wonderful! …Look at Zatorah still waving her little fingers at you. …Yes, this is Mr. Chappy, Zatorah. …She always knows nice people when she sees them. You can tell she likes you, Mr. Chappy."
Chappy:	"She's an angel, alright—just as happy and content as a little sunbird."
Torasine:	"Yeah, she's more precious than all the gold in the universe. She'll be six months on the 17th."
Chappy:	"Let's see how much of my brain I got left. She was born July 17, 1980—a mid-summer baby. And she's got the sunshine in her face and those sparkling eyes to prove it. …Well, I hope the situation that brings you two here wasn't too bad."
Torasine:	"Well, just between you and me—my husband, Zatorah's father, I've found to be a man with dark secrets and an *evil* side. [Whispering next] Among his secrets are a number of secret identities. These are things I had no idea were part of him.
	"Mr. Chappy—that revelation almost destroyed me. Honestly, I think if it wasn't for my little sunflower, here, it might have sent me over the edge."

At just that instant, the door of room 111 cracked open. The man behind it had heard the melodic voice and the effusive talk, filtering into his room, in contrast to the hotel's silence. He was Roman Almas, a visitor to Richmond on a 90-day business trip. On the windshield of his vehicle, sitting in the hotel's adjacent lot, was a discreetly displayed sticker. It indicated

Almas' affiliation with the military facility at Fort George G. Meade, Maryland.

Almas slowly opened his room door and stepped out lithely. He began his address of those standing in the hallway.

Almas:	"Excuse me folks. I don't mean to interrupt. Hi, there, Chappy. How's it going today?"
Chappy:	"I'm just having me a *high old time* chewin' the fat with these two beautiful ladies here. ... Roman, this is Miss...Torasine, I think she said her name is. And this other totally captivating young lady is Zatorah. And Torasine, this is my neighbor, sort of—name's Roman."
Almas:	"Torasine and Zatorah—how beautiful! Well... pleased and completely charmed to meet you."
Torasine:	"How do you do, Roman. Let's see if you get Zatorah's special smiley face, indicating her pronouncement of you as one of the special people of God's good earth. ...Well what do you know—she's just blushing and beaming. I think you have Zatorah's stamp of approval."
Almas:	"And as far as I'm concerned, there's no greater honor. Hellllo, Zatorah! I am not exaggerating, Torasine—she is the absolute most beautiful baby I have ever seen!
	"She absolutely sparkles and radiates with that beautiful smile. It's like you got the sun all dressed and wrapped snugly in that little pink and yellow blanket."

Torasine was pleased to see what appeared to be a wedding band on Almas' ring finger. She took it as a sign that he could make a good, trusted, *plutonic* friend. Inside, she was in emotional turmoil, but doing her best to mask it. Within that hotel hallway at that particular time, the very atmosphere seemed, to her, infused with an enchantment. It was as though the "magic" was associated with the special, mutual fondness that had sprung among the parties.

Almas:	"I don't mean to be nosy, but, I see you're standing at 109. Is that going to be your room here?"
Zatorah:	"Um-hm, it's going to be my and Zatorah's room for a few days."
Almas:	"I had hoped that whoever settled in next door to me would be a good neighbor. Clearly, that wish is granted. Looks like you haven't even settled in, yet. I take it that those are bags of your things, there, beside you."
Zatorah:	"Yes, I've been talking so much, bending Mr. Chappy's ear, I haven't even opened the door to see what the room looks like."
Almas:	"Well, here's an idea. How about you two ladies go in and check the room out thoroughly, while Chappy and I stand guard out here. Then, if it meets your approval, I say why don't the four of us plan for a nice, hot dinner, out, this chilly afternoon—on me.
	"I'm trying to get used to the cold sandwiches I put together, as a meal, and, also, eating out, alone, in Richmond's various restaurants. But, I'll tell you, it sure would be nice to have company sitting across a dinner table, now and again."

Merquan's latest exploration was solely for Zatorah's benefit. Therefore, he expressed his wish to relay his recall of it without the presence of the EIRI van driver and technician. It was a thoughtful gesture, for, as Merquan suspected, his information left Zatorah nearly in shock. But, it also left her with questions she'd had no reason to ponder before.

First, what, exactly, had driven her mother to seek shelter with Richmond Social Services? Second, how close a bond of friendship did Torasine share with Wilson and Almas, and to what extent did each play a role in her life? Finally, was either Almas or Wilson someone who might still be contacted for further information? As thirty-two years had gone by since their first meeting, Zatorah knew that Wilson might likely have passed, by this time.

Regarding Zatorah's burning questions, Merquan's most recent *past-time* "guide" seemed to know only this: Torasine and Almas did become friends, during the rest of Almas' stay in Richmond. For Zatorah, in present time, he took on a tremendous importance, suddenly. Outside of Torasine, Almas could be the only person, still living, with knowledge to solve the mystery of her father.

Clearly, Torasine was unwilling to shed light on her past, in Richmond. She had said only that she and Emrich Heinz decided, in mutual agreement, to go their separate ways. Each had concluded, amicably, that they would be happier—apart. Zatorah had always found her mother's account both odd and incomplete.

Faced with the rest of the evening and night to recover from Merquan's revelations, Zatorah fought to regain calm. She was obligated to meet, in conference, with the EIRI team and university decision makers to discuss the study's write-up. That was to last until seven this evening, and from there, the plan was to continue, in informal discourse, during a café dinner. It would most likely be after sunset this Friday when, alone in assigned quarters, she would have time to mull over the recent development.

Back, finally, in her room at nightfall, Zatorah's mind filled with pictures she constructed from Merquan's earlier descriptions. She visualized the hotel setting: reception desk just beyond the entrance and, to the right, a long aisle with numbered doors on each side. She envisioned "Chappy" Wilson,

Roman Almas, Torasine and herself, as an infant, occupying the space in the hallway, between rooms 109 and 112.

In an effort to interrupt the visions, Zatorah took the initial steps toward exploring an idea that came suddenly. Fully aware of the power of *internet* searches, she decided to see what would result from an inquiry of the name, Roman Almas. The laptop within her room was perfectly suitable for the task she set. To the extent that there existed a chance, at all, of making a search "hit," it seemed in her favor that the search *name* was so odd.

A simple *internet* "White Pages" search uncovered *nine* Roman Almases in the United States. For five of the individuals, locations ranged from the state of Texas to that of California. One was in Florida and two were listed as having resided in various locations of New York State. Zatorah actually gasped when she saw residential locations for the *ninth*. For the state of Maryland, the list showed Baltimore, Laurel, and Prince George County. The most recent residence cited an address within eastern Henrico County, in Virginia.

Employing the *Google Maps* search feature on her laptop, Zatorah was able to see the exact location of the Henrico residence. In addition, she was able to trace a route from her location near 2nd and Byrd Streets to the "flagged" one showing on the laptop screen. Long and hard she stared at the home in question, on the screen. *My God, what if,* she wondered, *the Roman Almas of that time in early 1981 actually lives there?* The welter of varying emotions she felt made her feel faint.

Burning within her, now, was the question of whether she would really summon the will to go the Henrico location. One full day remained before her flight back to Massachusetts, along with her Cambridge colleagues. She would have to "sleep on it" and decide, early Saturday, if she would let the opportunity for investigation pass. No phone number was given for the Henrico "Almas" listing. Therefore, taking the safe, but least revealing, route of a simple telephone call was not an option. It was either "brave up" or leave Richmond frustrated and defeated.

The following morning arrived, "on schedule." Zatorah thought long and hard on when might be the optimal time to arrive at Almas' Henrico address. Finally, she decided on two o'clock p.m. She hoped it gave her time to gain emotional composure.

In the drive to her Almas destination, Zatorah was as nervous and apprehensive as she might be if traveling to get results from a crucial medical exam. Parking in front of the home, she mustered the courage to amble along the long walkway and, finally, ring the doorbell.

In the preceding hours, Zatorah had rehearsed a hundred different greetings and preliminary dialogues. Each scattered in abandonment of her, when the door opened partially and the man, of sixty years, appeared. His look, at first, was bland, with a hint of annoyance, but gradually changed to quizzical.

Zatorah stood speechless, barely conscious of her own hope that somehow the man would recognize her and spare her a spate of disjoined mumbling. She watched him strain his eyes and shake his head in seeming disbelief. Finally she heard his utterance: "Zatorah?"

She determined that her expression must have answered yes, because she saw Almas smile widely. Next, Zatorah watched Almas step out to greet her fully, taking her hand in both of his. This time, she perceived that Almas didn't state her name in question, but rather in conviction: "Zatorah!"

In her beyond two-hour visit, Zatorah gleaned a wealth of information from Roman Almas. Unaware that it would bring her to tears, he immediately located and brought out pictures of her sent to him by Torasine over past years. Some were taken soon after Torasine's arrival in Cambridge, when Zatorah was eight months old. Others were in approximate two-year intervals, to the time that she was ten.

Against his inclinations, Almas revealed to Zatorah the reason the pictures stopped at that point. Without going into details, he conveyed that it was related to his past work with the *National Security Administration* (NSA), at Fort George G.

Meade, Maryland. In short, at times, his residences changed often and secretively. It was especially so, after Almas and his wife finalized the divorce that loomed over them from the year of Zatorah's birth. Astonishing Zatorah even farther, Almas told how his work with NSA promoted his investigations of her father, Emrich Heinz.

The more Almas talked, the more he saw how completely drawn into his revelations Zatorah became. Much of his tendency toward reticence and guarded expression melted away amid the obvious innocence of her inquiries. He could no more deny her answers, this day, than he could resist her bright-eyed smile and gaze, when she was five, six and seven months old.

Almas' attempts to limit his revelations met less and less success as his vision shifted from present to past. In Zatorah's face he saw images of the baby she'd been. Amused at his new "handicap," Almas allowed himself, gradually, to leak knowledge he had of Emrich Heinz's *experiments*. It was through that line of conversation that Zatorah discovered, with breathtaking shock, Heinz's link to Bonita Paler.

Two hours with Almas passed as though it had been ten minutes. Standing, now, at Almas' front door, Zatorah felt as though all time had stopped. Outside, she stepped, almost entirely backward, along Almas' walkway toward her car, waving. The whole time, she gazed with enchantment at the man who she felt had changed her life in a single sitting. This followed the great embrace she had given him, and accepted from him, in return. It had taken all her strength to hold back the tears until she pulled away, in her rental.

There would be no follow-up conference with the other EIRI team members this day. Zatorah knew already that she would tell them of her preference to spend the day nursing a headache, in her room. She only needed to stop crying long enough to execute the ruse and then end the tears, before the Sunday morning shuttle to the airport.

Chapter Fifteen

A T HOME, IN Cambridge, two things Zatorah was sure of: She could no more bear, *alone*, the knowledge she'd gained from Roman Almas than she could suffocate herself with a pillow. The other was that she was not of a sort to risk her mother's emotional well-being. Zatorah determined she'd be doing just that by making known, to Torasine, her discovery of the truth Torasine had gone to such lengths to hide. Therefore, her husband, Peter, and he alone, would have to co-manage, with her, the burden of her prodigiously dark secret.

Zatorah donned her most professional tone, when she phoned Merquan and Patrice to speak of her offer. She and her husband, Peter, she said, wished to further reward his work with her. The proposed compensation was four years of college for Merquan, with tuition, books and other maintenance expenses, paid by the Leemans. She further stated to the pair that Merquan's revelations had changed her life in an indescribably profound way.

Although disinclined to be sentimental, Merquan was almost as moved by the offer as was Patrice. As wonderful an opportunity as it was, however, explained Merquan, he was convinced there was no time for it. In his thinking, he was obligated to begin immediately trying to find the avenue by which to get his new-found message across. Both Merquan and

Patrice sensed Zatorah's disappointment but also saw that she felt it inappropriate to press farther.

Zatorah was not ready to *give up*, as is said, *by a long shot*. If Merquan wouldn't go to the mountain, so to speak, the mountain was coming to Merquan. Using her affiliation with the Richmond-based *Extranormal-Incidents Research & Investigation* team, she set out to implement a plan. Writers for Richmond newspapers and news magazines were made aware of the research, during its conduct. Many found it intriguing as did some television reporters. Zatorah designed to present to workers, within each of these media, the Richmond "marvel" discovered by the EIRI team, in the course of their study.

Calls Zatorah made to reporters, writers, radio talk-show hosts, and station managers were numerous. She urged and challenged them all to have audience with "young Mr. Paler." Only then could they experience, firsthand, the power of his *spiritual* revelations. As readers, viewers, listeners and ratings were the life blood of their institutions, she said, they owed it to themselves to investigate her claim. At every step, Zatorah kept Merquan and Patrice abreast of her campaign, securing their approval.

Finally, an enterprising Richmond radio talk-show host decided to investigate the "find" claimed by the insistent Cambridge researcher. Tim Brikhead of the "Brikhead Lunch Hour" convinced station managers to risk expensive radio ad time advertising an upcoming guest. Of course, he did so only after interviewing Merquan and being floored by his commentary. In forewarnings to his audience, Brikhead labeled his soon-to-be interviewee "Paler the *Impaler*." He added, emphatically:

"Folks, take my word: this guy is not for the *faint of heart*. Now, I happen to know my *typical* audience is not of the particularly *sensitive* variety. But, if any of you 'radio wanderers' happen to tune in, *on a lark*, I suggest you cover your torsos. Paler-the-*Impaler* will be throwing 'spears'—often *racial* ones—next week, and with deadly aim."

Informed, well in advance, of the scheduled hour of the interview, Zatorah arranged to be at home to get Patrice's call. At the start of Merquan's fifteen minute guest-spot with Tim Brikhead, Patrice adjusted the radio volume. Her aim was to make sure the voices carried well to and through her phone, to Zatorah's in Cambridge. Following introductions and the preliminary explanation, the discussion went forward.

Brikhead: "So, Merquan, you explained that you are given to epileptic seizures. But the state you achieve during those spells is waaay beyond the ordinary. Indeed, we are to believe that you communicate with the dead and that they've transmitted a rather startling message—one with *racial* overtones, no less."

Merquan: "Yes. The message is for those of us with clear *racial ties* to central and southern Africa. And the message is: *'Have a care about your future generations. Put an end to careless, spontaneous reproduction.'* Conditions in the future world will be extremely hostile to, and unforgiving of, both the *practice* and the *products*."

Brikhead: "Where did you go to school, Merquan? You got a nice delivery, there."

Merquan: "I did three years at Armstrong High School and in the last one, opted for GED as my goal. That was four years ago. Since then, I haven't so much as picked up a book, or made a single academic investment. So, you see, the change from my old speaking style can only be viewed as the result of those *life-segments* I've lived in the past. What you're hearing is a very recent phenomenon, not a culmination, over years."

Brikhead: "How many of those 'life-segments' do you believe you've lived? And were you ever anyone

	famous in history, like George Washington, or somebody?"
Merquan:	"No, I wouldn't say so. All my *past* experiences were with people whose lives taught *them*, in one way or another, what I feel *I* need to get across, now. As far as the number, I would estimate, maybe, eighty to ninety, which corresponds to the approximate number of seizures I've had in my life."
Brikhead:	"Um, hmm. Well, you've given us sketches of some of those *lives*, but you say you prefer not to talk, at any length, about particular identities."
Merquan:	"Yeah, actually, my objective is not really to focus on past individuals, but rather to relay their *collective message*. The closest descendants of the 'original people,' by the definition I gave earlier, have reached a two-pronged fork in the road.
	"We can continue patterns that will lead to a form of *holocaust* for our future generations. Or we can stop thoughtless procreation. The message is that simple."
Brikhead:	"It may be seen as a simple message, Merquan. Yet, it's one I suspect the *original people* all over the world will find disturbing, at best— and, at worse, downright *outrageous*.
	"In fact, we got a caller on the line, now. Go ahead, caller—you have a question or comment for our guest?"
Caller:	"Yes, I do. *Merkon*, or whatever your name is, you must not know your Bible. In *Genesis*, God told man to 'be fruitful and multiply.' So, what you're sayin' about black people is against God's command."
Brikhead:	"Thank you, caller. Okay, Merquan—and it's *Merquan*, caller—how do you respond?"

Merquan: "Well, for each of us who thinks like that, we're sending our descendants to catastrophe. I'd like to ask the caller, and everyone who *thinks* like the caller, this: Would you be *fruitful and multiply*, without a care, if you knew your offspring were headed for disaster?

"Unfortunately, I think there's a multitude of people on earth today whose backward thinking would lead them to answer 'yes'."

Brikhead: "I'm going to venture that most of our listeners would like to know where your *proof* is, that some *horrid end* awaits descendants of the *original people*."

Merquan: "What I have is not proof, exactly. I have a message *from the grave* whose reasoning, if understood, should make a person start doing some very critical thinking, at least.

"The *races* of mankind can be viewed in a way similar to the way we view the various animal *species*. Different species are in competition with other species, not only for survival but also for eking a comfortable existence. Any species threatening another's survival or comfort, and not strong enough to fight, becomes prey or what we call a '*natural enemy*.'

"Now, the weaker species has a couple of choices: either mutate into a stronger or smarter species, or become experts at *reproduction*. In that latter situation, the weaker species sacrifices a good number of its progeny to feed the stronger, with the understanding that some will survive. A *race* that consciously or unconsciously opts for the last *is pathetic*."

Brikhead:	"We got another enthusiastic caller, here, *Merks*. Alright, caller, you're on. Your question or comment for our Mr. Paler?"
Caller:	"Yeah, I want to say to Mr. Paler: You sound like you're full of self-hatred, and hatred of your own kind. You advocatin' *genocide* of your own *race*—that's what's pathetic!"
Merquan:	"Ha! This is an example of what is meant in the saying: '*A little knowledge is dangerous*.' The caller has taken an *incomplete* understanding of what I'm saying and has drawn a really wild conclusion.

"Curbing, or reducing, or even eliminating *careless* reproduction does not *kill* a *race* of human beings. In fact, it makes the entire group stronger. Here's a research idea for you: I say that in every society, the *products* of careless, irresponsible procreation—as a group—*cost the most* to the society and *contribute the least*.

"Now, I stress *as a group* because anyone with a brain knows that the argument does not hold up when you examine individuals.

"Here's another way to make the same point. Societies in which careless, irresponsible procreation is minimal will be found to be more progressive societies. Caveat: that's given the absence of other detrimental, or backward, traits of those societies."

Brikhead	"Hmm. ...Let's take another call. Caller, you're on the air."
Caller:	"I been listenin' to you, Mr. Merquan. I, myself, am white and neutral, so far. But, it sounded like you kinda' hinted at some'em *not good* comin' down the pike for descendants of the 'original people,' as you call it. Man, you even used that

loaded term, *holocaust*. You want to talk more on that?"

Merquan: "First, let me say: Obviously, I can't have *real proof* of what I've been shown by 'the ancestors.' But, I will state my understanding of what was relayed to me. I'll be blunt. Something as evil, as devastating, and as debilitating as black slavery, from the sixteenth to the nineteenth century, is on the horizon, for us who are closest descendants of the *original* people.

"It's sometime within the next sixty years. The amount, or degree, of effect it will have will almost completely depend on the proportion of our group—at that time—who are products of careless, irresponsible procreation. That means that, if this thing—whatever it is—happens, let's say, fifty years from this day, we would have had two generations, *time-wise*, to drastically reduce the numbers.

"Look, consider this: The *original people*— Africans who gave rise to all the *races*, over time—devised, probably instinctively, the strategy of prodigious procreation, in order to insure the survival of the *human* species. Okay, they succeeded. Now, it's time, not to *close* the 'valve,' but to throttle it down.

"Careless, irresponsible procreation is an *oil spill* on land. Whatever group is doing the most of it hurts itself more than it does any other group. We get to the point where we don't even value members of our own kind, in a twisted sort of *supply and demand* system, within our own *race*. There's no *demand* for the products of careless, irresponsible procreation, so the value of the product goes to *zero*. I know it sounds harsh—but the truth is the truth."

Brikhead:	"If that wasn't provocative, water ain't wet. Look at the board, *Merks*. It's a Christmas tree of lights. Here we go. Go ahead, caller, you're on."
Caller:	"God is gon' punish you, mister, for sayin' stuff like that about *His* special chi'ren. We done suffered so much and gone through so much and we gon' get our reward in *Heaven*. The *Lawd* wants us to produce as many followers of His word as possible.
	"You obviously don't know your Bible. God is in a contest with *the Devil* for souls. If you'd read or go to church, you'd know that. We are producin' souls for the *Lawd*, in our chi'ren. We teach 'em to love the *Lawd* and be *saved* and they get counted as followers of *Christ the Lawd*.
	"This earth, down here, don't mean nothin'! This is a proovin' ground. We only down here to worship the *Lawd* and every chile we bring into this world is a chile of God. God wants the whole world full of followers of His Word.
	"So, how dare you talk bad about the babies what come into this world and it ain't they fault. As long as the mommas and their daddies teach 'em to love the *Lawd* and be saved, it's all in God's plan. You sound like that *Devil* talkin' and…."
Brikhead:	"All right, caller—we're going to have to end it there. Your point is well-taken, and we thank you for your participation.
	"So, Merquan, how do you respond to the lady's opinion that people should just focus on *Christian salvation* and, otherwise, let the chips fly where they may?"

Merquan:	[After a chuckle] "Tim, letting the *chips fly where they may* is what led to 100 million black '*chips*' 'flying' into slavery, in the Americas, over a three-hundred-fifty year period.
	"Look, I happen to know that that's the same reasoning that was used to keep black slaves reproducing for white masters. His position was:
	'See, Sambo and Samboina, you're not only producing black babies for massa—new slave property that I might sell off, at any time—but you're helping God win a bet with the Devil. So, do it, enjoy it, and take pleasure in the fact that you're helping the Lord, thy God.'
	"I can't argue with people who opt for delusion over reality. My voice is for those who can consider that our ancestors realize, now, that they made a mistake in following patterns no longer beneficial to the group.
	"Careless, irresponsible procreation is a throwback to an ancient time. In the modern world—and I mean all time after the Middle Ages in Europe—it is foolhardy and just plain stupid."
Brikhead:	"Caller, you're on the air."
Caller:	"You're not a *Christian*, are you, Merquan? Do you even believe in God?"
Merquan:	"Like the vast majority of descendants of the 'original people,' since the 17th or maybe 16th century, I was brought up to believe in *Christianity* and in the *Christian* portrayal of God. By the time of my late teens I was as hypocritical as I now view all black *Christians*. For me, belief in *Christianity* was a safety net, just in case all that bullshit was true.

"You've heard me speak, a little, of my experiences in *past-time* visits. From the beginning, for the black slave, belief in that which was taught by, and acceptable to, the slave master, was a matter of both physical and *psychological* survival. By now, I dare say, that *poison*—that feel-good *hallucinogen*—is in our DNA.

"Only skillful manipulation and exploitation of religious belief could make a group believe that *careless, irresponsible* procreation has *spiritual* value and is a tool in God's arsenal to combat an imaginary *Satan*. It's really sad, because hundreds of millions of our ancestors went to their graves believing it. By the time of their demise, they had passed on a destructive trait to hundreds of millions more.

"And now, this very day, hundreds of millions of progeny of the *original* people are in the process of keeping that egregious pattern going. But, I'm here to sound the alarm. I, and no one else, as far as I see, have had the warning conveyed to me, by those who have passed.

"Wake up, my brethren, all over the world. As it is said, '*the hour is nigh.*' Put a stop to it, immediately. Stop sending the products of *careless* and *irresponsible* procreation into a future that will parallel—for those 'products,'— black slavery and incomprehensible *holocaust,* in its horror."

Initially, Zatorah had one word to describe her feeling, by the time the radio segment ended: "Wow." In her mind, she contrasted the young fellow in the grip of seizure at the *Dooley-St. Philip* memorial with the one in the radio. She welled with pride at the positive transformation. At the same time, though, she shuddered at what she knew was the initial reaction of the black audience. She saw Merquan as possibly destined for wide notoriety, but at what cost, early in his, sort of, ministry?

Talking long and candidly with Patrice, following the interview, Zatorah came close to confiding in her, the lineage she and Merquan shared. Her father, Emrich Heinz had been a researcher in *genetic science*. Clandestinely, he used the mothers of his two known offspring in his experiments. He had furtively injected, or promoted ingestion of, serums designed to cause developmental alterations within the mothers' fetuses.

It had all been conveyed to Zatorah during her visit with Roman Almas. At Fort Meade, in Maryland, the *National Security Administration* had been tracking Emrich Heinz. Almas' affiliation with NSA provided him knowledge of Heinz's activities. As Almas informed, the agency's interest in Heinz started in the middle 1980s.

But that was years after Almas met Zatorah's mother and her. To Zatorah, Almas revealed that both Torasine, and ten years later, Bonita, served as Heinz's guinea pigs. His aim was to instill characteristics in the nervous system of the developing embryo, which would translate to *psychic* abilities, later.

Once the process was perfected, the *products* of such a design were to be maneuvered into special work. They were to become specially equipped agents of espionage. The *psychic* abilities of these brain-altered individuals would be ideal for furthering the aims of secret service agencies, throughout the world. Heinz envisioned himself pioneering a new *business* in espionage. It was one wherein he supplied willing governments with altogether unique and valuable "players" to serve their interests. He believed a fortune could be made from sale of his secret processes.

Espionage and intrigue were integral parts of Emrich Heinz's scientific career. Over time, it was determined he'd employed a number of aliases and alternate identities, in the United States alone. Not surprisingly, he turned out to be well connected, both locally and overseas. It was, in fact, through these secret associations that Heinz learned of the surveillance being made of him. He fled the U.S. with authorities on his heels, just hours away from detaining him.

A number of times, in their talks after the radio interview, Zatorah was tempted to share knowledge that Merquan was her half brother. It took all her will to refrain from it, reminding herself of her earlier resolve to tell only her husband, Peter. If she shared the secret with Patrice, she would surely be obligated to do the same with Merquan.

And how could she justify leaving Bonita out of the informational loop? It seemed to her that Bonita should, perhaps, be told first, if the secret was going to be spilled at all, in Richmond. In the end, Zatorah decided it was best, for now, to keep the matter within its present confines.

Through that electronic process by which media stations determine the size of audiences, Brikhead became aware of something significant. His radio listeners on the day of Merquan Paler's interview climbed to soaring. But, the station managers were left with a *two-sided coin* situation. Additional sessions with Merquan Paler as a guest were sure to boost ratings. But, the downside was the continued expression of outrage by black audiences, from that first interview day.

The radio station tried to devise a compromise. Maybe they could get Paler to apologize for his earlier disparaging of religion, in the next on-air session. Perhaps they could even get him to say that, after further thought, he had made peace with Christian faith. After all, Paler's stated mission was shouting a warning about procreation, not the evils of religion.

Tim Brikhead's station gave Merquan fair recompense for the first guest appearance and was prepared to double it, for later sit-ins. When they approached Merquan with the compromise deal, he said he would try to keep his discourse on the main topic. He warned, however, that to the extent that a question required "essential enlightenment," he would say what he felt needed to be said. Warily, the station managers scheduled Merquan's second and third appearances.

Merquan's guest "spots" were a *hot potato* for the *Brikhead Lunch Hour.* While, again, listener numbers shot through the roof, so did outcry against what was perceived as the station's genocidal intentions. Brikhead's station discontinued Merquan's appearances, after the third, but aided in generating interest in him, by other radio programs. These were likewise of a kind willing to risk controversy. Thus, it was that Merquan did a circuit of radio programs, spanning a period of six months.

Zatorah's essential purpose, from the beginning, had been to find a way for Merquan to earn money, to support his family. Even while enjoying his present success, she continued to give thought to other possibilities. She and Patrice worked out a plan wherein Patrice recorded, or requested recordings of, Merquan's sessions. Receiving them in the mail, Zatorah listened raptly to what she considered her brother's eloquent elucidations. A few months into Merquan's "playing the circuit," she conceived another idea for furthering Merquan's enterprise. Without hesitation, she put a plan into action.

Instinctively, Zatorah determined that Merquan's radio appearances would, in due time, run their course and come to an abrupt end. Through connections facilitated by a media-wise friend of a friend, she arranged to speak directly to someone influential in *satellite radio.* To that person, she sent the recordings of Merquan's radio talk and question/answer sessions.

Zatorah's move was timely. At the end of six months of Merquan's delivery of his special messages, voices of objection within the public were threatening law suits. Targets were radio stations, radio managers, and even the talk show hosts who beseeched Merquan's insights.

Merquan discovered something Zatorah already knew: Similar to cable television networks, *satellite radio* does not contend with the same censorship that restrains public media. Largely through arrangements made by Zatorah, Merquan signed a contract to speak, at intervals, on various *satellite radio* shows. It wasn't long before he began getting calls from producers of cable TV shows. With actual and potential earnings increasing steadily, Merquan moved his two families out of Gilpin Court.

Strategically, the Palers and Keepers decided on homes within a mile of *Richmond International Airport*, and within the same subdivision. Merquan would now be catching flights to places all over the country. While he was away, Bonita and her two nieces would live just down the way from Patrice, Shar`dey, and Markee.

Merquan's past refusal to get treated for the seizures had led to full restriction of his driving privilege. In the absence of those seizures, of late, he worked to get the ban removed. In the meantime, he continued travel arrangements put in place over the past months. As a need arose, Merquan was driven here or there by Patrice or Bonita, both of whom worked part-time, now, and owned vehicles.

In addition, Merquan employed the services of two old friends to get him where he needed to go, when his mother and Patrice were at work. In fact, the Twine cousins, Trayon and Neil, found their new "positions" as Merquan's business and social *attendants* as, sort of, a godsend arrangement. The trio had a long history of close companionship. Merquan would never forget how Neil possibly saved his life that day, near Charity and 2nd Streets.

For their parts, the cousins would remember, always, that Merquan had valiantly stood between Neil and a likely arrest and conviction. Each additional second that Neil stood, frozen, with the "nine" in his hand would have aided in his identification, as the shooter. The charge, as it turned out, would have escalated to *murder*, since Ma'sahn Dixon expired after seven weeks in the hospital.

Chapter Sixteen

Not surprisingly, Zatorah and Peter purchased *satellite-radio* reception for their home and vehicles. In fact, they never missed a single one of Merquan's guest appearances on the radio talk shows. Their next plan, together, was to find a way for Peter to meet Merquan and his family. It was to be handled delicately, though. Zatorah had thought it wise not to show a level of interest in her Richmond relations, such as to arouse suspicions among those Richmonders.

Nevertheless, Merquan was her brother, and she wanted Peter to meet him, as well as the other members she had described so glowingly. They thought of a small vacation in Richmond, reserving a room at the *Massad Hotel*. In that way, Peter would be provided "visuals," to put with Zatorah's many descriptions of the place. Or, they thought, the Leemans could plan a festive gathering, in Cambridge, with the Palers and Keepers as special guests. Each seemed an excellent plan for achieving their aims. The couple's discussion of such plans would, later, play a role in addressing a crisis destined to arise.

Tim Brikhead's *lean* toward risk-taking made him the popular radio host that he was. The trick, for station managers, was knowing when to let him *go for it* and when to rein him in. When Brikhead requested having Merquan back, 18 months after that first sitting, for old times sake, they wavered and then consented.

The appearance was scheduled, and the day and hour arrived. Ten minutes into the segment, Merquan's commentary, again, stirred fervent interest, as well as indignation:

Caller: "Tim, I'm s'posed to be he'ppin' the old lady in the yard, and y'all got me glued to this radio. Now, my question for Merquan is: Ain't you seen no *white* people on the other side? You ain't tryin' to say there's a separate afterlife for us white folks, are ya'?"

Merquan: [chuckling] "Well...uh. As wild as it may seem, there are divisions among *spirits of the dead*, based on shared experiences. They are also based on special affiliations.

"You may have heard about the study conducted in Richmond, about two...two and a half years past, on what is called *'extra-normal incidences.'* The spirit *channeler*, Mr. Evan Nesset, from here in Richmond, made contact with a number of entities whose identities matched, in life, folks of European descent, or white. I'm told his contact of *spirits* of another race was limited.

"My experiences were mainly with people who, collectively, have a message for descendants with closest ties to the *original* people. So, I would answer you like this: Perhaps everyone who has lived and died has a presence on the other side. But *groups of spirits* have different and specialized agendas."

Brikhead: "Next caller—you're on the air with Brikhead and *Paler-the-Impaler.*"

Caller: "Paler, you from Gilpin Court, right?"

Merquan: "Born and raised."

Caller: [continuing] "I got family that lived in the back part of the Ward before anybody ever *thought* of a Gilpin Court. Now, you say you been goin' back in time and visitin' this one and that one. What you know about the history of the place you grew up it? And, hear me: I knows *Jackson Ward*, so don't try to blow no smoke."

Merquan: [with humor] "Yes, sir. Rest assured: I stopped blowing smoke when I quit cigarettes. But, about northern Jackson Ward—? I have memory of old times in the Ward that I can share. Maybe there'll be a link between something I say and something you know—that most don't know.

"I 'travelled,' in 1889, with an orphan who was adopted that year by a family who lived at 921 St. Peter Street. As you probably know, there *is* no 900 block there, now. When the 800 block got torn out to make room for the Interstate, the block north became a casualty, also.

"A group of us neighborhood boys used to roam Jackson Ward, from Leigh Street to *Potter's Field*, northward. *Potter's Field* was a hillside,[1] behind the Hebrew Cemetery that sits on the corner of Hospital and 5th Streets. For blacks who couldn't afford better burial, Potter's Field became their final resting place. Because it was a steep slope—and still is—the pine boxes, and corpses, used to slide downhill, in a big rain.[2]

"All along Jackson Street and Leigh Street there were venders of all kinds, and many of us boys used to wait for a chance to steal whatever we could get our hands on. We'd get chased all the way back to Baker, sometimes— across the 800 block of numbered streets that, now, are gone replaced by I-95. Once we got to Baker, we were *home free* because of the many small streets, through which to lose someone chasing you.

"Right across the street from my adopted family is where one of my buddies, Charlie, lived. The next year, in 1890, he got a job working for what was, then, called the *colored* newspaper.[3] I'm gonna' say he was about twelve, at that time. That's how old the adopted boy was that I 'travelled' with.

"Work at the newspaper put an end to Charlie's romping and doing mischief with the rest of us. After that, he kind'a graduated to more sophisticated shady activities—hanging around saloons and gettin' schooled by slicksters.[4]

"Of all things, ol' Charlie had an interest in *acting*. And he found ways to practice it among the set of vice-mongers, who were his new associates. He actually earned a little money doing performances along Second Street."[5]

Caller:	[continuing] "See, that's what I mean! Why should I believe any of that stuff you sayin' is true?!"
Merquan:	"I got you. But, you see, I'm trying to maybe hit on some little tidbits that you may have heard. Or I may say something that you can look up and find that it's *for real*.

"So…I was about to point out that Charlie's mom used to work at what was called the *Colored Almshouse*.[6] It was basically a poorhouse for addressing needs of indigent blacks, at that time. I don't know if any records from the Colored Almshouse still exist. Maybe I'll look into it, myself.

"Well, anyway, by his early twenties—and I found this out in a *different* past-time travel—Charlie and his mom moved north, New York, maybe, or maybe Philly, to live with extended family members. For any who have no idea of Charlie's identity at this point, I'll add this surprising outcome: He became a famous actor. Charlie's full name was Charles Sidney Gilpin. *Gilpin Court* is named after him." [7]

Caller: "Mr. *Merk*`on, you need to stop. I *know my* Lord ain't let you go back *in no past!* You might fool others wit' that crazy talk'a yorn, but I know *my* Lord, and He ain't gave you no more powers than nobody else. Why is you sittin' up there lyin'?!"

Merquan: [laughing] "Next caller, please."

Next caller: "No, you ain't gettin' away. I'm on the same page wit' that last caller. Who put you up to tryin' to *shame* black people? Talkin' 'bout we shouldn't have no chur'in—maybe you the one what shouldn't 'a been *bo'n!*

"I know your *mumma* is got to be shamed'a you. You need to go to *church*—and *join* the church—so you can learn to respect yo'self. And then, maybe you'll learn to respect yo'e people. Babies born in the *projects* is just as good as babies born rich. All we need is to be *good Christians* and be faithful to the *Lawd.* ... Amen!"

Merquan: "You referenced babies born in the projects. You're not talkin' to somebody who only *reads* about the projects. I *grew up* in *that hood.* I fought in *that hood* and hustled in *that hood.* To paraphrase a noted rapper: *I shot at niggas and been shot at*, in that hood called 'the projects.' And I can tell you that I—and all those I ever

213

knew—were brought up in the *Christian* faith, in *the hood*.

"Check this: You can search far and wide, in any *hood*, and you'd be hard-pressed to find one thug or killer, in *the hood*, that don't believe in *Christianity* and the *God* of Christianity. You said something about me not having respect. Here's some'em to think about. You can't find anyone, anywhere, with *less* respect for others, than *Christian* thugs and killers, in *the hood*.

"But, it's not just thugs and killers. I'm gon' come *up front* with it. There is not in the world today a race of people who shows less respect for its own kind than those I describe as the closest descendants of the *original people*. I'll estimate that, over the world, at least ninety five percent of that group is either *Christian* or *Muslim*.

"So, you tell me what attachment to either one of those religious labels has done for us, the closest descendants of the *original people*. Now, let's look at the evidence.

"In Africa, what do you see? You see people taught *Christianity* by their former rulers, who despise and fight one another in the most horrid fashion, based on tribal differences. What is the pattern of how women are treated there? Sex objects! Human beings to be raped in war just as casually as though they were inanimate items to be confiscated. These are *bona fide*, white-man-taught *Christians*, showing their Christian *dis*-respect for one another.

"So-called 'black Muslims' shouldn't overlook the fact that light-skinned, North African, Arab Muslims were instrumental in the capture or other retrieval of hundreds of thousand of black Africans to be sold into slavery. So, blacks throughout the world who run, out of dissatisfaction with Christianity, to other religions, need to be careful about finding solace—just anywhere.

"Now, let's turn the microscope lens here, to the U.S., specifically. In the very early days, the white man saw some things, *apparently innate*, in those of African descent. And he decided to exploit it. First, that ol' *Christianity* made, and makes, us Africans drunk with delusions of *pie in the sky*. Once drunk, the group is a target for easy manipulation.

"Second, the *Christianity-drunk* descendant from Africa will reproduce under the most horrific conditions of slavery. That, in itself, shows his disrespect for the women—in my thinking, it *clearly* shows it. Third, that primal tendency to despise rival tribesmen was exploited to keep 'the descendants' divided. Our forefathers and mothers were taken from various parts of Africa and brought together haphazardly. A blind man can see that *that* could, and would, work against development of cohesion among slaves.

"Unless you're so steeped in *Christian* delusion that you can't see straight, we can recognize versions of the same thing today. The difference is that there's no *forced* slavery of the mind. We're still acting out the past scenario, on our own accord and volition.

"You think *Christianity* stops you from being a hater? You better wake up. Christianity just *drugs* you, to where you can't look at yourself objectively. You'll do the sleaziest, sneakiest, rottenest, most underhanded and dirtiest of acts

toward someone of your own kind—and remain
convinced that you're a *'soldier of God.'* What
you are is a *spiritual drunk*, and one of the worst
examples of a *fool.*"

At the end of the segment, Tim Brikhead walked over and
shook Merquan's hand. He shook, also, his head and smiled
broadly.

"*Merk*s, old buddy, I'm sure I'll be able, at some point down
the road, to convince the 'wigs' to *do you* another appearance.
But, I'll be damned if I can say *when.* I'm scared to look out the
window, *Merk*s. I expect to see crowds out there with torches,
like in the old *Frankenstein* movies.

"And just between you and me, brother—I don't have one
damned regret. This was refreshing, stimulating, exciting,
exuberating stuff—and a mite scary, if you want to know the
truth. But *the Brick* loved every blood-draining-from-the-face
minute of it. 'Course, if I were black and Christian, I might
want to slug ya' one."

"And after that didn't work out, then what? Maybe you'd
start giving thought to my 'mad prophesies.'"

"What was the mold they made you from? You damn sure
live up to the moniker I've placed on you: Paler-the-*Impaler*.
Speaking for a couple'a thousand of my listeners today: *'Ouch!
Take thy spear from out my heart!'*"

"Ha! I dare say you're *a piece of work*, yourself, Tim."

The reaction Merquan received when he visited "the hood,"
on occasion, was mixed. Many of the denizens thought his
message was "on point." Others, even when they disagreed
with his viewpoint, strongly admired what they considered
his display of roguish audacity. Some were coolly silent but
thoughtful. Seemingly, as a bad omen, a minority seethed, in
private.

As before, Patrice preferred that Merquan not travel about
his old haunts in *the Ward*, without her. But, she worked a

steady job, now, and could not monitor his inclinations to travel, like in the past. It was of only marginal consolation to her that he enjoyed a sort of bodyguard-ship by his most trusted confidants. She was aware that Neil had likely saved Merquan from getting shot that day on 2nd Street. Nevertheless, she had mixed feelings about the Twine cousins' role in the incident.

At least, Patrice often mused, her Gilpin contacts were still in place. They were still ready to phone her to report any significant sightings of Merquan. And she'd find a way to take any and all such calls, whether at work or not. It was just a fact that her communication-chain of girlfriends, in Gilpin, was an element of her peace of mind, when it came to keeping tabs on Merquan.

For three years, now, Merquan had been giving his *satellite-radio* exposés, warnings, and broadsides. He had always told Patrice that his forte was making a living with his mind, in spite of his seizures and lack of higher education. His accomplishments, to date, confirmed it. Mortgages for the home he and Patrice's shared, and for the one purchased for his mother, were paid in full. He and Patrice were now saving money for their planned marriage and for the future.

With drivers license finally secured, Merquan, this day, treated Trayon and Neil to cruises about Richmond. After some time, the three returned to Gilpin Court, where the cousins still resided. Merquan parked in front of the residence of another good friend. It was his old Hill Street location, but the block just west of the one where Patrice's former unit sat. With Merquan the center of attention, the group around him showed a celebratory spirit.

In the midst of all the light talk and amiable moods, a black SUV cruised eastward, along the block, and stopped where Merquan and company stood. There were three young men inside, but, at present, Merquan had only clear sight of one. It was, he, the front seat passenger, who made comment toward Merquan:

"That's that nigga that's *down* on *Christians* and *Christianity*. What you got against *Christians*, nigga? My great-grandma listened to that shit you talked a couple'a years ago. That shit made my granny cry, nigga. She dead, now. I ain't go'n say it was you, nigga. But I remember how that shit you talked hurt her. What's up with that shit, nigga?"

Merquan saw Trayon furtively motion his hand toward his back. It was where his "piece" rested under his shirt. With equal subtlety, Merquan made a gesture that requested Trayon to "chill." To him, the situation required further assessment before setting a deadly defense in place. As yet, he still had not gotten a good look at the driver, or at whomever else might be a passenger in the vehicle.

"We can't discuss it with you sittin' up high in the 'short'. Why don't you and *the family* park and slip on out? Then, we can do some barkin' right out in the open."

"You don't want it wit' me, nigga."

"You're right—and I didn't ask for it. I'm just tellin' you how to do *business*…how to do things the *manly* way. Be out in the open, like me. In the 'short,' you might be tryin' to hide some'em. I can, and do, *say my say*, out in the open. You should be able to, too."

"You don't want it wit' me, nigga."

"Who is that mannin' the steering wheel on this *ship*? … Tariq? Damn! Look at you rollin' like the *big dog*, bruh! You weren't go'n speak to a homie? It ain't *like that*, is it?"

"Hey, *Merk*. What-up?"

"Chillin', *my dog*—takin'a break from the grind. *Pullin' coats*, tryin' to get the message across is *hard work*."

"Yeah, I heard about you."

"Who's in the back, behind the *smoke* glass? …Oh, snap! It's little George…done growed up. Damn, you 'bout big as a tree, sittin' back there. I know I shouldn't ask, but did you graduate high school, homeboy? I remember your mother used to say you were gon' graduate, if it killed you."

"Yeah, I made it. Graduated from Marshall this year."

"Good man, good man! ...I see y'all's homie, here, is got *mad beef* with the *Merk*sman. My experience has been, once I understand a thing better, sometimes it lightens the ol' mood.

"You want to have a chat, *young blood?* ...What's your name, bruh? You already know mine."

"I ain't got nuttin' to say to you. You be makin' fun of *God.* I ain't wit' that shit."

"I take it you're a *Christian,* huh?"

"*Motha-fuckin' right!* My family—we don't like niggas playin' wit' *God.*"

"You don't think God is big enough to handle His own business?"

"Man, you tryin' to be funny. I ain't *down* wit' niggas that don't respec' *God!* You fuckin' makin' me mad, now. Just get the fuck away from me, man. Go on back over there. I don't like niggas like you, up near me."

"You're afraid of your own God, aren't you? Maybe it's God that you got *beef* with. Maybe, if you look close, it's not me."

"It's *you,* nigga! I *hate you,* nigga! You from the *Devil.* Made my granny cry, nigga. You better get away from me, nigga!"

"I can't, I won't. 'Cause I know you're afraid of your own God. I say what I say to help free you from fear. Fear is makin' you hate. That shit's gon' eat you up inside, bruh. Let it go."

Noting his friend's heightened agitation, Tariq intervened: "We gon' roll out, *Merk.*" To Merquan's companions, Tariq gave his first address: "Hey, y'all niggas *be easy,* alright? ...Later."

"*F'sho',* my nigga."

"Bum-ass short you ridin', Tariq. That *johnson* is *royal.* Catch you later."

As the SUV pulled slowly off, Merquan turned back to his associates, shaking his head. He addressed them:

"Can you believe that? That shit is sad. You see, that's the very shit I'm tryin' to cure us of."

"Man, *Merk*, some niggas don't know they ass from a hole in the wall. They don't know how to try to analyze nothin'. They just fuckin' *zombies*."

"You *on* it, Tray. You hit it on the head. That's the proof that tryin' to enlightenin' is, sometimes, a totally uphill exercise."

"I didn't like the looks a' that shit, though, Merk. I'm gettin' me a bad feelin' about that hater. Maybe we should all go inside for awhile. Then Tray and me can keep a watch of the front, from the window or the front door."

"Believe me, I'm feelin' your caution, *blood*. But I think I've been given this special understanding of things, for the purpose of enlightening my brothers and sisters. And I think it's regardless of whatever dangers there are. Once I start hidin', bruh-man, that's when paranoia takes over. I'm not tryin' to go that route. But, I ain't discountin' your caution, Neil. Not one gram."

Ten minutes later, Merquan's troupe of friends were still standing about, enjoying each other's company. Suddenly, a green colored, old model *Seville* could be seen rolling, again eastward, through Hill Street. It stopped briefly and from a back window, a shot was fired. The round fired into Merquan's chest, at his heart, and he fell to the pavement.

The green *Seville* raced off. It passed where Hospital Street takes over from Hill and pressed, onward, to the eastern end of Shockoe Hill Cemetery. At 5th Street, the vehicle ran a red light and barreled down the Hospital Street decline, into the valley, heading toward 7th Street.

Zatorah was preparing dinner at home, when the six o'clock news broadcast a report, coming in from out of state:

"We have an alert, just in from Richmond, Virginia. Merquan Paler, a frequent guest on *satellite-radio* talk segments, who has recently stirred much interest in his commentary on race, religion and matters *beyond the grave*, was shot a few hours earlier. The incident happened in a Richmond public housing complex known as Gilpin Court. According to our affiliate station in Richmond, Mr. Paler was pronounced dead at the scene...."

Unable to control herself, Zatorah screamed continuously. She did so, until Peter rushed into the kitchen to console her and find out what was the matter.

All of Merquan's closest family members and adopted family members, that is, the Keepers, were devastated at the news. It reached Patrice first, via her *connections* in Gilpin Court. Just minutes after the shooting, a girlfriend was on her cell phone calling Patrice at work. All that day, on the job, she had had an odd feeling of unease. When the call came from Gilpin Court she came close to fainting.

For Bonita, the world had, in some ways, *come to an end*, realizing that Merquan was irretrievably lost. If not for the two nieces, who required her care, she felt she might just give up her own struggle with life. The girls were now nine and eleven and making excellent showings at school. Just as she had "lived for" Merquan, when he was a minor child, Bonita, now, felt her life had little meaning beyond care for the children of her adopted sister.

Instinctively, Bonita and Patrice knew that the family's well-being, at least in the immediate, depended on togetherness. Always, the two had felt a deep respect for one another. Now, their bond deepened, as they tried, as a family, to understand both Merquan's life and his death.

In their many reflections on Merquan's behavior and style over his twenty-five years, they concluded that he had lived an extraordinary life. Although far too short, they believed that his life had a meaning that would positively affect people far into the future.

Hundreds of miles north, in Cambridge, Massachusetts, Zatorah just couldn't seem to recover from the emotionally crushing blow. The fact that it seemed beyond her will, to regain composure and initiative, startled even her. Weak and drained, she could not, or would not, eat properly. It was as though she was trying to *will* herself to die. Only at the urging of her husband and Torasine would she carry out the rudiments of a daily routine.

Continuing her duties at work was, for the time being, out of the question. At the university, the Psychology Department "head," was obliged to find a replacement professor, to complete Zatorah's fall semester.

Patrice had held off calling Zatorah with what she knew would be demoralizing news. After some days, though, she took the plunge, only to find that Zatorah was already aware of the tragedy and in the grip of despair. The phone-line discourse was so depressing that they ended the conversation after a short period. Grief of the magnitude they each experienced did not make prolonged exchanges, via telephone, easy.

After two weeks of failed attempts to bring Zatorah out of her languished state, Peter decided on a course. Both he and Torasine now discussed having Zatorah put under extensive care of a doctor. First, though, Peter wanted to test an idea he conceived. The gamble, he thought, just might have the slimmest chance of ushering in a turning point for Zatorah.

Peter knew, well, his wife's anguish at keeping the secret of her father's unconscionable work, in *fetal nervous system mutation*. The fact that he, Peter, was a willing co-bearer of the burden apparently was not enough. In a flash of insight, he concluded that, likely, there was something to be gained from Zatorah's opening up to others, regarding the extent of her father's past practices.

Determined to forge ahead with his plan and risk whatever might be the consequences, Peter chose a tentative date for convention. It was to be a multipurpose gathering. For one, he thought a union of people central in Zatorah's life, for the purpose of celebrating Merquan's *passed* life, was in order. Secondly, and conversely, the gathering would be also to mourn, collectively, Merquan's passing. Finally, and this would be entirely Zatorah's decision, it could be the perfect occasion to *make known* family matters currently *unknown* to the guests.

By the time Peter told Zatorah of his designs, he had made all arrangements for a catered gathering. The time set was far enough in advance that it could be altered or cancelled, according to Zatorah's wishes.

Among the planned guests were Torasine, Bonita Paler and the nieces for whom she cared, Patrice Keeper and her two children and, finally, some of Zatorah's closest friends and associates from her research team. Peter even considered inviting the *psychic reader*, Madam Lu, whom Zatorah had spoken of, so often. But, again, that would be Zatorah's "call."

All the reservation Peter felt, at times, during the arrangement phase, turned out to be unwarranted. Zatorah expressed, lavishly, how considerate and insightful she thought it was that Peter had taken such initiative. She would not become aware, until the day of the gathering, that he hoped for her agreement to divulge "the secret," to their guests. As it turned out, Peter's intuition, there again, was *on the mark*.

The union and reunion was, for all intents and purposes, a true *family* gathering. For those who had seen Zatorah slowly fading away, it was like watching her being reborn. She was the mythical *phoenix* rising from the ashes of emotional and psychological demolition. Confiding to her spellbound family of friends the intricate details of her dark secrets freed her from all despair.

Adults and children, alike, knew that the bonds formed in that splendid gathering were not just temporary and expedient for the occasion. All would be, henceforth, as members of a family with blood ties. To a large extent, it would be the memory of both Merquan Paler and those messages he conveyed from *spirits of the dead* that held them all together.

References

Books

Anderson, Frederick J. *A People Called Northminster: The History of Barton Heights and Northminster Baptist Churches.* Richmond: Whittet & Shepperson, 1979.

Belsches, Elvatrice P. *Black America Series: Richmond, Virginia.* Charleston, Chicago, Portsmouth, San Francisco: Arcadia Publishing, 2002.

Case, Keshia A. (1) *Richmond: A Historic Walking Tour*: Charleston, Chicago, Portsmouth, San Francisco: Arcadia Publishing, 2010.

Case, Keshia A.(2) *Then and Now: Richmond.* Charleston, Chicago, Portsmouth, San Francisco: Arcadia Publishing, 2006.

Dabney, Virginius. *Richmond: The Story of a City.* Charlottesville and London: University Press of Virginia, 1976, 1990.

Davis, Veronica A. *Here I Lay My Burden Down: A History of Black Cemeteries of Richmond, Virginia.* Richmond: The Dietz Press, 2003.

Hoffman, Steven J. *Race, Class and Power in the Building of Richmond, 1870-1920.* Jefferson and London: McFarland & Company, Inc., 2004.

Kollatz Jr., Harry. *True Richmond Stories: Historic Tales from Virginia's Capital.* Charleston: The History Press, 2008.

Lankford, Nelson. *Richmond Burning: The Last Days of the Confederate Capital.* New York: Penguin Group, 2002.

Poe, Edgar Allan. *The Raven and other Poems*. (Many publications)

Potterfield, T. Tyler. *Nonesuch Place: A History of the Richmond Landscape*. Charleston: The History Press, 2009.

Richmond Historic Plaques (presented as "SA" with number, placed in various locations throughout the city). For a comprehensive list of plaques and locations, visit the *historical marker database* site (hmdb.org.) and search Richmond, Virginia

Rouse Jr., Parke. *Richmond in Color*. New York: Hastings House, 1978.

Salmon, Emily J. and John S. (editors, providing text and captions) & Library of Congress & Library of Virginia. *Historic Photos of Richmond*. Nashville and Paducah: Turner, 2007.

Historical Photographs Source

Most photographs cited and featured in books referenced in this work can be viewed at the Valentine Historical Center in Richmond, Virginia.

Newspapers

Richmond Dispatch
Richmond News Leader
Richmond Planet
Richmond Times Dispatch

Richmond Atlas Maps (Accessible at the Library of Virginia in Richmond)

Baist, G.W. *Atlas of the City of Richmond, Virginia and Vicinity*. Philadelphia: G. William Baist, 1889.

Beers, F. W. *Beers Atlas of the City of Richmond*. Richmond: Southern and Southwestern Surveying and F.W. Beers Publishers, 1876.

World Wide Web

encyclopediavirginia.org
nationalparksservice.gov (nps.gov)
virginiastatelibrary.org

Endnotes

CHAPTER ONE

1. Establishment of wards in Richmond is addressed in Hoffman, p. 116
2. Richmond's *ward* divisions, as drawn after 1870, were composed of the Madison, Marshall, Jefferson, Monroe, Clay and, Jackson *wards*. See Beers Atlas of Richmond streets.
3. A description of *Jackson Ward's* formation and development is given in Hoffman, pp. 114, 116, 118.
4. See Hoffman, p. 118.
5. See the *NationalParksService.gov* (nps.gov) site, concerning Jackson Ward.

CHAPTER TWO

1. To about the mid 20th century, 13th Street ran northward from Marshall Street and continued for three blocks but, today, is nonexistent. See Beers Atlas, Section G.
2. The described concourse, featuring the Dooley Hospital memorial, is shown in a 1970s photo, in Case (1), p.112.
3. The rate, for example, that Richmond blacks suffered tuberculosis was two to three times that of whites, up to the year 1920. See Hoffman, p. 106.
4. The "Colored Almshouse" was located just south of the corner of 5th and Hospital Streets. See Beers Atlas, Section A.
5. Richmond City Jail was located at Marshall and 15th Streets before

I-95 was paved through Shockoe Bottom. See Beers Atlas, Section G; Baist Atlas, plate 4.

6. An internet search of Richmond's *Dooley Hospital* reveals its opening and a history. Also, the slated 1920 opening of Dooley Hospital at 13th and Marshall is reported in the Richmond Times Dispatch, page 12, May 28, 1920.

7. A picture, from about 1941, of the adjoined Dooley and St. Philip Hospitals appears in Belsches, p. 79.

CHAPTER FOUR

1. For a striking account of the Confederate "defensive" burning of the old Mayo's Bridge and other, lesser, bridges near 7th Street's south end, see Lankford's *Richmond Burning*.

2. Built in the early 1800s, the Virginia State Penitentiary covered a space just over four city blocks, square, with its southwest corner at Spring and Belvidere Streets. It was demolished in 1993. Its location is referenced in Richmond Historical Plaque, **SA 62**, located at the southwest corner of Spring and Belvidere.

CHAPTER FIVE

1. For a street-map view of address 1540 Franklin Street, see Beers Atlas, Section L.

2. A photo reproduction of the 1600 block of East Franklin Street at the turn of the 20th century (just east of address "1540," given in the story), is seen in Salmon, p. 103.

3. Sections of Richmond predominantly inhabited by blacks in 1923 *and earlier*, are shown in a map displayed in Hoffman, p. 98.

4. The literal spelling of Richmond's numbered streets is to conform with the way they are presented in early Richmond maps. See the Beers and Baist Atlases of Richmond streets.

5. The old *Seale* section of Richmond was near to, and likely centered around, Union and Fifteenth Streets, and seems, by newspaper report, to have been in disrepute. It is estimated that *Seale House*, itself, was located along the odd numbered side of old Union Street. See *Richmond Dispatch*, February 25, 1890, page 1, column 1, under *Personal* 3. See, also, Baist Street Atlas, Section L.

6. Union Street, of old, is present-day *Ambler Street*. Ambler stretches a single block and borders *Main Street Train Station*

at its east side. It terminates, north, at Grace Street, at the early site of *Lovings Produce Market.*

7. The old *Navy Hill* section of Richmond was centered at 6th Street and Duval Street. See Beers Atlas, Section A.

8. James Bradley, referenced in the story, actually attended Navy Hill School, at Sixth and Duval. See *Richmond Planet*, March 1, 1890; page 1, column 1, first paragraph.

9. For a brief history of "colored" schools that blossomed from the post Civil War *Freedman's Bureau* in Navy Hill, see Belsches, pp. 59, 61.

10. See *Richmond Dispatch*, February 25, 1890; page 1, column 1, in *Personal* paragraph.

11. *Richmond Dispatch*, February 25, 1890; page 1, column 1, paragraphs 3-9.

12. See *Richmond Planet*, March 1, 1890; page 1, column 1, first paragraph.

13. See *Richmond Planet*, March 1, 1890; page 1, column 1, second paragraph.

14. See *Richmond Dispatch*, February 25, 1890; page 1, column 1, last paragraph.

15. Ibid., sixth paragraph .

16. *Richmond Dispatch*, April 20, 1890; page 11.

17. The path of Shockoe Creek, in the late 1800s, disappearing in drainage under Union

Street, can be seen in Baist, Plate 4 and in Beers, Section L. The extended view of its course is given in Beers' Sections A and G.

18. See *Richmond Dispatch*, February 25, 1890: page 1, column 1, fourth paragraph.

19. For a turn of the century view of *Union Station* and a brief description of its construction, see Salmon, p. 98.

20. For a synoptic history of Virginia *Union* University, see Belsches, p. 69.

21. The former *Ross Street* is given much focus in the story because of structures that, today, stand in its original path. Eastward from Governor Street these include the building that is the Division of Natural Heritage; a section of the Monroe Building; part of the on/off ramp for Interstate 95, off Broad Street; and a path along the MCV-VCU parking lot, south of Broad Street.

To view the course of old Ross Street, see Beers Atlas, Sections G and L.

22. Today, a brief section of Grace Street runs east from Governor Street but once was the western limit of Ross Street. See Beer Atlas, Section s G and L.

23. A view of Richmond, prior to the 1981 completion of the Monroe Building (looking west, from above East Grace Street) is shown in Rouse, p. 93

24. A winter scene of trolleys and horse-drawn carriages climbing Franklin Street from Fourteenth Street, at a time close to 1890, is featured in Salmon, p. 44.

25. For a pre-1896 view of the Ballard and Exchange Hotels and the pedestrian bridge connecting them, see Salmon, p. 29.

26. A brief mention of Locust Alley's notorious past is made in *Richmond Burning.* See Lankford, p. 176.

27. See Baist Atlas, Plate 4 (street map listing businesses).

28. For a view of Main Street, looking west from 17th Street, before the start of the 20th century, see Salmon, p. 68.

CHAPTER SIX

1. *The News Leader,* April 9, 1921; p.1, fourth column.

2. The statue honoring Bill "Bojangles" Robinson appears in a photo presented in Case (1), p. 114.

3. Bill (originally, "Luther") Robinson appears, with family members, in a photograph presented in Belsches, pp. 110-111.

4. The role of black officers in Richmond's *First Precinct* is mentioned in Richmond Historic Plaque **SA 65**, located in the 300 block of West Leigh Street.

5. The site of Richmond's *First Precinct* is shown in Beers Atlas, Section F.

6. The site of Richmond's First Precinct can also be viewed through an internet search of Richmond's *Smith and Marshall Streets,* via *Google Maps.*

7. Web sites such as *VirginiaStateLibrary .org* inform that the *Richmond Planet* was the first black owned newspaper publication in the South or, perhaps, the nation.

8. *Richmond Planet,* May 10, 1890.

CHAPTER SEVEN

1. Kanawha Canal and Brown's Island are both related to the James River in Richmond. Kanawha (begun and built in the late 1830s through the 1850s) was designed to allow vessels to bypass non-navigable sections of the James River and was proposed for construction as early as 1784. See Hoffman, pp. 18-19.
2. The building whose ground level establishment , today, is café "27" formerly was a furniture warehouse called the Jurgens Building. See *The News Leader*, March 14, 1921, front page.

CHAPTER EIGHT

1. Street maps of Richmond published in the 1970s and earlier show the original path of Coutts Street, from St. Peter to 2nd Street.
2. In earlier times, Nicholson Street did not terminate at the intersection with Williamsburg Road, but continued northward, where a park extends, now. The 300 block, odd, of Nicholson was located in the immediate block north of Williamsburg Road, and was on the east side of the street. See Beers Atlas, Section N. Page 117.
3. *News Leader*, March 12, 1921.
4. *Richmond Planet*, March 19, 1921.

CHAPTER NINE

1. News Leader, April 9, 1921.

CHAPTER TEN

1. See note 1, from page 70.
2. *Richmond Planet*, February 8, 1930; front page, first paragraph.
3. To view a photo reproduction showing the *Reformers Mercantile and Industrial Association* store, formerly at Sixth and Clay Streets, see Hoffman, p.155.
4. See Beers Atlas, Section A.
5. Ibid.
6. Ibid.
7. For a view of the "colored" medical and training center, at 406 East Baker Street, still in existence in 1830, see Belsches, p. 79.
8. A description of the founding of the "colored" Richmond Hospital, at 406 Baker Street, is given in Kollatz, pp. 78-79.

9. See note 2, on page 158.
10. For a view of the Hotel Reformer (owned by the Reformer Mercantile Industrial Association, formerly cited) see Belsches, p. 24 and/or Hoffman, p. 154.
11. Looking west from the bridge over I-95, on 7th Street, one can almost see the ghost of the Hotel Reformer, sitting atop the hillside, on the right.
12. For a description of the rise and accomplishments of one of Richmond's most noted black Fraternal Orders, the *True Reformers*, see Hoffman, pp. 151-156.
13. For a history of Maggie Walker's *St. Luke's Penny Savings Bank*, see Hoffman, pp. 160-166.
14. To view photo reproductions of the St. Luke's Penny Savings Bank meeting hall and business office, during its operation at Baker and St. James Streets, see Hoffman, p. 160 and/or Belsches, pp. 35,37.
15. For a discussion of the plight of black-owned financial institutions by 1929, see Hoffman, p. 147.
16. It is believed that two events most led to the decline in operation, for St. Luke's meeting hall and business office, located at St. James and Baker. One was Maggie Walker's death in 1934. The other was the St. Luke's Savings Bank survival-merger in 1928, leading to *Consolidated Bank and Trust*, still in existence. See Hoffman, p. 161.
17. To see reproduced photos of African American businesses during Jackson Ward's "golden age," see Hoffman, pp. 152-155, 159, 164-165 and Belsches, pp. 21-44.
18. See Hoffman., p. 170
19. See Hoffman, p. 175
20. See Salmon, p. 112.
21. For a comprehensive discussion of the establishment of a "black economic system" within early Jackson Ward, see Hoffman, pp. 144-146.
22. See Hoffman, p. 114.
23. To view the Robert E. Lee Home at various periods, see Salmon, pp. x and 47, and Case (2), p. 20.
24. Photos of Thalhimer's, Miller & Rhodes, F. W. Woolworth, McCrory's and other department stores, pre-1940, can be viewed within the collection by Salmon, pp. 135, 137, 151-153.

25. Ibid.

26. Ibid.

27. Ibid.

28. To view "Quality Row" and other upscale homes owned by blacks in early Jackson Ward, see Belsches, pp. 118, 119, 122, 123.

29. To view an early photo depicting the Hospital Street *Almshouse*, which made provisions for poor whites of Richmond, see Salmon, p. 24.

30. The point is made that white Richmonders still resided in the Hospital Street section of Jackson Ward, in the late 19th century. See Hoffman, pp. 123-124.

31. The *Almshouse* served as a Confederate hospital, during the Civil War. It is known that, from the 1880s, whites with sufficient funds in north-most Jackson Ward, and other areas of Richmond, migrated northeastward to Barton Heights. See Case (2) p., 81 and/or Anderson, pp. 15-18; and/or Salmon, p. 55.

32. *Richmond Planet*, January 17, 1920; second page, center column

33. See Beers Atlas, Section A.

CHAPTER ELEVEN

1. To view a map of Richmond's dimensions in 1749, see Hoffman, p. 40.

2. Ibid.

3. The description of present-day 17th Street as the original site of *First* Street in given in Kollatz, p. 24.

4. A photo from 1870, showing Shockoe Creek's floodwaters stretching from 15th to 17th Streets, slowly coursing toward the James River, is seen in Salmon, p. 32

5. Oliver Hill Parkway (earlier, 17th Street) was previously called Valley Street. See The Beers Atlas, Section G.

6. The original city of Richmond is described as covering only one-fifth of a square mile. See Hoffman, p. 38.

7. See Hoffman, p. 40.

8. See footnote "1" from page 139.

9. For a mid-to-late 18th century description of the area along present

day 17ᵗʰ Street, between Main Street and Canal Street, see Kollatz, p. 24.

10. For a view of Shockoe Creek's flow from Henrico County, north of Richmond, to an underground conduit on Union (Ambler) Street, between Grace and Franklin, before dumping in the James River, see Beers Atlas, Sections A, B, G, and L.

11. Regarding the *Robert Lumpkin Slave Jail*, compelling mention of it is found in Belsches, p. 69; Kollatz, p. 25 and Lankford, pp. 16, 90-91.

12. Realizing, April 2ⁿᵈ, 1865, that Union troops were marching from southeast upon Richmond, intent on capturing it, the government within Richmond ordered that stores of wares, that might be used to aid the Union cause, be burned. In the early morning hours of Monday, April 3ʳᵈ, windswept embers from burning warehouses and the burning Mayo's Bridge, set fire to Richmond businesses and residences from 5ᵗʰ to 15ᵗʰ Street and from the James River to just south of Broad Street. See Lanksford, *Richmond Burning.*

13. On the banks of the James River in east Richmond, escaped bondsmen following Union troops into Richmond, as well as newly freed slaves *of* Richmond, made encampments. To view a photo reproduction of these camp sites, see Salmon, p. 6 and/ or Belsches, p. 20.

14. For a description of blacks being freed from Richmond's "slave pens," see Lankford, p. 126.

15. For a description of the effort, aided by freedmen, to clear the James River of hazardous obstructions in early April, 1865, see Lankford, pp. 156-161.

16. For an account of President Abraham Lincoln's hazardous journey to Richmond on the James River, see Lankford, pp. 159-161.

17. Ibid., pp. 159, 161

18. For a description of the jubilation shown by blacks in Richmond, at Abraham Lincoln's arrival, on April 4, 1865, see Lankford, pp. 161(near end), 162, 165.

19. Lincoln's single boat is described as having made land near *Libby Prison*, formerly located at 18ᵗʰ and Cary Streets. See Lankford, p. 161

20. A picture looking at the southeast corner of old Libby Prison is shown in Salmon, p. 3.
21. A photo of *Castle Thunder*, the Civil War prison for Union Army officers, is shown in Salmon, p. 5. (The view looks at the present northwest corner of 19th and Cary Streets, where sits a parking lot, today.)
22. A picture of Libby Prison's southeast corner is presented in Case (2), p. 88 (The description of original location may be in error, as most sources say the prison stretched from 18 to 19th Streets.)
23. See Salmon, p. 7.
24. See Lankford, p. 161.
25. For a description of Richmond's *appearance*, upon Union control on April 3, 1865, as a town whose vast majority was black, see Lankford, p. 126.

CHAPTER TWELVE

1. The history of the *Richmond Colored High and Normal School* and Richmond's Armstrong High School can be accessed through internet searches, including Wikipedia.org.
2. A photograph from c. 1890, seems to show the *Richmond Colored High and Normal School*, standing above Shokoe Valley at Twelfth and Leigh Streets. See Potterfield, p. 46.
3. The Richmond Public Schools Website reveals usages for the building that once housed the *Richmond Colored High and Normal School*. Once there, search Armstrong High School.
4. To, about, the mid 20th century, 13th Street ran northward from Marshall Street and continued into the "valley" beneath the present-day Martin Luther King Memorial Bridge. Today, MCV buildings obstruct that path. See Beers Atlas, Section G.
5. A *Google Maps* search of Richmond's 4th and Baker Streets provides a conceptual view of the original path of 4th Street, from an aerial vantage.
6. To view a photo reproduction of the Richmond Hospital and Training School for nurses, formerly located at 406 East Baker Street, see Belsches, p. 79.
7. See later Kollatz references.
8. A picture showing a front view of the home-and-office, belonging to the early 20th century husband and wife doctors in Jackson Ward is shown in Belsches, p. 80.

9. Mention of the home and office of Drs. Miles and Mary Jones is made in Kollatz, p. 78.

10. See Kollatz, p. 78

11. See Kollatz, p. 88.

12. Kollatz, p. 88.

13. *Richmond Times Dispatch*, May 28, 1920; column one, page 12.

14. Synopses of the lives and accomplishments of Dr. Miles Berkeley Jones, Dr. Sarah Garnett Jones, and Dr. Mary Jane ("Janie") Jones are found in Belsches, pp. 78-81 and Kollatz, pp. 77-79.

15. *Richmond Planet*, May 13, 1905; front page, third column. Also see Kollatz, p. 79.

16. Kollatz, p. 77

17. Ibid., pp. 77, 78

18. Kollatz, p. 77

19. The splitting of Jackson Ward into northern and southern halves is described in Richmond Historic Plaque **SA 74**, located in the 500 block, odd, of 2nd Street.

20. For a description of the city's construction of a crematorium and incinerator on Orange Street in Jackson Ward in the 1890s, see Hoffman, p. 124.

CHAPTER THIRTEEN

1. That the Van Lews employed blacks as free servants is evinced in Lankford, p. 19.

2. A captivating view of the Van Lew mansion's left wing, with Elizabeth Van Lew posing in the foreground, is presented in Dabney, pp. 220-221, plate 42.

3. Photographs of the former *Van Lew Mansion*, in various states of elegance, can be accessed through internet searches.

4. *Loco foco* was the name of an early 19th century matchstick, ignited through friction.

5. See Richmond Historic Plaque **SA 69**, located in front of the Belleview Elementary School, in Church Hill.

6. Photos showing Elizabeth Van Lew are found in Lankford, pp. 120-121 (the last page of photos) and Dabney, pp. 220-221, plate 42.

7. Mention of Edgar Allan Poe's editorship with the *Southern*

Literary Messenger, formerly located at 1501 East Main Street, is made in Salmon, p. 164.
8. Further mention of Poe and the *SLM* journal is found in Lankford, pp. 17-18
9. Excerpt from Edgar Allan Poe's *The Raven*.
10. Enlightenment that Edgar Allen Poe was an esteemed guest at the Van Lew home, and recited his poems there, is given in Lankford, p. 119.
11. Visit *encyclopediavirginia.org* and search Maggie Lena Walker

CHAPTER SIXTEEN
1. For a compelling description of past black burial grounds, particularly Potter's Field within Richmond's Jackson Ward, see Davis, pp. 11-14.
2. See Davis, pp. 11-14.
3. See Kollatz, p. 100
4. Ibid., pp. 100, 101
5. Ibid., p. 101
6. See Kollatz, p. 100
7. Ibid, p. 100

Chapter Synopses

Chapter One
Pages 1 – 16

In Cambridge, Massachusetts Zatorah Leeman awakens from her dream; she gives first mention of her father and a plan for research in Richmond, Virginia. First descriptions are made of Richmond's *Gilpin Court* and surrounding *Jackson Ward*. A section of Gilpin experiences unrest and Merquan Paler and, later, the Twine cousins are first introduced. Black limousines roll along Hill Street and Priola emerges. Police arrive and escort limousines to downtown Richmond. Merquan reenters the housing unit wherein he stays, and Patrice Keeper is introduced. Back in Cambridge, Zatorah meets with other research members to discuss the Richmond, Virginia based study; there, Evan Nesset is first mentioned in the story. Focus shifts back to Richmond, Virginia. Mequan Paler is given further description, including mention of his epilepsy. He catches a transit bus to the fictitious Omega Suites Hotel and encounters the Twine cousins boarding the bus.

Chapter Two
Pages 17 – 31

The Richmond research is given broader description and addresses the preliminary investigations. Zatorah and husband, Peter, pack her luggage for the trip to Virginia; her mother, Torasine, calls and makes first appearance in the story, through phone dialogue. During the conversation, Madam Lu, the psychic reader, is first mentioned. Later, Zatorah catches her flight. In a following scene, Patrice, her two children, Shar'dey and Markee, along with Merquan, travel to the Richmond Department of Social Services on Marshall Street. From there, they walk, for sandwiches, to 13th and Marshall, where seizure overtakes Merquan, and Zatorah arrives in an airport commuter van to witness the scene. Merquan makes the first past-time excursion mentioned in the story. Zatorah and Merquan have their first communication when he comes out of the seizure. When Zatorah rejoins her research group, the first mention of the study's name appears along with added description of the research and the location of the team's operations base.

Chapter Three
Pages 32 – 41

Merquan "sees" the faint impression of what used to be Orange Street. Although he does not carry a cell phone, Patrice knows how to keep tabs on Merquan, as on this day when he walks to his mother's residence, not far away, in Gilpin Court. Bonita Paler and Merquan's cousins are introduced in the story. Mention is made of Merquan's father, Mercer Quinn Paler. Merquan's walk around Jackson Ward to lend money to smalltime drug dealers is described; it ends with his encountering Neil Twine, their ensuing dialogue and the call to Patrice by a friend concerning Merquan's location.

Chapter Four
Pages 42 – 52

The EIRI vans make their first excursions. Evan Nesset does "channeling" at the *Tredegar* historic site. Afterward, Nesset's group is called to Belvidere and Spring Streets in Oregon Hill; there he encounters a "spirit" from the old Virginia State Penitentiary. The researchers plan a search for corroboration of Nesset's report. Days later, Merquan and Patrice arrive home in a taxi with their groceries, and when the food is all put away they settle into dialogue about his work with Priola. The first mention of *Shockoe Bottom* is made along with the fictitious Club Celestine, located there. After the melee at the club, Merquan and friends scatter in different directions. Merquan ends up behind abandoned stairs of the *Main Street Station*.

Chapter Five
Pages 53 – 65

Epileptic seizure takes Merquan to the year 1890 and a place called *Seale House Corner* where he gains knowledge of places and people of Richmond's past. Dialogue between Tom McRoy and his "gramps," Donald Colver, is presented. After the description of Annie Taylor's trial, Tom McRoy makes the trek up Ross Street to Governor Street, southward to Franklin Street, and then eastward back to Franklin and 15th. There, Merquan "disengages" from his host, while his club buddies undertake a determined search for him along both Franklin and Grace Streets.

Chapter Six
Pages 66 – 80

The EIRI team breaks the code regarding Nesset's Spring Street reports; unexpectedly, Zatorah seems to have been referenced in the ghostly relay. Next, the team visits the site of what once was 318 West Leigh Street, where Nesset encounters the spirits of "LAJ" and "ATB." The EIRI team finds corroboration of Nesset's report in the *Richmond Planet* archival newspaper. Taking advantage of a break, courtesy of Nesset's schedule, Zatorah visits a few blocks of Monument Avenue, in Richmond's *West End*. While there, Zatorah talks with Torasine, in a long telephone dialogue, and mention is made of the EIRI team's upcoming two-week break from research. The following night, Zatorah compels the EIRI-2 van crew to drive around 4th and 5th Streets, near Main. A call comes in for all vans to meet at Adams and Broad Streets; there Nesset sees images of the Jurgens Building fire of the year 1920. After Nesset's relay of communication from ghosts at the scene, the accompanying policeman is relieved to see the researchers depart.

Chapter Seven
Pages 81 – 94

Back at home safe and sound with Patrice and the kids, after his Shockoe Bottom ordeal, Merquan settles into a compliant disposition. When Priola calls to set up another job for Merquan, Patrice cashes in on Merquan's accommodating spirit to negotiate a "new deal." She and the kids will ride the bus with Merquan to his job site but stay on the bus when he exits. The nature of Merquan's work with Priola at the Omega Suites Hotel is revealed. In Cambridge, Zatorah enjoys the final days of her two-week break from research in Richmond, Virginia and finds an opportunity to visit the psychic reader, Madam Lu. Zatorah tells Madam Lu about the Jurgens Building fire and of Evan Nesset's relay of messages from the spirits on the scene, at Broad Street; she tells how those conveyances led the EIRI team to discovery of George Nelson, formerly of 105 Coutts Street. Madam Lu gives Zatorah leads regarding sites of possible importance in Richmond, e.g., northern Jackson Ward.

Chapter Eight
Pages 95 – 104

With only three weeks remaining for conduct of the Richmond study, Zatorah prevails upon the team to investigate the possible presence of spiritual energy in northern Jackson Ward sites. When no significant finding is made by the EIRI vans' detection equipment, Zatorah decides to conduct her own investigation of northern Jackson Ward, and is seen by Patrice walking pass her public housing unit. Meanwhile, Nesset gives his next "channeling" effort in Richmond's Fulton Hill section, where the apparent *spirits* of past black folks give the EIRI team a surprise. One of their messages to Nesset is that he should discontinue "spirit channeling" efforts with the EIRI group. Afterward, in her own investigative travels, Zatorah visits a Henrico-based psychic reader and also drives to the site of the Richmond city jail. Traveling from the jail site, she spots Patrice and the kids turning the corner from Hospital Street onto Oliver Hill Parkway.

Chapter Nine
Pages 105 – 115

Patrice visits Merquan at the city jail. In this first mention of Ma'Sahn Dixon, he lies in a hospital bed, bullet wound to the head and under 24 hour watch by sheriff's deputies. A description is given of events leading to Ma'Sahn's being shot and Merquan's being charged as perpetrator. Merquan is bailed out of jail and, later, informed of Zatorah's research and belief that he is a key figure in a ghostly prediction. The EIRI study is now in suspension, with Nesset's decision to honor the "spiritual" request for him to cease his efforts with the group. Decision-makers in the EIRI study give a tepid response to Zatorah's proposal to have Merquan included in research procedures; they relent, with strong reservations, when she presents pertinent findings from prior research incidents that seem to point to Merquan's relevance to their work.

Chapter Ten
Pages 116 – 136

Merquan and Patrice join the EIRI researchers and the van is parked at Federal and 2nd Streets; there, Merquan goes back the year 1930, merging with his host Padrik Mews. An elaborate and loosely accurate depiction of Jackson Ward in the year 1930 follows. Merquan resumes consciousness in the van and relates his past-time experience. Afterward, his reports are confirmed by the research team, but project managers decide not to include his work in the overall investigation. Merquan is exonerated in court of charges related to Ma'Sahn Dixon. Zatorah decides to ask Merquan and Patrice to be part of her own smaller investigations, using the research vans, but first, she talks at length to Merquan, Patrice and Bonita. Zatorah's offshoot study gets underway with the EIRI van parked at Broad and 17th Streets.

Chapter Eleven
Pages 137 – 147

Merquan begins the experience with his host, "Cro," in the year 1749. The offshoot team finds verification of Merquan's past-time recall and the investigators go next to a site in Rocketts Landing; there, Merquan experiences a psychic merge with "Tess," recently released from the *Lumpkin Slave Jail*.

Chapter Twelve
Pages 148 – 162

After the usual verification of Merquan's report of conditions in Richmond in April, 1865, the researchers park the EIRI van near the corner of 12th and Leigh Streets. There, Merquan "travels," next, with host, Curtis Skimmer, in the year 1920. The same evening, the research group rides to the Dooley Memorial on Marshall Street where Merquan shares his memory of history there. The group goes, next, to Jackson and 4th Streets, where Merquan talks about the altered landscape, the old *Richmond Community Hospital*, and prominent blacks of his past-time memory. Following Merquan's reports, the researchers, again, find corroboration of them in archives and other records. Convinced of Merquan's validity as someone who has obtained knowledge through extra-normal means, Zatorah is nevertheless put off by implications of racial divisions, in the afterlife. Before their next investigative work with Zatorah, Merquan and Patrice talk about the change evident in his thinking and speaking.

Chapter Thirteen
Pages 163 – 184

Zatorah uses the final day of scheduled explorations for the EIRI team to continue her own offshoot investigation, employing Merquan. All members are aware that whatever findings made will not be merged with the earlier study. Known only to the EIRI van driver, the next area to explore is across the street from the Bellevue Elementary School in Church Hill. At that location, Merquan merges, psychically, with Ms. Minks. At the end of Merquan's seizure, as, again, induced by the van's radiations, he shares significant events that took place in the former *Van Lew Mansion*. Via internet searches Bonita, Patrice and Merquan find material that corroborates an interesting fact offered by Merquan, concerning Richmond's *Maggie Lena Walker*. The three engage in a long dialogue about the new meaning Merquan attaches to his past-time experiences. During the conversation, Zatorah calls by phone with her proposal for a final investigation, for shedding light on a matter personal to her.

Chapter Fourteen
Pages 185 – 194

The EIRI van stops in an alleyway between Main and Franklin Streets, just off 4th Street; there, Merquan connects with "Chappy" Wilson and experiences an evening at the corner hotel, on a cold Sunday, the fourth day of 1981. Upon Merquan's "return," within the van, he provides Zatorah a number of previously unanswered questions which, now, creates several more. After much personal deliberation, Zatorah decides to look up, and then to visit, Roman Almas. Almas and the revelations he provides leave Zatorah in a welter of mixed emotions.

Chapter Fifteen
Pages 195 – 208

Zatorah is back in Cambridge, aware that she is forever changed by her experience in Richmond. She also realizes that she must share her knew knowledge with someone and that it would have to be with Peter, exclusively. Zatorah offers Merquan a free college education and when he declines, she sets out to aid him in his plan to spread his insights to large groups. Merquan begins his career as a radio talk-show guest with his first appearance on the fictitious *Tim Brikhead Lunch Hour* radio show in Richmond. Merquan's unique brand of oratory in the expression of his new ideas gets much attention. Zatorah initiates the process of getting Merquan satellite radio appearances. Merquan moves his two families out of Gilpin Court, but continues the close relationship with the Twine cousins.

Chapter Sixteen
Pages 209 – 223

Both Zatorah and Peter follow Merquan's satellite radio appearances devotedly. Zatorah feels determined to find just the right occasion for introducing Peter to Merquan and the others in Richmond. Merquan makes his final appearance on the Tim Brikhead Show. Merquan finally gets his Virginia drivers license, free of former restrictions related to epileptic seizure. Merquan visits old friends in Gilpin Court, with the loyal Twine cousins at his side; there, he encounters an angry "hood" *Christian* riding as passenger in an SUV. In Cambridge, the TV news report she hears sends Zatorah into a downward spiral, emotionally and psychologically. Peter's gamble to bring together important people of Zatorah's association pays off.

Dooley-St. Philip Memorial

Baker Street School, looking E. along Charity from St. Peter

Abandoned entrance to Main Street Station

17th & Broad, looking west

4th & Jackson looking north; ahead, left, is United Network
for Organ Sharing bldg.

Historic Plaque, 9th and Main

Site of Lumpkin Slave Jail, formerly 15th near Ross

Historic Plaque, 300 block of West Leigh

Left corner of building at 316 West Leigh

314 & 316 W. Leigh, near fire station

Hill Street, looking west from St. John Street

Hill Street, looking west from St. James Street

Private property overlooking Gamble's Hill Park, looking SE

300 block of Federal, looking east at 2nd

S. 2nd running north, crossing Byrd

I-95 N & I-64 E overpass, looking from 4th Street bridge

Robert E. Lee Bridge over the James, looking west

SW edge of Shockoe Hill Cemetery

100 block of Ambler, looking N toward Grace from Franklin

Inside Shockoe Hill Cemetery

Looking N. along 4th Street wall of Shockoe Cemetery; Hebrew Cemetery and part of the former White Almshouse, in the distance on Hospital

Tredegar Road and base of R. E. Lee Bridge

Afton Building; corner of Belvidere (left-right) and Spring;
site of old Virginia State Penitentiary

View along the 2200 block of Monument

View along the 2200 block of Monument

Monument & Strawberry

SE corner of Monument & Allison

00 block of N. 4th (tall bldg. left of hotel was site of parking lot in early '80s)

YWCA in 00 block of N. 5th between Main & Franklin

Cafe "27" at SE corner of Broad & Adams.

In foreground, front section of former Masonic Temple,
across from Cafe "27"

Central Social Services front walkway

17th & Main, looking west; Main Street Station
with clock in the distance

Looking E. at Oliver Hill Pkwy and the west side of city jail

18th Street, looking east along Broad

Western edge of Belleview School (former site of, Van Lew mansion), looking N. along 23rd from Franklin

Edgar Allan Poe Museum, 1900 block of E. Main; oldest residential structure in Richmond

Business office bldg. of former St. Luke's Bank, at Baker
(fence and tree side) & St. James (bldg. face)

Jackson Ward Historical Plaque

Historical Plaque, Belvidere & Spring,
across from Afton Bldg. (left)

View north, from the intersection shown

Looking N. along 2nd as it intersects with Hill (left side) &
Hospital (right side)

N. 5th (right-left) intersecting with Hospital, which veers,
ahead, into part of Shockoe Valley

Bldg. in foreground, right of traffic signal, is sight of First Baptist Church (1780), renamed the First African Baptist Church in1841, when slave members outnumbered whites; stretches, westward, from old 14th to College Street